THE LADY OF TITLE:

A Tale of High Life.

BY A WOMAN OF THE WORLD.

"Think you there was or might be such a woman
As this I dream'd of?
Gentle Madam, no.
You lie, up to the hearing of the Gods."—SHAKSPEARE. *Antony and Cleopatra.*

THE DINNER-PARTY—A LATE ARRIVAL.—*page* 4, *col.* 2.

No. I.

THE AUTHORESS TO HER READER.

WE are about, reader, to look forth at human life in all its varied phases.

The atmosphere will not glitter. It will shine only when, throwing my eye over the face of Nature, I seize and detain those objects of beauty and sublimity which are there, and seeing we all admire. When I insinuate myself into the turmoil of life, there will be nothing but darkness. I shall tell of the PASSIONS, the woes, and the crimes of men and women; but men and women of heroic mould. All will be massive, vehement, stern, tremenduous. The prime fact of the world, SIN—huge, visible Sin—will be never out of sight. Is it ever so? It looms out from the universality of things colossal, ever during, ever present. It is as eternal, universal, and unbounded as the powers of nature without and the conscience of man within.

Once committed, guilt will be seen going on accumulating from minute to minute till the dire hour of fell explosion.

With these miseries immeasurable showering down from above, welling up from beneath, will be interwoven the delicate workings of the youthful breast in those luxurious woes which come to us all from the soft white hand of beautiful Love.

CHAPTER I.

CAPABLE OF GOING ANY LENGTHS.

Like as a wily fox, that, having spied
Where on a sunny bank the lambs do play,
Full closely creeping by the hinder side,
Lies in ambushment of his hopëd prey.
SPENSER.

The clock in Old-square, Lincoln's-inn, struck one.

A woman of an olive complexion, delicately-tinted, with ebony hair of pure and glossy texture, and a full black, soft, bright eye, that had a look of sleekness like velvet, rose.

A proud, wild-looking beauty it was, of a magnificent organisation and in vigorous womanhood.

It was Anastasia, Baroness Leone.

"And now," she continued, addressing Bother, the lawyer of Viscount Mirfield, "you will, of course, make an early appointment for Lord Mirfield to attend and settle with me. But stay," she added, "when I was last in England you promised to introduce me to him."

"Which I should have certainly done," said Bother, "had he not been absent from England. But to-day he dines with me"——

"Ah!" exclaimed Anastasia, in a quick, excited manner.

"And if you will honour me by being one of the company, Baroness"——

"With pleasure," replied Anastasia eagerly, her whole face brightening with delight. "Lord Mirfield and I will then settle this matter very amicably. You will see. You dine"——

"At six."

"At six, then, I will be with you at Fulham. Good afternoon.

"The door, Stork—open the door for the Baroness Leone," said Bother, immediately opening the door of his room, and addressing his managing clerk, who was perched on a high stool in the office, behind a very imposing fortification of timber work. Stork touched a spring, which had as magical an effect as the words "Open Sesame," in the nursery tale of Hadji Baba and the Forty Thieves, for the door flew open.

"Good afternoon, Mr. Bother," again said Anastasia, with one of her sweetest smiles, as she passed out at the office door which had opened so miraculously.

"Good afternoon, Baroness."

The elegant, shawl-enfolded form of Anastasia disappeared down the dirty staircase. In another moment the Baroness was stepping into her carriage—a chariot of gaudy appointment, with a leopard skin hammercloth, and pannels as azure as a Venetian sky—and telling her footman, a gay young fellow in shining shoes and the whitest possible stockings, to direct her coachman to drive her home.

The lady thus introduced to the reader had the placid, enigmatic countenance of the Sphynx. She sat in her carriage, looking as Coriolanus might have looked when he rested immoveable and undaunted on the hearth of his enemy, with eyes as black as death, fixed steadfastly on vacuity:—sat as pale as monumental marble, and with a mind no more to be deciphered than the hieroglyphics upon an Egyptian obelisk; and, but for the heaving of her bosom, she might have passed for a masterpiece of Phidias—her cheek was so colourless, her form so motionless.

Gradually the lassitude, the corpse-like inanition, which, in the company of Bother, had been distinguishable in her manner, gave way to fast-flitting, yet strongly-marked expressions of countenance, indicating the ever-changing and violent moods of a susceptible, energetic, and intensely working mind. But it was peculiar to her that, in society, an indurating influence passed over her like a crust, confining and crushing the genial impulses of her nature. It was only when alone that she displayed, in their true colours, her heart and head, and brought out in strong relief her peculiar tastes and talents, her inner principles and powers.

The flood-gates of her soul were opened. The least observant eye could have seen how currents of thought were sweeping through her brain.

Any one who had seen her at this moment, with all her grace gone; with nothing prepossessing left in her appearance; with her mien harsh—her movements abrupt—her face, which recently shone in the light of beautiful beneficence, now darkened by mingled rage and remorse—would have imagined that some sudden change had taken place in her fortunes, and that her fancy was peopled with the ghostly phantoms of despondency and disaster. She was the prey of baneful feelings, under whose mischievous influence she was hatching plots of villanous intent, pursuing the dark, half-hidden paths of vice—the crooked, devious ways of crime—and, in the deep solitude of her own bosom, succumbing—giving way to her passions, instead of surmounting and mastering them.

Zeno, Panætius, Posidonius, and the other Stoics of antiquity taught the total eradication of the passions. One of the greatest men of the seventeenth century said: "No! To think of entirely annihilating the passions is to wish to make yourself a god or a stone, by placing yourself too much above or too much below feeling." Truly, we should not seek for an imaginary mental strength to destroy the foibles incident to humanity. What we should strive to acquire—and it is possible for us all—is a rational wisdom which shall teach us to regulate and subdue them. Now, Anastasia, Baroness Leone allowed herself to be carried impassively along their torrent. Like the petrel, which floats on the billows in a tempest, she rose or sank with the waves that bore her. She yielded to occasion, which to her was either poison or steel. At times it ogled her with the smiling mien of a Syren: at times it inflamed her with the rugged frowns of an ogre. No female Socrates, she could exhibit no placid countenance, no equable disposition in wrongs and reverses. Borne away by circumstances, she was now fostering in her soul a venomous, an implacable hatred against a man whom she looked upon as a deadly foe.

Clenching her delicate fingers, and corrugating her gracefully-shapen brow into frowns—

"I am here in London," she thought, "to put down this man of ample means, powerful connections, and great prestige of birth—this Viscount Mirfield. Ah!" she continued, crumpling in her hand the documents she had received from the lawyer, "I have him here! in this will—these papers. But soft! I shall see him to-day. First, I must ascertain his weak point; then will I set to work to storm it. May success attend me! Success attend me!" she added, almost shrieking, and bursting into a scoffing laugh. "IT WILL. It is the great leading feature of my life. I believe in Destiny; and *that* tells me success is written in my brilliant horoscope.

"I must mature my plans alone," she went on musing intently, and laying one finger on the other. "I must execute them alone. No living being sympathises with me. Not even Sebastian Leonard. I must utter my speeches to myself, and keep in my own bosom the thoughts with which it is laden. Never was there but one man whose emotions and sentiments corresponded with mine—never but one man who ever made my heart beat with a quickening pulse."

She drew from her bosom the miniature portrait of an energetic-looking, sanguine, red-headed, sort of William-the-Conqueror-looking man, on whose features she gazed for some minutes in silence, evidently with pleasure—even with rapture. Still, fixing her eyes on those apparently beloved features, she continued—

"We were alike in nature. Many salient points in our characters stood forth in bold relief and resemblance to each other. We were like two structures agreeing in all proportions. Yes, we were terribly similar. And what was he?" she continued, fiercely. "Oh! he was ravenous in turpitude; merciless in ferocity; unpitying in intent; revelling, like a wolf, in the agonies of others; a real devil; pre-eminent in demoniac sentiment and conduct. Compared to the slaughters which took place daily at his command, what are the sacrifices to Juggernaut? What were those to Moloch? Positively merciful. Yet, in spite of all his depravity, fury, and mocking character, I loved him. Oh! yes, Zejugah," and she pressed the miniature to her bosom, energetically, passionately, "I loved you—loved you! Oh! how I loved him! He was a true man, loving war for war's sake. Even I, a woman, feel a lifting up of my spirit at the roar of cannon and the flash of scimitars. I loved him for he was bold and chivalrous. Ay, the bravest of the brave; as I have seen him, among the vast and intricate islands of the Indian Archipelago, making his attacks in the shadow of night, and in the broad daylight, assisted by his native Illanuns and Malays, and his brave Dyaks and natives of the Nicobar Islands.

"I do not shut my eyes to his dreadful assassination," she resumed, with savage bitterness of tone; "nor clear my memory of the unsightly picture of his being shot down by musketry and cannon-ball; of his ship being destroyed by fire, and myself nearly taken in captivity. The English hero returned here, to this England, with all the dignity of complete success, to receive a splendid appointment and promises of increased power, himself a man of influence and a member of the native aristocracy—even this Viscount Mirfield. Ha! To-day I shall at length obtain a sight of him again. He will have forgotten me. So, with a tongue of oil I will deceive him; with looks of softness I will charm him; I will betray him with false promises, and with gross deceits lure him into toils where death alone shall await him."

Uttering the last words with increased energy, she paused for a few seconds, and then added in low tones:

"I must ponder over this matter most narrowly. It is an act which must not be committed rashly and hastily."

In this manner this unrelenting woman serenely meditated the cold-blooded assassination she thus deliberately forecast in her mind. No inward struggle disturbed her reflections: she did not turn away from the horrible thought; on the contrary, she encountered it with seeming delight, and, like a practised murderer, looked to the heart of it. Great, almost supernatural, surely, must have been the reward she expected would result from the crime, for, after communing with herself for a few minutes longer, she determined to be as severe as destiny—to continue steady and true to her purpose, and in no faint, weak kind of way to halt or falter in her career.

In a short time she was interrupted in her self-communings by her carriage driving up before the splendid mahogany portal of one of those capacious and gorgeously decorated mansions in Arlington-street, where real princesses are reared in the hot-house atmosphere of luxury and refinement.

She made a lengthened stay in her princely residence, for it was not till five hours after that she came out of it in more glossy glare and glitter of attire than when she entered it. In a few minutes more she was being drifted in her carriage along the breezy Piccadilly, going at full speed in the direction of Knightsbridge. On her left stretched the Green Park, worthy of its name; beautifully and refreshingly green, the tints of the declining sun falling over and mellowing its vivid hues.

CHAPTER II.

BEAUTIFULLY DRESSED AND COMPASSED WITH OBSERVANCES.

> "So shoots the morning forth,
> Spangled with pearls of transparent dew."
> FORD. *The Broken Heart.*

So Anastasia pursued her way as gaily and happily, in a carriage as richly painted, and with a speed as great as a sheriff going to a hanging.

In a short time Knightsbridge and Old and New Brompton were left behind, with their uniform lines of barrack-like buildings, that are so characteristic of this old Jerusalem. Still the carriage spun along, the wheels whizzing in their whirling flight, and the horses tearing on with rapid strides, as if they were trying to step out of their harness, or trot off their tails.

Soon the road became lonely. Only a cart filled with carrots, and driven by a little old man in a brown hat and with a broken whip, passed. On the right lay fields, secluded lanes, and market gardens. Over all shone the solemn sun. Anastasia looked at her watch. It was half-past six.

"I am late," she murmured.

She was very late. For it was about half-past six when Bother and his wife and daughter, and his two partners, Squeeze, in his white waistcoat, and with big bows in his pumps, and Crush, with his gold seals, and the parson of the parish, the Rev. Abraham Drawler; an extraordinary eater, Spinks, and a prim maiden lady, Miss Perkins—long past the years of discretion—with a grim relaxing of features, and a pair of large, bright gold spectacles, and Lord Mirfield, whom they had all assembled to meet, retired from Bother's drawing-room to Bother's dining-room.

Bother had given up Anastasia, and hoped she would not come.

What, not come! The she-dragon breathing vengeance! In form and look, a white and harmless seeming angel; but, under the epidermis, black and abominable—a gorgon! a harpy! though wingless to behold.

Just under the famous old oil painting of his father—with the diamond studs, the frills, the silk stockings, and the shoe buckles—Bother, as happy as an Irishman, was sitting at the head of his table, in an arm-chair, like an ox in a stall, with his guests around him; and the very best light from the brilliant chandelier was shining on his spectacles, his bald temples, his soup, and his sparkling decanters of East India sherry; and he was talking, with a smiling countenance, to Lord Mirfield, who was sitting on his right hand, and he was hoping that his noble guest—*his* great Lord Viscount—for, at least, that day, would be relieved from the tormenting presence and persecution of the Clytemnestra of 1850, when the sound of wheels was heard without, and, rushing like a Russian-driven drosky, the chariot of the Baroness Leone was pulled up short, with immense importance, by the fat coachman, under the pillared portico of Bother's Tusculan abode among the *periœci* of Fulham.

"Papa, dear, are you ill?" inquired Miss Susan, the eldest daughter of father Bother. "How pale you are!"

"Nothing ails me, my dear," replied Bother. "I am all right."

"But indeed, Papa"——

"The Baroness Leone," exclaimed the servant, flinging open the door, and swinging himself, like a parrot on a ring, behind it, to make wide room for Anastasia.

Bother, looking frightened—though there was nothing to frighten *him*—it was not *he* who was to be nervous—rose, and, soaring above his silver tureen and his silver soup-ladle, looked along the table, peeping over the centre ornament, a heavy base and column of silver, supporting an immense Bohemian glass bowl, intended for fruit or flowers, sugar-plums or crackers, to adorn his dinner, and in this, if not elegant, at least pictureque, posture he was ready to salute Anastasia immediately she entered.

And soon Anastasia did enter, with a natural and graceful attitude and bow, which the most accomplished person in Europe would not have been ashamed of imitating, and dressed in all the peculiar finery of the opulent and luxurious ladies of the Western nations. A large ruby brooch on her bosom was as prominent as the Dragon—the imperial badge—on the breast of a Chinese Mandarin, and there was such a glitter scattered over every part of her person and apparel, that she was an object like a portrait by a Persian artist, or the initial letter in a monk's illuminated missal, gorgeous from a profuse application of gold and flaming colours.

> "The freshest, fairest, bonniest beauty was she,
> A very bona roba, and a bouncer,
> In yellow, glistering, golden satin."

Everybody was thrown by her into the shade. "Beautiful"—"lovely"—"unapproachable"—"wonderful"—was all you could say of her, as it is all you can say of the turkeys and cocks, apples and grapes, daisies and butter-cups, of Mr. Hunt, the water-colour artist. On her back she bore a fortune; on her shoulders lace that might deck a queen's; round her throat pearls; on her fingers diamonds, the price of which I hardly dare to whisper, lest I should mention a sum that might seem exorbitant; yet, whatever sum I might name, I believe, would fall far short of their value. Wanton, luxurious, meretricious was she, half-draped, with jewelled bracelets and jewelled hair—her hair, silky and raven, was plaited, braided, and piled up in the Grecian mode of head-dress, and about every rich fold of the satin drapery there was a ruffling grandeur, as if it was imperial purple that billowed about her rounded limbs and her snowy breasts.

CHAPTER III.

THE BALL IS ROLLING.

"The banquet waits our presence—festal joy
Laughs in the mantling goblet; and the night,
Illumined by the taper's dazzling beam,
Rivals departed day."
REV. DR. BROWN'S *Barbarossa*.

How Miss Susan Bother stared at the Baroness Leone's costly clothes, her rings, her smiles, her fine neck, and her soft round arms.

"I am afraid," said Anastasia, "I have mistaken the time."

"Six, Baroness. I said six precisely," replied Bother, quickly — impatiently; his head seeming to Anastasia, where she stood, as if it was resting, like John the Baptist's, in a large silver waiter, that, behind him, was standing upright on a carved side-board, among knives, cucumber-cutters, fish-slices, sugar-sifters, forks, spoons—a whole dinner-service.

"We are too crowded here, I am afraid," continued Bother. "Baroness, take care—your elbow. Shall I place your bouquet on this stand? Can you squeeze a little lower, Crush?

"Oh! there—by Lord Mirfield—Ah! let me introduce you. Lord Mirfield, the Baroness Leone—the Baroness Leone, Lord Mirfield."

Up rose the Viscount, and down went his head in the very lowest inclination; so struck and charmed was he already by that woman of first-rate pretensions to that qualification so attractive in the fair sex—beauty; and Anastasia, bowing graciously, and smiling sweetly, seated herself by the side of her *new* acquaintance with regal magnificence.

"The Viscount, Baroness," said Bother, also sitting down, "has been a great traveller in Spain, and can talk to you of that country, of which you are so fond and proud."

"Ah! to be sure! The Baroness Leone!" observed the Viscount. "Were you not in Madrid, Valentia, and Valladolid four years ago? I galloped over three-fourths of Spain in my search for you."

"I wish you had overtaken me," thought Anastasia, with a pang at her heart, and then she said aloud with her most fascinating smiles: "While I had put half-a-dozen mules to my carriage, and had bade farewell to the soil of sarabands for the next ten years to come."

"Perhaps the Spanish people weary you. They weary me. They have such a natural genius for doing nothing, playing dominos and the guitar."

"All they do has the appearance of child's play; but I take the world as it comes," said Anastasia, with a careless indifference.

Thus she conversed with the Viscount in a natural and easy manner, in a voice not loud, but distinct and well heard; calm, grave, earnest, feeling, mild, dignified, and impressive, accompanying her observations with striking expressiveness of looks, and graceful gesture; commanding stillness and attention, and arresting deeply the admiration of Lord Mirfield.

As a man walking in an Indian jungle, comes suddenly into the presence of a splendid yet dangerous reptile—say, a rattlesnake—all but steps upon it as it crawls nearly under his feet from lying coiled at the bottom of a shrub, and, beholding the dreadful enemy of monstrous shape and amazing power, unfolding himself slowly and gracefully from his folds of glorious hues, gathering himself into his muscular masses, and glaring upon him his beautifully bright and piercing eye, stands paralysed, transfixed to the soil, in the full consciousness of danger, with all his execution defeated, and escape denied him—so Viscount Mirfield, when there thus burst upon him unexpectedly at that bright banquet Anastasia, Baroness Leone, with her fascinating powers, the extraordinary assemblage of charms, mental and personal, possessed by her, though, like the Indian traveller, aware of all the peril that surrounded him, overcome, spell-bound by the miraculous might of that singular woman, could not fly from her, but with her image momentarily finding its way deeper and deeper into his heart, felt a subtle and obscure agency at work, like magnet upon iron, drawing him towards her, and there holding him fast, so that he could not tear himself away. This was not love. No! It was cataleptic rigidity of the heart.

Perceiving how successful she was in her attempts to fascinate the Viscount, Anastasia continued to talk to Lord Mirfield with beaming smiles and gleaming eyes, coquettish looks, and all that play of passion and feeling, that pleasing and exquisite variety of nature common to continental people.

Lord Mirfield suddenly started, changed countenance, and exclaimed eagerly and abruptly—"Good God! Is it possible? I cannot be deceived. You are — " and he whispered in her ear.

"Hush!" said Anastasia, with amazing self-command, and without a muscle moving in her face. "What I know you know."

"And your present elevated position in society?"

"Elsewhere ask me—not here, or now."

The dinner was going on. Incessant was the clatter of knives and forks, and loud and general the conversation.

"Once so bright, joyous, and admired," said the Viscount, in tones low enough to be heard by no other ears than Anastasia's, "still bright and lovely—as beautiful as in your early morning"——

"Shake off the reminiscences of the past, Viscount," said Anastasia, playfully.

"May I not woo you?"

Anastasia laughed in tones like silver.

"I beseech you by the authority of love"——

Again Anastasia stopped him with a light musical laugh, and, placing her hand in his, said gaily—

"Love! You are dealing in romance. Look on the past as a fiction. Other dreams have been realised."

"Ah! Again I must ask you whence this present elevated position?"

"Are you willing to help me to purchase a couple of quiet, country estates, one in Berkshire, the other in Kent, Viscount?" said Anastasia. And, as she spoke thus, she looked at him with a side glance, laughingly, but jeeringly, and with a serene face, as if her mind was quite at rest, and everything about the Milsington property was fair and upright, honestly obtained, and securely possessed.

"I feel I could do a great deal for you," replied the Viscount.

"You shall," said Anastasia; "I look forward with real delight to the future. We will talk of this hereafter."

And she rose, laying her hand on his. The ladies were moving from the table.

"One moment! said the Viscount, detaining her by a slight tug at her dress.

"Not a word!" said Anastasia, assuming a kind of wild look in the eye, and speaking in feigned tones of terror. "If you expose me I am ruined."

"Do not be alarmed," said the Viscount, as if amused. "I declare to you on my honour I will not say a syllable to a soul. But when can I speak to you alone?"

"This evening," said Anastasia, her eye sparkling. "I see a terrace outside the window."

She dropped her handkerchief purposely.

The Viscount picked it up, and, in presenting it to her, stood by her side: his face being close to hers, she said to him, in all but a whisper—

"I will seek an opportunity of seeing you there, in less than a quarter of an hour."

She took the handkerchief, and, moving on, vanished from the room like a sylph.

The Viscount took but little interest and no part in the conversation of Bother and his friends after the retirement of the ladies, so wholly absorbed was he in reflecting upon his good fortune in having met with the Baroness Leone. Suddenly he beheld before the window drapery hanging in graceful folds, with freedom in its bends and creases, imparting the idea of the exquisite flexibility of supple, and, *he knew*, lovely limbs. He availed himself of an almost immediate opportunity to leave the room. He went forth upon the terrace to meet Anastasia.

She looked up in his face with a smile as he approached her.

"How it delights me," he said, bending down and speaking in fond tones, "to see your bright eyes condescending to shoot additional rays when I happen to appear."

"Always gay and graceful, I see," said Anastasia, in her blandest voice. "It is not possible to put on a face of frowns against your elastic good-humour." And then added, "I am, moreover, one of those who have never been able to resist importunity; and, least of all, that importunity which comes armed with kindness."

As if under the influence of a tenderness of past days, the Viscount here, without giving any warning of his intention to his companion, threw his arms round the Baroness, pressed her to his bosom, and kissed her.

"You are entitled to insult me," said Anastasia, with well affected modesty, but without any indignation though disengaging herself as rapidly as possible from the Viscount's embrace. "I must submit to it, or you would think it theatrical affectation. But rather than increase the contempt you must have for me, I should prefer death."

And she turned away, raising her scented, delicate, and richly embroidered handkerchief to her eyes. It had a pretty and stagey effect, and was still more pretty and stagey from there being no tears to wipe away.

"Here's a jolly lark," said Bother, leaning over to Squeeze, and speaking to him in the lowest tones from behind the back of his hand, for the window being open enabled him to hear voices without. "There's the Viscount on the terrace making love to the Spanish Baroness," he continued in a whisper. "Listen."

And all Bother's guests grinned, winked their eyes, put up their hands to each other, as if enjoining silence, and, placing themselves in attitudes of the profoundest attention, listened eagerly.

"Do not pass such a lamentable decree upon me," continued the Viscount, tenderly, to the Baroness. "My life depends on a word from you; and I have come here to hear that word from your lips. Promise me that you will meet me again to-night!"

It was clear from the kiss, and from these words, that the Viscount had made a mistake about Anastasia. He treated her as if she was a gay lady, who spent half her life in amusement, and the remainder in rambling and sleeping. An idler she was, but a showy idler; and having come to England loaded with the wealth of India, was likely to be welcomed to the saloons of the leaders of society.

"No," said Anastasia, firmly, but kindly.

"To-morrow, then?"

"No."

"Then I cannot answer for what I shall do to myself," said the Viscount, half seriously, half jestingly. "If you knew the mad thoughts that are careering through my brain," he added insinuatingly, "you alone can save me from the sinister act I meditate."

"Do not speak so," said Anastasia, with well-feigned offended feeling and fright. Then speaking loud enough to be overheard by Bother and his guests—"Suppose any one should overhear you," she added.

"Hush!" said Squeeze, as Crush knocked his gold seals against the table.

"Grant me but one more interview," said the Viscount.

"I cannot," replied Anastasia.

"Then there is no knowing for what you may be responsible," observed the Viscount.

"Here'll be work for Payne, the coroner," said Bother, in a low tone. "We shall have the Viscount slitting his carotid artery, or blowing out his brains before the morning."

Though spoken low, this speech of Bother's reached the quick, attentive ears of Anastasia. Her eye suddenly lighted up with a bright and strange expression of mingled delight and surprise. She turned round abruptly, and hastened from before the window in an apparently very indignant manner, but immediately pausing beneath the shadow of the wall, said to Lord Mirfield in a singularly kind and mild voice, and in the lowest whisper—

"Yes, you shall see me again to-night."

"When? where?"

"Leave the house at the same time as myself. Let your carriage drive on first. I will follow, and overtake you."

The Viscount caught hold of Anastasia's hand. The Baroness tore it from him, passed on quickly, but entered the drawing-room quietly and calmly.

The only two very bright objects to be seen outside Bother's house were now the Viscount and the evening star.

CHAPTER IV.

HARDER TO BE WON THAN A STRONG CITY.

> "So her disembowell'd web
> Arachne, in a hall or kitchen, spreads,
> Obvious to vagrant flies: she secret stands
> Within her woven cell; the humming prey,
> Regardless of their fate, rush on the toils
> Inextricable; nor will aught avail
> Their arts, or arms, or shapes of lovely hue."
> PHILIPS.—*The Splendid Shilling.*

The clock had for some time struck twelve, when a couple of orbed lights, that had all the appearance of the eyes of a firefly flitting through the dark air, could be seen in the distance along a winding lane leading to Parsons' Green. Presently after a rumbling sound gradually became louder and louder. Then the outlines of Anastasia's chariot, that seemed harsh under a light that fell perpendicularly upon them from the bright disc of the fair full moon in the zenith, could be seen approaching at a moderate speed.

It was a lovely night, the stars shining brightly, and no cloud to be seen.

A moment after, and another carriage could be heard approaching at a rapid pace in the same direction. In less than five minutes more, both the vehicles were standing side by side.

Out of the latter descended Lord Mirfield. He stepped up to the first carriage, in which was Anastasia, whose handsome figure, dressed apparently in white, though it was golden yellow, made her look, through the darkness, like a nymph. They spoke to each other in subdued voices. Then Lord Mirfield got into the same carriage with the Baroness, and they drove off at a careering speed towards London.

Several seconds passed without their interchanging a single syllable. Perhaps they were at a puzzle what to discourse about. Certainly, they did not seem disposed to chat over strikes and mutinies, the condition of the poor, or an increase of the income tax, the inconvenience of an armed peace, or Major Beniowski and his printing machine. As for Lord Mirfield, who was always an ardent admirer of the other sex, and who appeared inclined to deliver to his fair companion his dicta upon love, while irresolute as to his course of conduct and the tone of conversation he should assume, at this commencement of the anxious amatory interest he took in Anastasia, kept earnestly gazing at her face and form; and the thrill of joy with which he contemplated her beauty distinctly showed itself in his sparkling eyes. At length he caught her by the hand, and squeezing it, said—

"I am perplexed how to address you."

"Call me Anastasia," was the reply.

"But that is not your real name," said the Viscount.

"Admitted," said Anastasia.

"Oh! I see," said the Viscount laughing, "you have disguised yourself under a fictitious name."

So she had, like some of the licentious ladies of antiquity, Mysachne, Borborope, Anasystopolis, Pandosia, Leophoros, Maniocepos, Ilipos, and others mentioned by Athenæus, Suidas, and Eustathius.

"As I thus sit by your side," continued the Viscount, quietly winding his arm round the lithe waist of Anastasia—and it did not seem at all disagreeable to her, for she made no signs to repel the advance—"and discern all the glowing graces of youth and beauty in your person, a soft and transporting emotion seizes on my whole frame, and my heart flies to my eyes with an ecstacy that resolves every sense into sight."

Anastasia bent her head forward with the most bewitching coquetry, and gazed at him sideways, but would not, or could not make an answer. It was but for a second, for before the Viscount resumed, she observed with a calm grace and a careless charm—

"You have taken it into your head to pay me a great deal of attention. And do you really love me?"

"I am dying for love of you."

She smiled even more roguishly than before, and again peeped up in his face.

"You, certainly, have nothing of death from grief about you," she observed.

"Ha! ha!" laughed the Viscount. "Well, that's good. Ha! ha! just like you—never know how to catch you—like a puff of smoke, up the chimney or out at the window."

And the glowing warmth of the Viscount's laugh resounded cheerily through the atmosphere. Then, resuming his gravity, he went on—

"Well, there's something unreadable, too, about you."

"It seems there must be magic in me to fire

you to this," she said, casting an arch glance at his arm round her waist.

"And, candidly, there is a magic in you forcing me to this," said the Viscount, drawing closer to her side. "In short, Anastasia, I love you to distraction! Absence has, indeed, scattered ashes over the old flame; but the treacherous embers are still alive, and blaze with the slightest fuel."

"Or, rather, without any," observed Anastasia, quietly. "A lover's ardour, Viscount, is a sort of phosphorus, which will kindle on mere air. But I hope the flame with you is of so harmless a nature, that it may play on your heart without any danger of impairing it."

"Would you have me infer from that you seriously refuse me?" said the Viscount, dropping his arm from round her waist.

"It is not in my nature to be serious for a moment," said Anastasia, arching her eyebrow.

"I am inclined to believe the rejection proceeds rather from your pride than from your heart," said the Viscount, dropping back in the carriage. "But then, flattered, followed, admired as you must be by every coxcomb, I prove myself the most absurd of the group, when I think for a moment of engrossing you. But your objection?" he added, raising himself eagerly in his seat.

"Amidst the real ones," replied Anastasia, placing the tip of the forefinger of her right hand on the tip of the forefinger of her left hand, "pride is the first; but the ostensible are as numerous as my caprices," she continued, dropping her arms by her side, and speaking with striking levity. "They change with the cast of a man's countenance, the cut of his coat, the dressing of his hair, the polish of his boots, the shape of his hat, the buttons on his waistcoat, and his very neck-tie. In short, I rise and fall alternately in the thermometer of my heart, till the chilling atmosphere of vanity drives me to the very freezing point."

"Oh!" how I flattered myself I had forgotten you," exclaimed the Viscount, in a tone as of bitter self-reproach. "But I cannot, and never could, quit the pursuit. Strange! that it should have been you that, hearing of in Spain, I hurried after, and fled to Valladolid, in the hope of overtaking you.

"Yes," said Anastasia, with sparkling eyes, and in a very singular voice. "Fortune has amused herself with keeping us in perpetual chase. But let us not complain," she continued, placing her hand in the Viscount's. "We have once more blundered upon each other in the gay precincts of the great metropolis:" and she shook Lord Mirfield by the tips of his fingers.

Her eyes, as she was speaking, were attracted towards a dead wall by which they were passing. Along it was placarded a large bill with this announcement, in letters so gigantic that you could have read it with facility from an express train, flying along at sixty miles an hour:—

THIS EVENING.

VAUXHALL GARDENS.

GRAND BAL MASQUE.

A sudden thought seemed to strike Anastasia, for, turning quickly round towards Lord Mirfield, she said to him with much friendliness of manner—

"And now, Viscount, what are your plans for the evening?"

"I have none," said the Viscount, moodily.

"Psha!" said Anastasia, gaily, and trying to rally him, "you are not going to fall into a fit of gloom. Surely you can rescue mind and body from despondency. It's fit only for a foolish young fellow. Pluck up your spirits. If you are so enamoured, this is my advice," she continued, with a slight and silvery laugh: "follow your nymph. In mere fatigue, she may give up the chase."

"Oh," said the Viscount, bluntly, "if you are proud, where's the use? What hope can I have of silencing your pride? If I had the wit of all the fellows who write plays, the money in the Bank of England—"

"A thought strikes me," said Anastasia, interrupting him, and assuming all the airs of a syren. "We have but just come across each other, after very many long years of separation; and our characters—altered, as they must be, by time—are yet equally unknown. What think you if my objection may be all consolidated in a single point? Shall I tell it you, Viscount?"

"Well!"

"It's a very freezing one to a woman." And then a slight pause.

"Viscount—we are *strangers*."

"Is that all?"

"Why, of course it is," said Anastasia, merrily. "So then, borrow a title of friendship. Let us become better acquainted. A few hours' conversation will show us if we have sympathies together."

"If so"—

"Why, then, rally my rejection of you. Appear in a point of view that shall not alarm my pride, and give yourself the chance of knowing whether you have touched my heart."

"The plan is promising, I must confess," said the Viscount, with a pleased smile, and with sparkling eyes; and sitting upright, took in his own the hand of the Baroness, which she did not draw away, but allowed to lie passively in his own. "But the execution"—

"Oh, the easiest thing in the world," said Anastasia; "there is a masked ball at Vauxhall to-night. Let us go and spend a few hours there together."

"Vauxhall!—A masked ball!"

"Oh," said Anastasia, guessing at the thoughts of her companion, "I see your objection. Our acquaintances in London, it is true, are very numerous; but they will not be there. Those that are will be only a set of thoughtless young fellows, who will readily countenance a frolic so common." Seeing Lord Mirfield still hesitating, she added—"If you like to stand upon punctilio, well. But"—and now she threw out the bait—"in a scene of dissipation, you may not find me so indifferent. If you do, why, you will be but where you are. But my life upon it, Viscount," she continued laughing, and shaking her fore-

THE BARONESS LEONE AND PEKRA, THE DWARF—THE FATAL RING.

finger at him, "when you peep at me through the medium of such laxities as a masked ball, you will discover a thousand charms which are lost at the present immeasurable distance."

What a speech! It was like a spark to a train of gunpowder. It lit up all the fire in the heart of the Viscount. He squeezed Anastasia's hand, and observed:

"I like your scheme, and am half determined to adopt it."

"Adopt it wholly," said Anastasia, in a firm voice of determination, and, without waiting for a reply, gave such a tug at the check string, that it almost wrenched off the little finger of the fat coachman, who pulled up his horses in less time, as a schoolboy would say, than you could cry "Jack Robinson." Then his red ears under his powdered wig quivered, stiffened, and stood erect in his speechless amazement on hearing the clear, ringing voice of his grand, fashionable mistress calling out to him in unmistakeable tones:

"Vauxhall Gardens!"

The carriage drove on.

CHAPTER V.

SHAKING OFF THE SEMBLANCE OF SERVILITY.

"I fear your disposition:
That nature which contemns its origin
Cannot be border'd certain in itself."
SHAKSPEARE.—*Lear.*

Scarcely had the high-mettled, long-barrelled blood bays pranced a hundred yards, before Anastasia, with the air of one struck by an idea, turned to her companion, and, addressing him with the ease and freedom natural to her, said:

"Viscount, we—at least, I am not in the costume suited to the sort of people we shall meet at Vauxhall. If we returned home and changed our dresses, it would delay our visit but for half an hour at the most."

"It is for you to order, I to obey," said the Viscount, with his ready and customary gallantry, and continued: "I think it would be advisable. The wind has much increased; it is almost cold; and I shall fancy myself all but freezing in this light coat and vest."

A counter-order was given to the coachman to take the shortest road to Arlington-street, and to drive quick.

The Baroness and the Viscount now lapsed into reverie.

Was it from the beauty of the night? for we are all so disposed to muse beneath the misty beams of the pale, grey pilgrim of the night. Those soft beams are so much more conducive to pensive meditations than the dazzling rays of the sparkling god of day. Brown was the landscape; deep blue the sky; the dark azure firmament was studded with numberless stars, that twinkled and glistened like diamond grains on a dark ground: here and there voyaged in empty space vapours so thin and translucent, they seemed like snowy gauze veils that had fallen before the face of the moon to receive additional lustrous beauty from her silver effulgence. A fresh and balmy breeze had risen.

Something is so imposing in the sight of a beautiful night, it involuntarily leads to muteness and to contemplation. Vivacity, gaiety, has nothing in common with the vague, indefinite gloom that broods over slumbering nature. The tongue is held for the ear to listen to the stillness.

It was not the sanctity of the night, nor its stilly impressions, that caused Anastasia no longer to laugh and to jest, and for no more to be heard ringing and joyous tones in her voice when she addressed an observation to her companion.

She was involved in momentous considerations—thinking how imperative it was before she went with Viscount Mirfield to Vauxhall Gardens that she should see ONE person.

On arriving in Arlington-street, she bade a brief and hasty adieu to the Viscount, who was to go on in her carriage to his home in Charles-street, Berkeley-square, and when he had changed his dress, to return and accompany her to the masked ball in Vauxhall Gardens.

Entering her splendid mansion, Anastasia traversed a superb vestibule, paved with large slabs of marble, in diamond-shaped patterns of alternate black and white, and supported here and there by soaring light columns, terminating in gilded Corinthian capitals; she passed by luxurious sitting-rooms, and, going up a gently ascending, broad, carpeted staircase, went into a front room on the second floor, her bed-chamber, which was fitted up in the most elegant Gothic fashion—if the term "elegant" can be applied to any style of Gothic employed in the bed-chamber of a beautiful young woman.

But then Anastasia, with that taste for which a woman has such genius, had corrected all that was unbecoming in that chamber. By having recourse to subterfuges with an art quite her own, she had changed furniture, that, fragments of the antique looked like ruins, into a curious and captivating museum; and breaking in upon the Gothic in, Heaven knows, how many thousand ways, she had, by falling into a goodly number of anachronisms, so mixed up Mediæval, Renaissance, Gothic, and Rococo as to give to her chamber an enchanting and feminine air quite delightful to the eye; so that chamber of her's, instead of being, in its antiquated Gothic dress, as dark and as dismal as a tomb, was as shining and as smiling as a little Paradise.

Into this elegant room, to assist her in her toilette, Anastasia summoned one of her waiting women, whom she dismissed as soon as she had changed her magnificent dinner dress to one less simple, but equally picturesque. Now, from her beautifully formed head hung a costly black lace veil, partially covering an ample robe of sombre-hued silk, and over her rosy shoulders, that were at once so plump and so firm, was carelessly laid a soft woven Cashmere scarf.

She placed herself in a high-backed, sculptured, Gothic chair, which should be considered the most inconvenient in the world to sit upon, but which it is the fashion now-a-days to think the most comfortable and the most delightful. Her eyes gazed into vacuity—rather, she kept them fixed on a large ebony-framed glass-case, filled with nameless, priceless curiosities, which people with a passion for the rare and the antique pay for by their weight in gold. She kept her eyes fixed so long and so intently on this case, she seemed to be taking an inventory of its contents—of its ivory cups and vases, its silver plate, curiously and marvellously inlaid and wrought, glasses of a variety of colours, gilt chalices, rock crystal, rich enamels, and, amidst these rarities of Middle-Age Europe, things monstrous, hideous, and grotesque, the baboons and chimeras, that are the inventions of the Japanese and Chinese—things so rare and valuable that any dealer in old curiosities, even though of Bond-street or Piccadilly, would, in spite of his riches and his respectability, have felt a great itching at his fingers' ends to purloin.

After she had sat thus for several minutes she turned away her eyes; and, covering her face with her hands, looked as if she was going to say a long prayer, though I am certain she did not; she was only pondering over matters of a wicked nature. Then she rose and rang the bell five times.

In about as many minutes—not before—the

door was slowly opened; nobody was seen to enter; it might have been some very small animal like a cat or a dog; but whatever it was it made no noise; and it discreetly remained in the same place, without stirring a limb. On looking down below the handle of the door the eye caught a glimpse of an immense head—almost as massive as that of the Spanish giant who was exhibited some years ago in Regent-street; and a bigger head, I think, I never saw on the shoulders of a human being. Piercing, glittering eyes were also seen, not fixed in one direction, but wandering about all over the person of Anastasia, as if the beholder was under the conviction he was surveying the Baroness Leone fast asleep.

All on a sudden a singular noise was heard from that end of the room. It was a hoarse, panting respiration, followed by a sort of a low growl which burst into a light bark like that of a dog. It was not a dog, however: it was a man; the dwarf that Anastasia had got possession of when she was travelling in Russia in the summer of 1847; for dwarfs are about as common in Russia as negroes are in Africa and monkeys in France. In the reign of the Empress Catherine no Russian prince was without his dwarf, as no French lady of high rank was without her ape in the reign of Louis XIV., or her poodle in the reign of Charles X.

Pekra, as this mannikin was named, was of an age that nobody knew, not even himself, for no date was kept of his birth, but he must have been under twenty at the time he was taken off a remote Tartar village of a Russian prince to be made a present of to Anastasia. He knew not the fate in store for him, which was to be prime pet of a wealthy, pretty young woman, who had a far greater hankering after a dwarf than the most superb diamond necklace which the greatest jeweller in Europe could fabricate. I say, he knew not the lot that awaited him, whether it would be good, bad, or indifferent; but, believing that any change in his fortune must be for the better, he congratulated himself, being exceedingly rejoiced to part company with his village and the people with whom he had lived; for the peasants had run away from him, as if he were a dreadful wild beast; his father was always twitting him for not being worth the bread and salt he ate; and his very mother would thrust him away when he asked for a kiss, and curse the day he was born. Nobody loved him; nobody even cared for him.

In sooth, he was hideously ugly. Talk of the gorilla, found in the wilds of Africa by Du Chaillu! Never was there anything so monstrously strange in the form of humanity.

In *his* case excessive deformity was highly advantageous; it made a *thing* of him instead of a *being;* as a thing he was a positive beauty, just as a Skye terrier is the handsomer the uglier he is. Nothing in her whole house did Anastasia consider prettier than Pekra—nothing did she think of greater value, not the most superb porcelain vase in her whole rare collection of Delft and Dresden china.

I must endeavour to place this dwarf before the reader.

Fancy to yourself, then, my reader, a little man, scarcely three feet high, perhaps two feet ten inches, a sort of land urchin in the social strata, looking so much like an extinct animal that in the list of the palæontologist he would have assumed an important place, even as on account of his diminutive size the naturalist might have included him among insect life. Not one of those pretty little organisms that star the forests with their elegant forms, that are leapers among the leaves and herbage of groves and meads, or hunters along the river bank and over its sunny waters, or gaudy flutterers over the flowers of the lily and the lilac; but of the uglier, coarser order, the beetles, cockroaches, grasshoppers, and dragon-flies. He was a brachiopod, or splay-footed animal, and rose in complexity of structure with a spine as curved as a fish's, and a back like a camel's, with a hump just below the shoulder, with arms like fins, a knob for a head, and eyes like a barrow-pig's, as little and as wrinkled at the corners; and his mouth, which was so wide it seemed to stretch from ear to ear, was, like that of the Australian cestracion, paved with broad crowned corrugated teeth that seemed meant for the crushing of crabs and lobsters, crayfish and cocoa-nuts. Had he been in a state of nudity and crawled on all fours, Professor Owen would have taken him for a restored form of the Labyrinthodon; and his foot-prints would have been the same as Cheirotherium.

"Ah, Pekra! Is that you, my beautiful little pet?" said Anastasia, without turning round her head, for she saw him by casting a glance at an immense mirror immediately in front of her. "You came into the room so quietly I did not hear you."

"How could you when you were fast asleep?" said the ungallant little man.

"I was not asleep, sweet little Pekra, I was dreaming of you. Oh! you are such a charmer, you must come here at once and let me have a kiss at you."

The dwarf did not move a step.

He stopped still as if bewildered, bewitched; as if not rightly understanding what had just been said. He was all eye and all ear to hear more.

"Why do you stand there, devouring me so with your beautiful green eyes, Pekra, dear? Come here, and let me eat you up with kisses. I long to devour your rosy, stony cheeks. What! are you afraid of me?"

Here the dwarf, as if to show that he had no reason to be afraid of Anastasia, walked forward with what dignity he could command, and, placing himself gravely at the feet of the Baroness, kissed her hands; nay, covered them with kisses.

"Tell me now, Pekra, what I can do for you," continued Anastasia. "I will do anything that lies in my power. If you are in want of money, name the sum."

The dwarf sprang to his feet with one indignant bound.

I should here mention that Pekra was as passionate as a monkey, as savage as a baboon;

and that his greatest happiness consisted in being wicked and cruel; and all this arose from the poor creature knowing that he was despised; a buffoon; a plaything; less than the least of men; a machine; and from his knowing further that there was nothing but insult in the attentions bestowed and the caresses lavished on him; and that every word, every look, every smile was a sneer at him, a sarcasm, a bitter irony: so he hated everybody about him,—except *one*—ONE ONLY. The result of this temperament was that he occasionally flew into fits of impotent fury, and took a delight in being revengeful: it did him good to do others harm. On such occasions they would order him to be whipped; and when they set about carrying the sentence into execution he would become frantic, fling out his arms like the vanes of a windmill, and throw about his legs like those children's toys of harlequins; bite and kick; and when the punishment was over he would roll on the floor and give vent to the most lamentable and hideous cries of rage and grief.

"Money!" he exclaimed, "which is given only to servants!"

And on his breast, from despondency and shame, he drooped his head, which the moment before had been raised with dignified pride.

There was a moment's pause. Anastasia stretched out her hand to him, and tapping him gently on the cheek—

"From this day," said she, "I will count you among my friends. I have made you the offer of a favour which you have refused to accept; I will now, in my turn, ask you a favour which it is in your power to grant."

The dwarf's eyes sparkled.

"Give me that emerald ring you wear on your thumb; and take in exchange this gold chain, which consider as the badge of our future friendship."

As she spoke she flung over the neck of Pekra a massive gold chain which had been adorning her own neck, and was still warm from resting on her beautiful, white, protuberant bosom.

The dwarf trembled in every limb. He turned as white as a sheet.

CHAPTER VI.

GIVING A PASSPORT TO A LAND OF PROMISE AND BEAUTY.

"But that my bosom
Is full of bitter sorrows I could smile
To see this formal ape play antic tricks;
But in my breast a poisoned arrow sticks,
And smiles cannot become me."
MIDDLETON.—*The Roaring Girl.*

Anastasia knew that a scene was about to ensue; for she was aware of all the ill humours of her dwarf. But, object as he might, she was resolved to gain her point. To be in possession of that ring she would, at that moment, have been almost induced to give in exchange the whole of her property. On the other hand, to give away that ring would have been a greater sacrifice to Pekra than to give away his life.

That ring contained in the cavity of its setting the deadliest known poison in the world. Where Pekra got it Anastasia knew—from a wild tribe of Calmuck Tartars inhabiting the fastnesses on the banks of the River Amour. It was a poison unknown to the chemists of Europe.

Pekra kept this ring in order that he might always have his life at his disposal; of late, too, he had felt a greater aversion to the world than ever. The following circumstances will explain the reason of this:—When he first went to Anastasia, and was warmly received by her, his nature, which from the disgust he occasioned in his native village was savage and sullen, became all on a sudden mild and sociable. The first kiss Anastasia gave him made him gentle and tractable; and the first three months that followed his abode under her roof passed away with him like a dream of fancy. Attached, from a feeling of gratitude, to the Baroness Leone, he had nothing to do but to serve and amuse her, and she was so kind to him that he thought he had been born only for those three months, for it was then that for the first time he thought he knew what it was to have a mother. Unfortunately experience of life coming at the same time as happiness, he soon became disenchanted, and slowly fell into a state of greater despondency and wretchedness than ever. Sometimes he conceived the notion of being loved by somebody; it was only confusedly; the material comforts by which he was surrounded seemed to him like a sort of love; but when, by keeping his eyes and ears open, he observed things as they were, the world burst upon him with a blaze of light which completely illuminated his apprehension; he awoke out of a dream; he saw what he was;—what I have already described him,—a poor, degraded being; a mere toy and plaything. Persons who are wretched require so very little to make them happy. One kind word from Anastasia, and all the malice of Pekra vanished; one act of tenderness from her, and he became reconciled with all humanity. By kind words and tender acts alone had Anastasia attached that soul to her for life; Pekra was more to her than a slave; he was as devoted, faithful, and submissive as a dog; she exercised over him a kind of magnetic power, and when he was worried and about to give vent to one of his tremendous fits of fury, a mere look from her would restore him to calmness; he would be charmed, and with a low growl would either slink out of her presence, or—which was more frequently the case—place himself humbly at her feet. Anastasia had given him happiness; Anastasia had shed joy and hope over that joyless and despairing spirit. The first day he crossed the threshold of her home, she behaved to him with a kindness which made him love her like a mother. The first day she defended him from insult and annoyance, he worshipped her as a superior being. But when the world appeared to him as it was, when he saw that he had to play a part in it as a mortal, when he perceived that he was on the same level with the rest of humanity in thoughts and passions, his feelings and ideas burst forth with the greater violence because he had not the mental power to subdue them; at one bound he overleaped the intervening distance, and his mother, his divinity, was nothing more to him than an angel, a woman. Above that filial love, that sacred worship, arose insensibly another love—a love as monstrous as himself; an impossible love—a love at the consequences of which he trembled, and yet which made him cling to life; and though he had the courage to aim at the realisation of a mad hope, and to be indebted for a new existence to the fostering of an impossible desire, hundreds of times he felt as if his heart was breaking in the dreadful conflict, and death appeared to him sweeter than one hour passed under the dominion of such an overwhelming conception. Hence it was that Pekra carried about with him the means of instantaneously depriving himself of life, if, as he feared would be the case, circumstances should occur which would render his existence for ever after an intolerable burden. To be asked, then, for his ring which contained that amulet of what he considered bliss; to be asked for it even by Anastasia, aroused all his fury; with the fire and energy of his impetuous nature and his indomitable temper, he shrieked rather than said, as he stamped the floor with his foot:

"I won't do it;—I won't do it. I say I won't—I won't. My freedom shall be at my disposal. You shan't check me, shan't curb me—no! shan't curb me! You shall miss your purpose—ha, ha! miss your purpose—not do the thing you have a mind to!" And again he chuckled savagely,—"Oh, ho! oh, ho!"

"Who has bewitched you?" exclaimed Anastasia, raising up her form indignantly, and speaking in a powerful voice, and with an air as if her bosom was nerved with manly strength, and not with the weak sensations of a female spirit. "What devil or drug has wrought upon your weakness that thus you address me? Are you mad? Or do you mean to mock me? Do you forget I am your mistress? Do you think I shall crouch beneath your wishes?" Then softening her tone, "Think not I fear Pekra," she added; "spiteful and malicious as he is." And in a winning manner she continued:—"I have faith in his discretion and prudence as much as in his devotion and attachment, and that is the reason why I ask this ring of him; and he must give it sooner or later. Then why does he not give it at once with a good grace? Pekra knows he is a being over whom"—

"Ay," quickly interrupted Pekra, suddenly changing his tone and becoming wonderfully calmed on hearing the mild, insinuating voice in which Anastasia's last words were uttered;—"Ay," he said, interrupting his mistress in a melancholy tone, "over whom you exercise a power I cannot understand."

"Nor I either," thought Anastasia. "But, verily, I can do what I please with him," she added to herself; and went on thinking:—"According to my fancy, I can give him one day the sharp hearing and the quick sight of the American Indian, and another day make him as deaf and blind as a door post and a mill stone."

Then reminded, by his own admission, of the power she possessed over him, she seemed inclined to exercise it.

This little scene was going on between them with the dwarf standing at a slight distance from Anastasia, hesitating, as if he was meditating to turn on his heel and quit the room. Anastasia, by merely keeping her eye steadily fixed upon him, worked a wondrous change: he stood as stiffly and firmly as if he were a plant rooted in the floor; she transfixed his soul; she soothed him into a drowsy enchantment wherein his spirit sat flattered and prisoned with a golden dream.

I have read in the book of a traveller who visited the United States of America that, on one occasion, he witnessed in the woods of Pennsylvania a foolish little squirrel fascinated by a rattlesnake, which lay at the bottom of a tree, with its head continually upright, its mouth wide open, and its eyes fixed upon the fluttering little innocent, which, making a doleful chirping, ran up and down the tree, leaping from branch to branch, and getting lower and lower down the bole, till in the end it hopped into the mouth of the snake, which, lubricating it with its tongue to make it fit for swallowing, gorged it whole.

So Anastasia kept her eye fixed upon Pekra with a steadfast look; dimples were on her cheeks; smiles played round her lips. From that moment Pekra was beyond his own control; he could not escape from the indescribably potent spell with which Anastasia swayed his soul. Instead of retreating he commenced, after a moment's pause, to advance towards her step by step; he began first a doleful outcry, then a piteous wailing, which any one aware of his ways would, on hearing, have immediately known was indicative of his being charmed by that beautiful young woman. He advanced a little way, then retreated again; then went on again, and then went back again; but always going on more than he went back; still Anastasia remained in the same position, keeping her eye fixed upon him with the steadfast look with which his attention was so entirely taken up, that a person accidentally coming into the chamber might have made a considerable noise, without the dwarf so much as turning about. Nearer and nearer he came always, till, at length, with a piteous cry, he leaped towards his mistress, grasping her hand, while from his throat came the most unearthly noises, and a low gurgling sound as if he was choking.

"Now you have called your wits together and are sensible, I can speak to you with no fear of your mistaking me," said Anastasia in the most charming and mellifluous tones she could command. "You know that I am here in England to search out a great secret, in which, let me tell you, Pekra, I have succeeded. And it is in your power to favour me in my success. I wish for your assistance, and trust that I may depend upon your aid. This is a cause wherein I may not,—nay, I dare not dally."

And again she transfixed his soul with a lubricious eye and a wanton smile.

"What can I do?"

"I never loved an ape or a poodle," continued

Anastasia, without heeding him, "with half the love I have for you, my little pearl. Kiss me, my dainty."

And she moistened his lips with one of her sweetest kisses, making his ribs thrill with joy at the touch of her fine lips.

"What can I do?" again asked the dwarf, this time with a cooing noise like a pigeon dove.

"Exactly as I bid you. Give me this emerald ring. Let me with my own hand remove it from your thumb. There's a good Pekra. And now sit close to me—closer still, Pekra. So—"

And she removed the ring from his thumb, immediately saying with a preternatural vehemence:

"You are my raven, on whose wings revenge comes flying to me."

Pekra started on hearing the word "revenge" fall from the lips of Anastasia, and for a moment remained, with an expression of suspicion, looking in silence and fright on his mistress.

"I am lost without my Pekra; and would not have had this night pass without his coming."

"You would not have cared, now, a straw if I were at the bottom of the sea," said the little man.

"If you were," observed Anastasia with fervour, "I should wish that I could run with the speed of a train of gunpowder beneath the world that I might blow it all up, and free you from the depths of the ocean."

"Even though you killed yourself?"

"Even though I perished in the chaos I myself created."

"I listen, but believe not what you tell me."

"I see then I must fall back to my old practices and tell you, Pekra—tell you how I love you."

"Love me?"

And the dwarf, frowning, sprang from her side, and, standing away from her, chuckled with the horrible leer and the ferocious grin of an ogre or a chimpanzee.

"Why, you little, blasphemous, misbelieving hippopotamus," said Anastasia, speaking in quick, hasty tones. "You foul-mouthed, ignorant, mischievous rat, you miserable churl, you"—speaking slower, and changing her tone to one of fondling—"sweet, little, beautiful curmudgeon, to abjure my fond affection."

"I only believe not in its existence, because it were too precious."

"And doesn't he know," continued Anastasia, chucking him under the chin, and with a lascivious look about her mouth and in her eyes—"doesn't he know that I will do him other good offices, and never more readily and speedily than if he will forget all this, and mention to no one what he has done, and if he will leave me now with his good wishes."

The dwarf made no promise, said not a word, but hearing his dismissal from the lips of his mistress rose and obediently bent his steps towards the door.

"He is gone!" said Anastasia, following him with her eyes as with a smooth and servile look in his rugged face he waddled, rather than walked, with a deliberate dignity, down the chamber; she saw the door close on his diminutive form. Then, springing from her seat and laying hold of the ring which she had placed on her finger, she exclaimed with a fiery energy:

"Now he shall swallow this like a mineral! Yes, the Viscount shall swallow it before the dawn of another day has broken along the sky. Ha! it will work with a precipitant and deadly certainty. I will not shrink. SHRINK! No! I will be resolute, since I can sink no lower."

While she was speaking thus a reverberating ring at the house door bell, accompanied by a prolonged, clattering knocking, announced the return of Viscount Mirfield in her carriage.

CHAPTER VII.

A PATH THAT WINDS BY STEALTH.

"If my fortune
Runs such a crooked byway as to wrest
My steps to ruin, yet thy learned precepts
Shall call me back and set my footings straight."
FORD.—*The Broken Heart.*

"My cloak! my mask!" cried Anastasia, hurriedly flying to a winged wardrobe and extracting from it a green domino and a black mask fringed with lace, and preparing hastily to leave the room.

Pekra was then pausing on the first landing.

The horrible impression flashed across his mind that his mistress, like the cunning devil of Bunyan, or a politic assassinating spider, went about ensnaring pleasure-loving pilgrims in her deceitful net; and that her passions were, like Goliah's stature, of a vast and majestic growth, unknown to the multitude in these feeble days of our ordinary world. The still more horrible impression flashed across his mind that, like a soldier of Cæsar, attacking the Massilian grove, she levelled to the ground everything that had for ages been counted sacred. True, Anastasia was of opinion that a woman who got a reputation for the name of virtue might sin at pleasure and never think of shame. It was the most difficult thing to discover her character because she always acted as if she thought herself observed.

The blood of Pekra mounted, not to his face, which always remained pale, but to his nose, which, hooked like the beak of a hawk, became as red as the crest of an angry turkey cock, giving him an appearance far more ludicrous than alarming.

"Ha!" he mused. "The Baroness speaks of revenge. Revenge!—on whom? On what ill-fated lover is she now about to wreak her vengeance? On whom is she about to burst in rage and agony? Ah, ha! She is a lioness who lies down among lions and nourishes whelps. I am one of the whelps she has brought up, and, like a young lion, must learn to catch the prey. I must nerve myself for a mighty and most dangerous mission, preventing Anastasia from devouring men, and thus save her from heinous sin and carking repentance hereafter. Oh! what a wild, burning tenderness for her maddens my heart!"

At this point of his soliloquy the ring at the house door bell fell on his ear.

He touched the tip of his nose significantly with his forefinger.

"The carriage returned!" he said. "And at this late hour! What can be the meaning of this?"

Slowly he continued his progress down the stairs.

In the hall he beheld a man servant as tall as one of the royal carriage servants, attired in a large, warm, outer livery coat—the footman who had been attending the carriage of the Baroness Leone.

"Ah! Mr. Mac Guffen," said he, going up to him. "It was with difficulty I saw you."

The idea of a dwarf with difficulty seeing a man of a lifeguardsman-like stature, who looked down upon such little men as Pekra as a great dog of the Mount St. Bernard mastiff breed looks down upon a diminutive Blenheim, so pleased the fancy of Mac Guffen that he smiled complacently.

"Where are you preparing to take the Baroness to at this unholy hour?" continued Pekra. "Were it not for such a galliard as you, six feet high as you are, and strong and bold too as you seem to be, our mistress might pay dearly for foolishly going out so late."

"True, Mr. Pekra. But don't excite yourself. You may leave the Baroness safely to our care."

"'Our' care! Who else then is there besides you and the coachman?"

"Viscount Mirfield, who is now in the carriage."

"Viscount Mirfield!"

Pekra pricked up his ears at the name.

"And is it any secret where you are going?"

"None, I believe. Mistress has taken it into her head to go this evening to the masked ball at Vauxhall Gardens."

"Vauxhall Gardens!—Viscount Mirfield!—my ring! my ring!—POISON!" mentally ejaculated Pekra. "My head is troubled now—troubled with no other business than the guarding of this lady. If I fail, I am cut into atoms," he further thought, and lapsed into a mysterious silence.

He turned on his heel and left the hall.

"Let the irregular north wind sweep me up and blow me into nothingness, but I will follow my mistress this very evening to Vauxhall Gardens. By the quick idea of my mind I see it all. It were idle here to question mischief. 'Tis plain!—palpable! Out of her brain with it! The object shall be removed. A woman dreaming awake! meditating revenge! So, then, we have here to deal with tombs and death-beds, funerals and tears. But it shall all end like an old woman's story. Come, to the weighty business. A tragedy must have some mirth in it, else it will never pass. I'll do it rarely—very rarely I flatter myself. Ah! it will be seen. Away! The engine for my business here is craft; craft alone is fit for the encounter."

These were the thoughts that, had they shaped themselves into words, passed through the brain of Pekra as he proceeded to his own private apartments in what architects call a "mezzanine" storey between the first and second floors of the mansion. There he set about divesting himself of his garments; for he was always decorated with excessive pomp and state as became the especial doll or baby of a fantastical lady; he wore the costume of a Highland clansman, and looked the very picture of a Middle Age servitor-herald about to step forth on the ramparts of a castle to give voice to a brazen horn to summon the lieges to their lord. Opposed to the whim of his mistress he thought to be thus attired was absurdly out of taste. So he donned the clothes of a gentleman of the present generation. And when he left the house in a few minutes after, he was as spick-and-span as if he had just come out of a band-box; or, to adopt a still more appropriate figure, out of the hands of Donald Nicoll, of Regent-street, or any other of the leading artist-tailors of the metropolis. He was dressed, too, according to the latest Parisian fashion, and was the prettiest caricature imaginable of a dashing, high-toned aristocrat, of the best blood and breed and the most unexceptionable style of fashion.

Thus he set out on a night pilgrimage through the streets of London, playing the part of Haroun Al Raschid in the "Arabian Nights' Entertainments," for he was wandering *incognito*.

Well, he *was* like Haroun Al Raschid; for he was *really* a prince.

What! Really?

Yes; of the Sons of Despair, and of all who are in the last degree of exhaustion from sickness of heart.

He could not have reached the top of the street when Anastasia came out of her house and rejoined Lord Mirfield in the carriage, which immediately drove off in the direction of Vauxhall.

CHAPTER VIII.

A SCENE A PAINTER MIGHT COVET.

"Hellish sprites
Love more the fresco of the nights."
PRIOR.—*Hans Carvel.*

And the elegant carriage of Anastasia, Baroness Leone, stopped, in an hour afterwards, before the principal entrance to Vauxhall Gardens.

The people standing outside to watch the masqueraders going in, stared again when they saw a fashionable female form, wrapped in a large silk cloak and hood, and with a mask covering nearly the whole of her face, descend from that costly equipage, and followed by another of the opposite sex of an equally distinguished air, attired in what seemed a loose riding coat, a broad-brimmed hat, and also closely masked.

Anastasia and the Viscount paid their money, received their tickets, and, threading their way along a dungeon-like passage, emerged into the blaze of the gardens, as the catgut of the fiddles of a large band stationed in the Temple of Apollo, shrieked and shook as if a whirlwind were amid the strings. But for the motley exhibition of spangles, and the fumes of bad tobacco everywhere, they might have imagined, from the smooth gravel walks and the clumps of majestic trees, with the starry eyes that looked down brightly upon them from the deep, dark vault of heaven, that they were in the country, in the midst of a lovely landscape scene.

The saying is trite but true, that "God made the country," and "man made the town." God raises stately groves; man rears superb cathedrals; yet, the religious gloom of a grove is more intense and is holier than that cast by Gothic aisles. For music God made trees; for music man made the fiddle; yet the winds of heaven whistling through foliage awaken loftier and more devotional feelings than the mellow tones of an old Cremona. No one would have ever accused God of having made Vauxhall Gardens, who had found himself buried in the recesses of those rural domains on the evening, or rather the morning in question. Seeing the rampant and prevalent intoxication, and masquerading in all conceivable forms that grossness can assume, he would have rather suspected the maker to have been God's most potent foe, the gentleman with hoofs and horns, claws and a tail. And some of that far from respectable old gentleman's people were there, in the shape of fair ladies, too; spirits of evil, to be sure; but for spirits composed somewhat too palpably of flesh and blood, with too well-painted roses, and too well-chalked lilies, and with a too passionate certainty of motion to be suspected of living upon air, like chameleons, or upon dew, like grasshoppers, or of disdaining to touch the earth, like birds of paradise. Here, paying her addresses to Momus in masquerade, was an all but naked nymph, a Hamadryad of the Alley, or a Naiad of the Fountain; there a syren, in an almost equal degree of nudity; and in other directions, aspiring to a similar amount of modesty, a goddess, a shepherdess, and a flower girl, in extremely short petticoats. Some scorned the silly sameness of scented, fringed, and furbelowed female attire, to overwhelm you with the multitude of their perfections in the kilt and socks of the Highland Laddie, or the jacket and trowsers of the Wapping sailor boy, or the Sheerness midshipman. Now the dancers mingled in confusion; now couples hurried away with velocity. Here a zany, all in white, and his companion, a debardeuse in cambric and velvet, distinguished themselves with inventive pirouettes, extraordinary swinging of the arms and convulsive distortions of the legs, every now and then separating, then falling into each other's arms, and suddenly bounding apart like a couple of India rubber balls. A masked pair, a pierrot with a lightly-dressed and light-minded shepherdess, danced soberly, languidly, with a cadenced and ceremonious march, contrasting singularly with the greater part of the multitude, who, excitable and undeniably lively, were gliding and revolving with joyousness and spirit, with a real movement to the sound of the music of a sonorous brass band. Along the avenues, where promenading was not a little impeded by quiet pedestrians being every now and then nearly upset by giddy throngs of dancers engaged in the captivating whirl of the waltz, or the equally seductive gliding of the polka, much laughter and diversion were occasioned by a gigantic Turk with bushy brows and a thick black beard, flourishing an immense scymitar and fiercely demanding a little beardless brigand in pink ribbons and a sugar-loaf hat to restore his partner, "that lovely damsel," the said "lovely damsel" being well stricken in years, and remarkable for an elongation of the chin and a peculiarly fiery nose, and whom he pronounced a favourite slave stolen from among the beauties of his harem. All was gaiety, to the disregard, perhaps, of taste and elegance, and of propriety and morals; but still it was pleasant to see so many young persons united together for their pleasure, or that of others, laughing, singing, dancing, playing, kissing, or quarrelling.

The gardens were crowded. Head arose above head, and the living mass heaved like an agitated sea. Anastasia and the Viscount could scarcely penetrate the throng. As they moved on, waves of people closed instantly behind them, like waters in a vessel's track.

Down an avenue, splendid with lamps pouring forth myriad rays, and alive with a motley, boisterous crowd, shaking their tinselled trappings, and uttering loud shouts, Anastasia and Lord Mirfield made their way, the Viscount all the while holding the Baroness on his arm, and, with his eyes fixed in passionate admiration on her face, making to her very silly and bombastic speeches.

"Charming Anastasia," said he, "your beauty has set my heart in a perfect blaze. By heaven I adore you. Do not look so scornful, though positively it makes you appear handsomer than ever."

Shameful and intriguing Anastasia insensibly enticed him into a deserted part of the gardens, that he might be better able to indulge in his love speeches, free from interruption.

"This morning, dear Anastasia," resumed the Viscount, "you will be mine, as you were years ago, in person and in heart. Do I not know it from your eyes?"

"But you forget, Viscount, that I am keeping up a deception. I am playing, as we all play, parts."

"As you please. But are you, then, dallying with me? What! so smiling? And answering, too, my sighs?"

For just then the Viscount heard the Baroness, who seemed—which he did not perceive—in an abstracted mood, heave a deep sigh.

"Oh! don't keep teasing me," said Anastasia, quickly and peevishly, for a moment quite forgetting herself; but amazed beyond expression at having been detected in so weak a mood she added, "In good fortune's name do not plague me with these eternal recollections of my past history. I would lose these memories of past frailties and subtitute memorials of true excellence. If you would speak of the past, be yourself the theme. Tell me about your naval career. I like anecdotes of wars."

LORD MIRFIELD AND THE BARONESS LEONE AT VAUXHALL GARDENS

CHAPTER IX.

SHADOWS STILL AND COLD DESCEND.

"My husband still
Runs in my mind, reads all my thoughts, and doth
Mingle himself in all my cogitations."
CARTWRIGHT.—*The Ordinary.*

Viscount Mirfield paused for a moment, and then said to his companion,

"There is nothing interesting in my career, except the last time I was in commission, when I was sent on an expedition to the Eastern Archipelago, for the purpose of extirpating piracy."

"Indeed!" exclaimed Anastasia, and she clung closer to the arm of the Viscount, and listened with interest depicted in every line of her countenance.

"Yes," replied Viscount Mirfield. "The Lanoons, or pirates inhabiting the small cluster of islands between Borneo and Magindano, each year brought out their fleets and waited for the prows bound for Singapore. With the Dyaks of Sorebas and Saharran they swept the shore, even to Celebes, and, while murdering men of all nations, and capturing women and children, rendered the communication along the coast dangerous, and prevented the cultivation of the soil near the sea-shores."

"And were they so cruel?"

"Cruel! After capturing the vessels, they reduced the crews to slavery—not of that mild description often ascribed to the Asiatics, but of that miserable character inflicted on board African slavers, for they bound their victims for months, and crowded them in the bottom of their vessels."

"Well!"

"Well, it was believed that vigorous measures might suppress in a few months all this work which had been going on for years within a few days' sail from Singapore. On my arrival in the Archipelago I found that the great nests of piracy were Magindano, Gillolo, and Sooloo; that the devastations and misery these pirates inflicted were incalculable, and yet no measures for their suppression had been adopted by any European community, Dutch, English, or Spaniard. I found that to attack them with success, they must be attacked on their own coasts with two or three steamers. A little money gained every intelligence as to where they were preparing."

"It was at Sooloo"—

"At Sooloo, where the Bulan, or chief of the whole fleet, a man of rank, resided."

"His name?"

"Sejugah."

"Ah!"

"A young man scarcely thirty years of age, active, clever, and intelligent, to whom were attached his family and his people. At a moderate computation, the number of his fighting men might have been reckoned at from five to six hundred. His captains were thirty-seven in number, stern, dark men, who had not the distinctions of uniform, each arraying himself in a manner as warlike as his means afforded, or his taste dictated—a truly rugged-looking band, wild, hirsute, and grand, with a sort of banditti-like ferocity of deportment. What was more, Sejugah was exceedingly rich. But then these Illanun chiefs, rich or poor, are incorrigible pirates. They are pirates by descent, from pride as well as taste, and they look upon the occupation as the most honourable hereditary pursuit. They are indifferent to blood, fond of plunder, despise trade, and look on their calling as the noblest occupation of chiefs and free men. Often have I heard of Sejugah showing his sword with a boast, as belonging to ancestors who were, in their day, renowned and terrible pirates, and deeming the wielding of his ancestral heir-loom as the highest of earthly existences."

"And his character?"

"He was of a haughty and reserved bearing. This fine athletic man had been, on my arrival, absent from Sooloo upwards of three years, during which he had cruised amongst the Moluccas, haunted Celebes, beat up the Straits of Macassar, and made constant visits to New Guinea and the easternmost islands, to procure the woolly-haired Papuas and sell them at high prices amongst any Malay community. During that cruise his actions equalled anything on record for military conduct and successful daring; but these brilliant acts were suggested by unworthy motives, and effected and disgraced by cruelty and all that makes war inglorious, even to the brave. It is a mistake to believe that cruelty is allied to cowardice—courage is her companion; it was at least so in the case of Sejugah; and the union begat villanies and horrors which humanity shudders to contemplate. If any man ever existed more cruel, history has not yet mentioned him in all her voluminous pages."

"And had he no natural kindness?" asked Anastasia.

"I have heard that being at one time in a deadly skirmish, he, nevertheless, found opportunity to conceal in a place of security a poor terrified English girl, whom he overtook, and who, by an imploring look, touched his heart."

"She became his wife?"

"She did."

"Did you ever see her?"

"But for a moment. She was sitting on a mat-floor with her back partially turned to me, richly and prettily dressed in a sarong suspended from her waist, and a silken scarf worn gracefully over her shoulder, just hiding, or, to speak more correctly, just exposing as much of her well-shaped person as she thought most becoming. This elaborate specimen of human beauty, I have been told, had all the tendencies of nature towards the good and beautiful; but accustomed to witness the infliction of torment, and to see life wasted more prodigally than water, she had come to have a total disregard of human life, and to look upon the tortured without pity. Sejugah felt for her great admiration, so he fed her luxuriously, dressed her splendidly, and beat her brutally."

"'Tis false," cried Anastasia furiously, her eyes flashing, and her nostrils dilating. "He doated on her, even as she doated on him—aye, even from the first moment she beheld him. When he appeared all her faculties surrendered themselves to him at once and for ever; for she had never seen nor conceived anything so glorious in the human form. She held the sun less resplendent than the manly beauty of his countenance: in the sound of his voice she recognised the tone of command to which it was impossible not to render instant and absolute obedience; and when that voice was softened to her, and with *love* to her, she would have died on the spot, by the mere effort of his will, had he bade her to do so."

"You knew her, then?"

"I know her now. But go on with your narrative."

"I confess, I somewhat dreaded an encounter with Sejugah, for he had never experienced a single defeat in a long course of years of command. It was a great contest between us. On the issue of it depended the security of the South Pacific Ocean. He was a formidable man. No treaties could bind him, no adversity could amend him; no considerations of justice or humanity could soften him, and no laws, human or divine, restrain him. But I had the good fortune to carry conquest and dismay into his heart, and check his rapid and unparalleled career of conquest."

Lord Mirfield knew not, as he spoke thus, how Anastasia's heart swelled with indescribable feelings of hatred and revenge.

They had now entered again the crowded part of the gardens. How different, now, was the countenance of Anastasia! Marked with anxiety and grief, it formed a striking contrast to the faces of the other gay young women that sparkled with hilarity and mirth.

Anastasia, Baroness Leone, did not seem to see, hear, understand, think, or talk about the masquerade. Her mind appeared altogether absorbed in the disclosures of Lord Mirfield. Listening to them intently, she moved about the gardens restlessly.

CHAPTER X.

CAREFUL ORDERING OF TEMPER AND CONDUCT.

"Thou cans't not play,
With the severity of fate; this change
Of habit, and disguise in outward view,
Hides not the secrets of thy soul within thee
From their quick piercing eyes, which dive at all times
Down to thy thoughts; in thy aspect I note
A consequence of danger."
FORD.—*The Broken Heart.*

"I remember," continued Lord Mirfield, "that it was the 7th of September, five years ago, when Sejugah with eleven ships and six hundred men sailed from Sooloo, assigning the south side of Magindano as the place of rendezvous. When he arrived there so desirous was every one who had a roving turn of sharing the dangers and the sport to which they were sure he would carry them, that he was joined by vessels of all descriptions, including armed boats and even mere canoes. This fleet, if it had had all the convenience and assistance of a king's dockyard, could not have been more magnificently equipped. It set sail on the 14th of October for the north-eastern extremity of Borneo, in order that they might plunder the country in all directions and carry off everything valuable. I made my way directly to that part of the island, and, anchoring some miles up the river, waited there for two days, prepared to give Sejugah a warm reception the moment he might attempt a landing. At daybreak, on the third day, I heard the rumour of the fleet being off the coast, and that the Bulan's object was to capture the *Bombardier*, the frigate I commanded. I therefore put myself into a complete posture of defence, with a determination neither to show backwardness nor suspicion. The morning wore on, bright and sultry; towards noon the pirates swept up the river—eighteen prahus, one following the other, decorated with flags and streamers, and firing both cannon and musketry. We immediately pushed on, our pinnace and gig had already passed up, when the report of a few musket shots told us that the pirates had been fallen in with. As we advanced, the increased firing from our boats, and the war yells of some thousand Dyaks let us know that an engagement had already commenced. On reaching the scene, I found about twenty boats jammed together, forming one confused mass; some bottom up; the bows or sterns of others only visible. Headless trunks, and heads without bodies, were floating quietly upon the blood-stained surface of the stream in all directions; parties were engaged hand to hand, spearing and krissing each other; others were trying to swim for their lives. Sejugah, his own boat sinking, was in the act of boarding the pinnace in which I was with twenty-nine others, when I met him sword in hand, overpowered and wounded him. I think he must have died almost immediately."

So excited was Lord Mirfield by his own narrative that he did not listen carefully, or he would have heard Anastasia gnashing her teeth.

"Yes," he went on, "I think Sejugah must have died instantly, being cut along the back and side, across the body from the side nearly to the back bone, a ghastly, gaping wound, besides having his arm slashed through."

Anastasia could have yelled; she only groaned.

"And what became of Sejugah afterwards?" she inquired in faint tones, as if sick at heart.

"The Illanuns, who have a horror of their dead falling into the hands of an enemy, carried the body away in a canoe, with a flag for a pall, and, at sunset, in the presence of his weeping wife, performed the last sad ceremony of committing the body to the deep, with all the honours that time and circumstances would allow."

Anastasia trembled in every limb.

They were again in a retired and dark part of the gardens, near the fountain of Neptune and his horses.

"What a terrible story!" exclaimed Anastasia. Then, with a nervous energy and wildness, she continued: "And to think that you should have conquered the Invincible! Oh! how I admire the heroic! and love heroes!—Mirfield, I love you!"

"Will you give me a proof of it?" said the Viscount.

Anastasia stopped. In a quiet manner, she turned round to the Viscount, and took off her mask leisurely; leisurely, too, she placed her veil over her bonnet; then laying both her hands slowly on the shoulders of the Viscount, she raised herself gently on tip-toe, and—KISSED him!

"Shall we retire?" said Lord Mirfield.

"By all means," replied Anastasia. She took his arm and walked on with him, clinging closely to his side, feigning well the passion of tenderness.

They retraced their steps to quit the scene of revelry.

Among natives of the city of London, Cockneys; inhabitants of the provincial towns and rural districts, visiting the metropolis, bumpkins; swell mobsmen, other Calmucs and other eccentricities, and the whole Nomadic race, who lead a careless life, that found themselves struggling with that crowd of a very miscellaneous description, was Pekra.

At one moment he was with the multitude, eager to see the dance and gazing with bewilderment at the noisy excited throng, apparently so insane, who in return stared at him with equal amazement and with galling jests. Now he was jostled by couples who were exciting every nerve to reach the boarded platform, allured thither by a brass band and young ladies in men's dresses. At another moment he was completely hidden out of sight by the upsoaring forms of the surrounding vast assemblage.

With that turbulent population he had nothing in common—nothing with those sons of Bacchus and Momus, whose pervading spirit was the love of pleasure—nothing with those daughters of Venus and Plutus, whose prevailing object was the all-powerful and engrossing pursuit of gain. He was eagerly watching his mistress, diligently concealing himself behind a crinoline or the bole of a tree, whenever she made the slightest motion of her head, for fear she should turn round and see him.

He beheld Anastasia and the Viscount pass by the supper-room.

"They are about to quit the gardens," said he. "I will anticipate them."

And, losing himself like a diver in deep water in the waves of the swaying multitude, he made his way to the gate of departure.

Just as Anastasia and the Viscount were passing by the supper-room, the Baroness caught a glimpse, unseen by her noble companion, of her host of the evening, who was accompanied by his friends, the two other leading members of the legal firm of Bother, Squeeze, and Crush. They had all come to the gardens, merely, of course, out of curiosity, being professional and married men, to see what a masquerade was like.

"Holloa!" exclaimed Bother, nudging his comrades who were hanging on to his a-kimbo arms on either side of him, "here's our gallant, brave, brilliant sailor-lord still running the career of his daring land enterprise of making love to the Spanish Baroness."

"And he seems uncommonly down in the mouth," subjoined Squeeze.

"Perhaps his fight is more desperate than victorious," suggested Crush.

"It's a habit of the Baroness," said the instructive Bother, "in engagements of this description, first to wound her victim, then take him prisoner, afterwards torture him by keeping him in durance without any enjoyment, and rarely restore him to freedom."

"In that case our gallant noble adventurer may tarnish a merry life with a little bloodshed,' remarked Squeeze.

"Oh! yes," added Crush, "it's too often a dangerous game—this love-making. Many will send a bullet through the brain when in an affair of the heart they have to sing the hymn of despair."

The eye of Anastasia, Baroness Leone, glistened like the stars of night as she listened to these speeches: to her they were like bursts of sunshine; they caused her countenance to brighten as if lit up by the blazing God of Day.

Now more than ever, she seemed to be all impatience to leave the gardens. Yet she listened attentively—earnestly, to what more might be said.

What further fell from the lips of the three friends was effectually drowned by the frantic efforts of the high priest of minims and crochets and his Levites. They were at their posts: the leader gave the signal, the orchestra burst forth into a deafening peal of music, and the shrill clamour of brass horns floated with ear-piercing strains through the crowded gardens. At the sound of the first bar, the formidable rows of dancers who had ranged themselves in order of polking, whirled away, twisting and intertwining, stamping and shaking the platform, and, with wild cries and wrenched limbs, meeting in violent contact amid shouts of laughter. Sons and daughters of toil were they, casting a veil over the morrow's labour, and giving vent to Terpsichorean festivity—drudgers of detested labour—victims of vampire machines—dwellers in sombre garrets—Magdalenes, whose smiles were deceit, and whose bread was purchased by shame—sultans of casinos and Cremorne Gardens—Jacks and Gills of Jessop's, in Catherine-street—Cyprians and syrens of the Turkish cigar divans and the oyster shops of the Haymarket. Seeking forgetfulness, they had no other object in view than to profit by the flitting yet pungent pleasures within their reach, and seize the happy moment as it flew. So the lustrous and silken Baroness, carefully masked in a black domino, attracted no attention as they passed around her, some with bravados, some with jests, some with shouts, and some with cigars.

"This is the scene for every kind of mischievous trick, which is practised here with impunity," said the Baroness, as she left the land of falsehood and delusion.

It was long past two o'clock, when she retired from the gardens in company with the Viscount, overpowered by foul odours; and, to do Lord Mirfield credit, he was quite disgusted with a scene that spread itself out before him as revolting as the orgy of Raphael and his companions in the "Peau de Chagrin" of de Balzac.

CHAPTER XI.

THE BILLOWS SURGING OVER HIM.

"Well managed knavery is but one degree
Below plain honesty. Give me villany
That's circumspect and well advised, that doth
Colour at least for goodness. If the cloak
And mantle were pull'd off from things, 'twould be
As hard to meet an honest action, as
A liberal alderman or a court nun."
CARTWRIGHT.—*The Ordinary.*

Hurried onward by Anastasia, the Viscount left the gardens. The two hastily made their way to the gate of adit. There a man of athletic frame, a footman in livery, who seemed to be waiting at the gateway for them, hastened before them to open the door of a carriage.

Had Anastasia looked behind her equipage, she would have seen, seated on the iron attached to the footboard, a man, so diminutive in size that she could not have mistaken him: she would have known again her dwarf. But, evidently bent on no ordinary errand, and acting in no ordinary way, she looked neither to the right nor the left. She could not think how any one could presume to act towards her as Pekra had done—intrude into her presence, or on her privacy.

She made her way with a determined air direct to her carriage.

There was something resolute in her attitude. Certain of success—for she knew that she was certain of always inspiring the emotion of love, and enchaining her victim—she walked on smiling, and with her eyes shining brilliantly beneath her mask.

Viscount Mirfield looked delighted; his eye gleamed—his step was light.

The faculty of forecast was inwoven with the texture of Anastasia's mental being, as the warp, not as the mere selvage to be torn away from the cloth for homely use; the Viscount, on the other hand, was one of those superficial men frequently found in large cities, who look at life as a moving panorama, careless of what has gone, indifferent to what is coming, looking neither before nor after, but vividly appreciating the present.

Aware of his weakness, and relying on her powers of craft, Anastasia was availing herself of every little minute and every trifling incident to mount her companion to the height of passionate adoration!

"Where are we going?" asked the Viscount, gaily.

"You will see," was the cold, curt reply.

The servant let down the steps.

"The colonnade in Pall Mall, stop at the corner of the Haymarket," said Anastasia to her coachman as she stepped with Lord Mirfield into the carriage; "and drive quick."

Her earnest, business-like appearance was striking. She had staked her all on the results of that evening's transactions. The time she had allotted to herself was brief, and was every moment getting still briefer; nor was she in any humour to trifle with it.

Her coachman obeyed her order.

They drove off at full speed.

The Viscount made an observation to which Anastasia replied in a dry tone and with a haughty mien; and then, with a peremptory gesture, as if enjoining silence, she sat wrapt in abstraction.

Rocked by the monotonous rolling of the carriage, deafened by the noise of the wheels upon the paved stones, immured in gloom and wrapt in silence, the Viscount mused over the manner of Anastasia;—her dry tone, haughty mien, and peremptory gesture appeared but little in harmony with the usual signs of a tender passion. Suddenly he thought to himself: "If I were the victim of a frightful machination!" But the youth and beauty of the Baroness dispelled his fears: his ideas took a different direction: the clouds became tinged with rose again; and, sinking his head upon the soft cushions, with an air of beatitude, he invoked the most smiling images. His imagination had scarcely displayed its wings, when he started up, and again addressing his companion, was about to try gestures, which have their eloquence as well as words, when the carriage stopped.

They had arrived at the colonnade. It was all but deserted.

The steps were let down. Anastasia was the first to descend. When on the pavement, she said in the same brief tone which had already sounded so harshly in the Viscount's ear:

"Descend, sir."

The Viscount did as he was bade; and Anastasia, ordering her servants to go home with her carriage, took Lord Mirfield's arm, and walked with him up the Haymarket.

Behind them walked Pekra.

His own heart, with which the Viscount was communing, bade him stay where he was. But he would as soon have taken counsel of birds that chirp on a window sill or on the top of an apple-tree.

The Haymarket had the look of keeping holiday.

The constant movement, the ceaseless gaiety carried the Viscount out of himself. The lighted shops of the pleasurable street; the trades, tradesmen, and customers; the taverns, restaurants, oyster shops, coffee-rooms, and divans; the crowds; the jest, and the laugh; the very dirt and mud; the lights shining upon houses and pavements; hats and bonnets beyond number; the pantomime and the masquerade—for both is the Haymarket;—all these things worked themselves on the mind of Lord Mirfield, and fed him without the power of satiating him.

Was it wonder of these sights which had impelled Anastasia into a night walk about that crowded street? And was she ready to shed tears in the motley Haymarket from fulness of joy at so much life?

Verily, Anastasia seemed as if she felt quite glad to get to the Haymarket; and there was something, truly, in the aspect of the street to produce that sensation. It looked laughing and light-hearted; it was gay and pleasant; withal business-like, yet without the air of business; for business was mingled so much with amusement; and then the Haymarket was full of life without being too crowded.

Even at that late hour they passed now and then a damsel with painted cheeks and in tawdry drapery, moving perfectly upon joints, not with a swim of the whole person, and with her arms but hanging on to her frame. There was no mistaking her for what she was—a plain, downright English girl—some Jenny, Sally, Annie, Peggy, Betty, Lizzy, or Molly—saucy, too, with the liberty which Britons enjoy.

"Whither are you leading me?" asked the Viscount.

Anastasia laughed, replying:

"Are you afraid?"

"Though your conduct is adapted to excite suspicion," said the Viscount, "I am not."

"And you need have no fear of violence," observed Anastasia in a soft tone, and at the same time in a tone of such frankness and with such candour in the expression of her countenance, that had the Viscount really felt any apprehension, he would have been entirely reassured.

In a minute more Anastasia and Viscount Mirfield stopped before the door of Moppy's Hotel.

Anastasia pushed a swing door open and entered.

Close at her heels followed Viscount Mirfield.

Close after him followed Pekra.

Anastasia and the Viscount ascended one flight of stairs, and, at the top of it, met on the landing-place one of the Dii Anculi, in the shape of a waiter, who ushered them, with the impetuosity of his craft, into a room, cool, lofty, and of considerable extent, with plenty of light and air. Gas, blazing in burners, cast brilliant reflections upon simple but solid furniture, walls covered with paper of a fantastic pattern, and a carpet of arabesque devices. The art of living comfortably was clearly understood in Moppy's Hotel. On a very large table in the centre of the room were placed sundry dishes of a cold collation, a tongue, a well-roasted pullet, a lobster salad, and pickled oysters. To these were soon added minced meat and marrow-bones, steaming with heat.

Of these Anastasia and the Viscount ate, after which they were supplied with delicious fruits, figs, and a pineapple. Both supper and dessert were attended and followed by Sherry and Champagne.

After supper,

"I will leave you for a few moments," said Anastasia.

And she disappeared into the adjoining room.

The Viscount, finding himself alone, collected himself, and endeavoured to arrange his ideas. He raised anew the problem, whether he ought to consider himself the victim of treachery; but the fear of a snare appeared absurd. The impulse which prompted Anastasia could be but love; her air, in truth, little resembled that of a daughter of Eve whose aim is amorous enticement, but she had, perhaps, a fashion peculiar to herself of declaring the tender passion. It was true, however, that, during supper, they had loved each other like brother and sister, and agreed most admirably.

While he was occupied with these reflections, the lock of the door stirred.

Wondering who his visitor could be, he turned quickly round, and a faint colour rose in his cheek as he gazed upon a figure that to his benighted vision seemed superhuman; for the figure that stood in his presence, though anthropomorphous, was singularly small, scarcely so high as one of the chairs. On his face pallor and emotion were visible.

"Who are you? and what brings you here?" asked the Viscount.

"Ask no questions, but heed my counsel," was the reply of Pekra. "Fly!"

"But for the cause of your advice—give me some reason."

"You are as helpless as a child—have not the power to defend yourself—fly. Thousands of miles she has swept rolling oceans over for revenge. Years has she had a longing thirst of hatred in her heart. Now the hour has struck for her to have her revenge, and she will have it, but for one wise step on your part—FLIGHT."

The Viscount rose from his chair, and, looking fixedly on the earnest and excited face of the dwarf, inquired,

"Pray, tell me who you are?"

"You would not know me were I to reveal myself. Fly! She looks so calm and still—so like peace—it is but to lull you to sleep. Beneath her face of beauty is a merciless heart. Meet her again, and you fade into livid death."

A visible shudder passed over the frame of the Viscount.

"Sir!" continued Pekra, laying hold of his hand with a fervent grasp, "Look upon yourself here as a poor, lone man—homeless, shelterless, unprotected"—

"I have done injury to no one."

"Hush! she is coming! Be afraid to cross her path again to-night. Let me see you safe. Come—this way—the stair's before you—the doors are all wide open."

The Viscount turned his head half towards the door: he stood in the middle of the room as if in the attitude to fly, doubting whether he should go or stay.

"What can she do?" he asked.

"POISON!" shrieked the dwarf.

CHAPTER XII.

THINGS PAST OUR HELP MUST BE BORNE WITH PATIENCE.

"I know not yet what grief is, yet have sought
A hundred ways for his acquaintance; with me
Prosperity has kept so close a watch,
That e'en those things that I have meant a cross,
Have that way turned a blessing."
ROWLEY.—*A New Wonder: a Woman never Vext.*

At the word "poison" the Viscount gave a violent start. He said not another syllable. All his secret misgivings flashed across his mind: he recollected all the unaccountable ways of Anastasia. In the dwarf he believed he had a good, guiding friend. He paused no more; but proceeding out of the room, descended the stairs rapidly, and the next moment was out of the hotel.

The dwarf looked at the door by which the Viscount had taken his departure; and, knowing that he was engaged on an errand of difficulty and danger, looked cautiously round the room.

"Good!" he soliloquised. "That is the best way of acting. Heaven knows how good my thought has been in saving this poor victim—this last entrapped man. She is a woman of strong nerve and fixed resolution; an unholy thing—desecrating a fair creation by acts unworthy womankind. I have made myself master of facts, and no one is safe with her—no one, when she has poison in her possession."

And Pekra walked about the room half mad; then pressed his hands wildly to his brow.

"She comes!" he murmured.

And, placing himself upright in an attitude of dignity, he, to look at her as she entered, turned round calmly and assumed a smile of perfect ease.

With a quick but easy step Anastasia re-entered the room.

She looked around surprised, for she thought herself alone. She missed the Viscount; and, as to Pekra, she did not for a moment see him.

When she did,

"You here!" she cried, her eyes flashing fire, and her thin, pinky nostrils dilating from the excessive indignation that was breathed from her passion-charged heart.

Her face indicated intense emotion; her feverishly expressive eyes wandered about, now at the door by which she had entered the room, now at the portal leading to the staircase, and then rested in wild anxiety on Pekra's face. Her countenance said as plainly as face could say—"What does all this mean? And if I am right in my conjecture, what does your interference signify?"

Mastering her emotion she went up quietly to Pekra, and, stretching out her hand to welcome him, said, smiling blandly:

"How is it that my darling Pekra has left his home to come here? and how knew my little dainty that his mistress was in the abode of gaiety?"

"That I knew it my presence is proof enough. How I knew it is a secret I shall keep to myself."

"Naughty Pekra! to be so pert! And—and—the gentleman who was here this moment. He has not"—

"Yes, he has"—

"What?"

"Gone!"

"From what motive?"

"Ah! ha!—oh! ho! *Not to see you again.* What motive, eh? Ask your own heart—you have one. Ask it, and it will answer for the motive—*not to see you again*"—

"What mean you by addressing me in this strain? To mock me? To treat me with indifference? To laugh at me? Answer me plainly, little tadpole—why went Lord Mirfield?"

"Because I told him."

Was there any rush of blood to the heart of Anastasia? Any unusual beating of her bosom? No! there was not even a change in the calm expression of her eye. If there was one faculty more than another strongly developed in Anastasia, it was the power of dissembling; but who shall say that that power is not one of the prime characteristics of the whole female sex? For if dissembling be not as inseparable from women as heat from fire, weight from mud, moisture from water, thinness from air, it is, at any rate, quite as common as spots upon pigeons, moles upon skins, caterpillars upon fruit, and cobwebs upon windows. With firmness, even with coldness of voice, Anastasia said:

"Pekra, my mind is made up. I must see the Viscount this night again; and I must see him instantly. You know where he has gone. Seek him. Bring him back."

The dwarf laughed.

"I can bear this no longer, Pekra; and I will not," said Anastasia; and her face, as she spake thus, was harsh, cold, and stony in expression. She continued in a determined manner, almost fiercely: "Do as I bid you. Go, and bring back the Viscount."

Pekra, according to his custom, said not a word in reply. He turned on his heel, and, obeying the injunction of his mistress in tacit submission, walked demurely out of the room.

Any one would have been amazed at his manner, after his scene with Lord Mirfield.

But, on leaving the hotel, he bent his steps, not towards Charles-street, Berkeley-square, but directly to Arlington-street; reaching Anastasia's house, he entered it, and retired to his private apartments.

As the last sound of Pekra's footstep struck upon the ear, Anastasia said:

"I have an all-engrossing idea at heart which banishes the reflection of other things. I have set my purpose before me, and will stride over all till it is attained."

Then she waited patiently for the return of Pekra and Viscount Mirfield.

She waited till her patience was exhausted. Reconciled at length to act as circumstances forced her, she cast from her memory the few past hours as if they had never struck, and the deeds and thoughts that had accompanied them as if they had never occurred and existed. But nothing seemed to her as if it was a phantasmagoria—nothing as if it had been all a dream: she saw things still in the same light; though their accomplishment was now another thing.

"Events like those of the past evening," she thought, "cannot slip away like a vision: they will burst forth, and speedily too, in another form still more startling. But now there is one thing to be done—to sleep and wait. Pekra is the cause of much trouble to me. I am sorely perplexed why the little monster has imposed upon himself this onerous charge. Well, well! No matter! I will see Viscount Mirfield to-morrow. I will write to him—I will appoint an assignation—here—at the same hour—or earlier—at midnight. Will he come? Come! Is it madness to hope that? What! When he expects that happiness will be the certain result of our interview?"

And she laughed a credulous but jeering laugh.

With these and such wearying thoughts in her brain, but with as much calmness of demeanour as if nothing obstructive to her views had happened—nay, as cheerful as she had been seen of late, perhaps more so, for there was a gleam of hope in her eyes to which they had long been a stranger—she rose and left the hotel. She felt no compunctious visitings of conscience with respect to the imprudences she had been guilty of that night as she proceeded homewards, all the way under the influence of one governing thought:

"Mirfield is charmed with me, and thinks that I am fascinated with him. If I ask him to meet me again to-morrow, he will—and then"——

A smile of satisfaction passed over her countenance.

CHAPTER XIII.

IMPOSSIBLE TO DISCHARGE THE SUM DUE.

"Every good admits
Degrees; but this being so good, it cannot:
For he is no friend is not superlative.
Indulgent parents, brethren, kindred, ties
By the natural flow of blood, alliances,
And what you can imagine, is too light
To weigh with name of friend: they execute
At best but what a nature prompts them to;
Are often less than friends, when they remain
Our kinsmen still: but friend is never lost."
SHIRLEY.—*The Maid's Revenge.*

When Pekra, instead of going in search of Viscount Mirfield, went straight to Anastasia's, and retired to his private apartments, he found himself in a small room immediately beneath the bedchamber of his mistress.

It was a room that had not much the appearance of being a portion of such a palatial residence as the mansion of Anastasia; on the contrary, it had more the look of a dungeon of a mediæval castle, or a cell in a modern prison.

The whole furniture consisted of a bed, a chest of drawers, a board on which a few books were ranged in a row, a copper lavatory fixed to the wall, a couple of chairs, a mirror nailed up in the darkest corner, and, lastly, and apparently principally, a holy image—a sort of a Roman Catholic's sacred figure of the Virgin, before which burnt an oil lamp, suspended by a small silver chain.

THAT IMAGE WAS THE IMAGE OF ANASTASIA!

Curious was it to observe the care that Pekra took of his apartment: he never allowed anything to be out of its place, and he wiped away every stain of dirt and every speck of dust. He thought as much of his little room as a young man of the girl he is in love with; and whenever he went out of it he locked it, and kept the key in his pocket, as if he was jealous of any one getting into it during his absence. From the day when Anastasia had made him a present of it, and had said to him, "This is your own room, Pekra," he had never allowed any one to enter it. He had arranged everything with his own hands according to his own particular fancy; and, whenever he had a leisure moment to himself, he would go and shelter there as in a sanctuary.

The passionate affection he cherished for Anastasia—a love more mysterious than the tomb, and which he kept secretly shut up within the inmost recesses of his bosom—gained redoubled strength and energy every time that her conduct caused him fresh shame and horror.

"This is hell I feel within me," he said to himself on his way that night from the Haymarket—and it was a speech he had often made to himself before. "It is a hell which prevents me from dying, and which condemns me to an everlasting burning."

And yet, though he thought thus, with what happiness he followed that road to which he saw no end, and even no horizon to mark out a boundary!

Every fresh dark deed committed by Anastasia convinced him more and more of one thing—that she loved nothing—nay, that she hated everything in the world. In his ambition to be loved by her he passed the whole of his days and nights in watching her: with an untiring vigilance he spied out her every step and proceeding: he kept his eye fixed on her every look and movement. In order to watch over and protect her the more, he made himself a greater puppet and plaything for her than ever. His sorrows and unhappiness he reserved for his solitary moments when he was in his chamber at night. During the day he was very merry and happy, and, giving way to a sociable humour, would, in his communicative disposition, answer those who spoke to him with sportive sallies and pungent repartees. Such had been his conduct ever since his love had sprung up for Anastasia; and when she saw this change in his conduct she was pleased—rejoiced; for when she first had him she thought him so low-spirited and moody, she was actually afraid of his dying of melancholy and hypochondria; and, as she said herself, she was "passionately fond of her dwarf."

Half an hour after Pekra's return to Arlington-street, Anastasia reached her home.

On getting into her chamber she was about to summon Pekra into her presence; but before ringing the bell, she ensconced herself comfortably in a soft arm-chair, and sat there languidly, and evidently musing. The few moments that she paused before touching the bell-rope, a vision passed before her, the incidents of which will perhaps sustain the attention of the reader, and which will certainly explain to him sufficiently and satisfactorily the whole of Anastasia's partiality for Pekra.

And this was the vision that passed before the mind's eye of Anastasia.

She looked back in fancy two years—to the summer of 1848, when she was staying on a visit at a Russian château in the neighbourhood of Moscow. A never-to-be-forgotten scene rolled itself out before her in its every little circumstance.

She saw herself and a party of Russian ladies and gentlemen—princes and princesses—enjoying themselves on a silver lake in the depth of a tranquil wood. In the far distance was a faint hum of voices chanting a popular gipsy song, that had a semi-barbaric, yet harmonious effect. The chorus at the end of each stanza took possession of her soul in spite of herself, and lifted her up into the realms of the sublime. Night was descending: here and there the twilight was casting its dim shadows over the stilly landscape: the evening was fine; the sky was clear; the moon was just rising; the stars were peeping out by two's and three's; the misty vapours crept and curled before a gentle, balmy breeze; three pleasure-boats floated on that silver lake; their white sails bulged with a graceful curve impelled the gilded skiffs that seemed, like gigantic seabirds, to be skimming the surface of the water with their snowy wings. The party, rejoicing in laughter and song, insensibly yielded to the influence of the pacific evening. Out of the silence suddenly arose the voice of a Russian—that of the Prince, the host of Anastasia, saying to her:—

THE BARONESS AND THE VISCOUNT AT MOPPY'S HOTEL.

"Is it not time for us to return home? 'Tis past the fisherman's hour. Look yonder!—at the back of us! There are the torches of the men coming this way."

Anastasia heard him not. Her cheek was resting on her palm: her bright black eyes were raised to heaven; and, as she gazed upwards, she looked as if she was wishing to follow with her thoughts the fleeting, floating clouds. Far away was her soul: no longer seemed she an inhabitant of the earth. Nature had drawn her into a dream of external life. Unconsciously she was laying bare to the outer and visible world a page of her inner and hidden life.

A handsome young Englishman of the party, Sebastian Leonard, never took his eyes off her, as she sat wrapt, as if she was chilly, in the Russian Prince's cloak: he looked at her as if she was too pretty for him to keep his eyes off her; he seemed to peer into her countenance, as if he was trying to get at her thoughts; then he turned away his head sadly, as if he was downhearted at not having been able to succeed.

"What shall I offer you for your thoughts?" asked the Russian Prince, with a smile.

"Excuse me," said Anastasia, starting out of her reverie, and sorry at being caught in so absent a mood; "but for the moment I really know not where I am. What were you saying?"

"That it is time for us to return home."

"Well, so it is. But you are our cicerone, and we place ourselves under your orders."

Thereupon the Prince gave directions to the men in charge of the boats to veer about.

The man at the helm of the boat in which were Anastasia, the Prince and Princess and Sebastian Leonard, ordered the sail to be shifted. As the attempt was made to do this the rope caught in the thwarts. The voice of the man at the helm rose loud and strong:—

"Quick—quick; let go the rope, or she'll capsize. Lower the sail."

The wind here caught the sail, which flapped violently in the breeze.

"Quick! quick!" again shouted the helmsman, in a louder and stronger voice than before. "Down with the sail at once, or we're over. God have mercy upon us!"

The ladies screamed.

"We are going over!" they cried and shrieked again. Then their voices rose once more in accents of indescribable fear, as they shrieked: "Save us, oh! save us! We shall all be drowned."

It was too late to save them.

The wind caught the sail just as the boat was veering. The skiff heeled over: another puff of wind came, forcing her over still more on her left side: the water rushed over the gunwale; and they were seen sinking rapidly.

It was a trying and a fearful moment.

From the other two boats that were following in her wake, and had been more fortunate in getting about, came a loud scream of anguish and terror.

All on board strained their eyes in search of the boat that was before them. Where it had been floating there was now but vacant space.

All was a blank.

Nothing again appeared on the smooth surface.

At this point of her vision Anastasia shuddered and turned deadly pale; the perspiration stood cold and clammy on her brow.

Cries arose of "Who can swim?" "Who can save them?" "Will no one try?"

No one answered.

They pulled and tugged at their oars with might and main: they puffed and strained their muscles in trying to hasten to the spot. They hurried to it without the loss of a moment's time. But though no time was lost, nothing was done.

At this instant the helmsman of the sunken boat showed his head above the surface of the lake, and caught hold of the side of one of the boats. He had something in his hand: it was a woman, whom he was holding up by the hair of her head.

"Here," said he, in his native tongue, "is the *barinia*"—by which he was supposed to mean a lady of high rank, the Baroness Leone.

"Thank God for this!" was the general exclamation. "We shall now find the others."

But it was not Anastasia.

It was the Princess, the wife of the host.

Anastasia was nowhere to be found.

Something at this moment was heard to fall into the water from the other boat. No notice was taken of it; for the splash was so slight, it was thought to be nothing more than a scull or an oar at the most which had fallen overboard.

Again on the surface of the lake appeared the helmsman of the sunken boat. He had hold this time of the Prince, who had twice caught him by the leg.

Then it was Sebastian Leonard's turn to be saved. He was senseless.

Three others were also saved. They were the men who had had care of the boat. They had been saved by an oar which had been shoved off to them.

But Anastasia could not be found! Nowhere—nowhere!

Now the whole sky became enveloped in clouds. Black as pitch was the night. It seemed as if the happy twinkling stars had been all on a sudden covered with a gloomy funereal pall. Bright torches gleaming in the distance were showering their light across the lake, while the night fishermen were singing merrily.

Anastasia could nowhere be found.

Suddenly they thought they heard a noise a short distance off.

They listened.

Sh!

Yes.

There *was* a noise.

It was a hard drawing of the breath—that peculiar panting which is made by a retriever, or any other large water-dog when swimming.

"Out with the oars! Lay to! Let us row to it!"

Such was the general exclamation.

And the men rowed in the direction of the noise.

Louder grew the noise; and distinctly was heard the splashing of the water, stricken quickly, evidently, by the palm or paw; and the quick succession of blows was every moment growing quicker and quicker, as if the strength of the swimmer was being exhausted. Another second! and they might arrive too late!

"Who is it? Is it the Baroness Leone?"

Such was the eager, anxious, and universal cry.

No answer.

But at that moment something monstrous and deformed was seen floating on the water—an orbicular, massive head, with eyes that gleamed like a firefly's.

This thing was holding in his mouth something white.

"'Tis the Newfoundland dog belonging to the castle!" exclaimed the Prince. "He is holding in his maw the Baroness by her dress. She is saved! she is saved! Pray God she is only still alive!"

"'Tis not a dog, gentlemen," exclaimed a loud, manly voice—the voice of Sebastian Leonard—who, in his usual strain, went on: "In your eyes 'tis something less than man; but in the eyes of God 'tis perhaps something more. With you 'tis a puppet; with God, a being predestined to eternity: and he has saved the Baroness Leone. 'Tis the dwarf, Pekra."

By the time Sebastian Leonard had finished this speech Anastasia was in the boat, and Pekra was lying at her feet breathless, exhausted, half dead. He listened not: he heard nothing that was said: he looked not around: he saw nothing but his mistress, for whose return to life he was anxiously watching.

Anastasia awoke out of this vision with a sigh; and she mused as follows:—

"Since that terrible evening when Pekra, in the presence of all, showed his courage and his love for me by risking his life to save mine, a great change has been operated in him. He has ever since forgotten what he is—my servant—my slave. He has placed himself on an equality with me. He has measured himself by a rule and standard of his own making—the deathless benefit he has conferred on me—the boon of life. He has the audacity to dream of another soul being his; and the thought drives him to the very verge of madness—the extremes of bliss and joy. Well—well! I suppose I must forgive him all the ill he does me for all the good he has done me."

She rose, and, placing herself before the ebony-framed glass case, began writing.

While she was writing Pekra was throwing himself on his knees before her image—which we have seen he revered as the image of a sacred being. In tones of the utmost gratitude and of fervent piety, he cried out:

"Thanks to you, oh, Lord! Thanks to you, that you have conferred so great a boon upon me as to make me the humble instrument of saving her this night from a most heinous crime. The effulgence of your heaven is shedding its blazing light into this room, and illuminating everything about me. 'Tis a blessed night—the brightest, the best, the most beautiful."

Then he arose from his knees, and lay down on his bed to court sleep.

Anastasia went on writing.

CHAPTER XIV.

MORE SPECKS ON THE VERGE OF THE HORIZON.

"The curse of human frailty,
Adding to our afflictions, makes us know
What's good; and yet our violent passions force us
To follow what is ill."
MASSINGER.—*The Great Duke of Florence.*

As Anastasia wrote, a smile occasionally passed over her lips, and a glance came into her eyes; that smile was coquettish and that glance, half-doubting, half-arch; they seemed emanations of a mind that can admit light thoughts in the midst of important emprise: they appeared to be the results only of that state of mind which attends those who have dashed into enterprise—who, to a certain point, have succeeded, whilst the event that must crown the whole is yet suspended—and who, in striving to grasp at the object at which they aim, have passed beyond a gulf between them and the heaven they long after—who cannot retreat—and who, having proceeded a considerable distance in their perilous career, are propelled by an irresistible force within to go on still further. Any observer, even the least keen, would have pronounced this lightness in Anastasia the prevailing character to which her mind was inclined by its original bias; and the deeper passions that darkened her brow, the artificial result of misdeeds. Hers was, indeed, a red and threatening evening, that had resulted, naturally but not indispensably, from a laughing morning and a glowing noon.

While she is writing we will look over her shoulder.

Ah! she keeps a diary, then; for the book that she opens, and in which she is preparing to write, is a manuscript volume, in which are noted down the events of each day of her life in her own hand. She has had every moment of the past eventful Monday and of the preceding four-and-twenty hours occupied; accordingly, she must be now about to record, in addition to the incidents of the day just passed, with which we are already acquainted, those of the day before—the Sunday.

What she puts down we must know.

Reader, keep me company, then. Quietly we will enter her chamber together. Here!—Here! We will place ourselves on this spot. Here we will listen to her; for every now and then she makes observations. When she writes we will step close to her side and look over her private journal.

Hush! She is speaking even now!

She is holding her confidential self-communications.

First a slight silver-toned laugh rings through the room; then her voice is heard—

"Ha! ha!—Ha! ha!" she laughs; and then she says: "Lord Mirfield thinks I love him. Oh! how vain those men are to be sure, to think we women entertain an affection for them, when, in nineteen cases out of twenty, we have not so much liking for them as for a favourite ape or lapdog. Ha! ha! ha!—Heigho! There *is* a man, though—and a superb young fellow he is—whom I picture to myself as eminently fitted to create, in *my* bosom, love—such a love as will justify itself. Yes, Bruce St. Aubyn—beautiful Bruce!—whom I saw yesterday for the first time. *You* realise to me the perfection of your sex. You are fitted to be the mate of my spirit. Yes; he shall come to be my chosen, my delight: he shall win and keep my heart. Keep it? Not quite. For a certain time, at least, he shall be the one in whose presence I shall find content, whose love shall be the richest flower in the chaplet of my life, and the dearest hope that shall reconcile me to—to—ha! ha!—this *world of troubles*—I think that's the proper phrase."

And taking up her pen gaily, she set about writing rapidly.

"The day before yesterday I arrived from Boulogne, in company with Sebastian Leonard, at that quaint-looking, demi-cinque port and limb of Dover—Folkestone.

"What a brilliant May morning it was! Spring seemed to me as personified by poets and painters —with her sunny brows crowned with garlands, her beaming eyes beckoning with joy, and her fresh, fair form glowing with fay-like grace. As Sebastian Leonard observed to me, the morning, with its soft sky, limpid waters, and rarefied atmosphere, seemed to have dawned expressly in revelry and laughter to welcome us back to this glorious shore of old Albion.

"It was an early hour as we drew up alongside the quay. The steamer was pouring from its deck its swarms of passengers, when the bells of Folkestone Church, having just chimed the half hour after ten, had begun pealing merrily for Divine service. It could not be said, as it has been so often observed, that the hallowed morning was gliding away in the current of time the same as on other days—being so perfectly like its fellows that human reason could not conceive, or human senses discern, any difference; for, independently of that external sign which made it known as Sunday, the pealing of the church bells, the whole scene, which, like a picture by Wilson, was glorious in colouring, varied in aspect, and instinct with the spirit of peace, was pervaded by all that stillness of sacred joy which to me—though it must be but fancy—has always seemed peculiar to Sabbaths.

"No signs of human labour were visible in the quiet landscape, except among a group of trees, whence occasionally, as from a furnace or an altar, ascended smoke from tenders, now stationary, and now flying along the rattling iron roads, fuming to the skies, and guided cleverly by swart, begrimed men, who, riding on the wings of steam, looked almost as black as the mineral heaped up about them.

"The Government officials, with whom Folkestone abounds—the Custom-house officers—were attending, with their usual punctuality, the arrival of those whom the billows and the blast, steam and sail, had flung on the civilised and cherished coast of England; with pomp and ceremony they were examining the baggage, in their laudable anxiety that no untaxed article should escape its contribution to the revenue, when a group of four—a family party of father and mother, son and daughter—the Earl and Countess of Milsington, their future son-in-law, the Marquis of Madcham, and their only daughter, Lady Rosalie St. Aubyn, came sailing grandly along the gravel walk, the elder couple, holding their heads in the air with Olympian grandeur, looking as awful as Jove and Juno, and the younger pair, as merry as Fauns, talking and laughing with exceeding gaiety.

"Well, that Lady Rosalie St. Aubyn is, certainly, a fair bud of promise, a maiden brilliant as the Houri of a Mussulman. Poetry is in her motion, music in the fall of her footstep.

"She was passing, as light as the spray of the ocean, by the bench on which I was seated, when Sebastian Leonard stepped forward to greet her, and entered into familiar conversation with her, while in a similarly cordial manner he conversed with the other members of the family, his demeanour towards the whole party being deferentially polite and unobtrusive. After remaining in conversation with them for a few minutes, he rejoined me.

"'Do you know, Sebastian,' said I to him, 'that all the while you were talking to that beautiful girl, I could not take my eyes off her. I admired her so much for her calm smile and placid manner.'

"'And her smile and manner,' he replied, 'give assurance of a mind at ease, and of kindness and mildness not contradicted by her humane and charitable character.'

"'Yet I question,' I continued, 'if Lady Rosalie St. Aubyn will possess happiness long.'

"'Eh?' he exclaimed.

"'Being the daughter of the Earl of Milsington,' said I.

"'You know the family, then?' he observed.

"'I am here in England, among other things,' I replied, 'to give the Earl of Milsington warning of his ways. But he will not heed me. His lust of rank and riches will bring misery to himself and family.'

"'You speak as if some mystery hangs about this peer.'

"'So there does.'

"'Well, what is it?'

"'Did I ever tell living soul what I know?'

"'Certainly,' he replied, 'I have known you now for three years; and, though I have been your constant companion during nearly the whole of that time, I must bear testimony to your bosom being a perfect hiding-place of secrets.'

"Rightly he spoke thus.

"He then moved towards the noble group which was now standing before the door of the Custom-house—the Earl directing the movements of a servant."

Here Anastasia laid down her pen, and, leaving off writing, said to herself as follows:

"A marvellous being that Sebastian Leonard! And a mystery to me—to every one. Who is he? What is he? I know not, beyond his bearing the name and superscription of Sebastian Leonard. Yet I have been his intimate friend, his almost inseparable companion, for three long years. Strange! wondrously strange! that this man, gifted with everything that should make him happy—an Antinous in face, an Apollo in form, a Scaliger in might and majesty of mind and extent of learning, an Admirable Crichton in elegant accomplishments; enjoying the robustest health; as young and blooming as the Adonis of the ancients; with ample means at his command (it matters not how it comes to him, he has great wealth); esteemed, admired, courted, envied—should have a soul gay but in sarcasms, revealing what dark thoughts agitate his breast silent ever as to his feelings; and, while affecting in all his speeches an invariable calmness and a cold indifference, should—as is clear to me—to everybody—when such a delight to others, be, in the rush and excitement of gaiety, a torment to himself, concealing with his hand the burning heart within, like Vathek in the Hall of Eblis. From what can it originate? Oh! what a marvel and what a mystery is Sebastian Leonard!"

Then, taking up her pen, Anastasia went on writing again.

"I watched the retiring form of Sebastian Leonard, and saw him shake hands with a young man whom I did not observe join the group, but who now formed the fifth person of the noble party. He was a tall, and slightly, but elegantly formed youth, about twenty years of age, with a fair complexion, and with regular features, that made him seem yet younger. In his countenance of almost feminine softness, his mother's beauty was still to be seen. But with the softness of his expression spirit was blended. From under a foraging cap a quantity of soft curling flaxen hair fell all over his brow and cheek. I fixed my eyes upon him with an expression of interest, more than of curiosity; but, perhaps, there never was a woman who did not try to get a look—and, when she got it, looked long too—at the Honourable Bruce St. Aubyn.

"After a few observations to him and the other members of the Milsington family, Sebastian Leonard returned to me, observing, as he did so:—

"'The person, manners, and accomplishments of Bruce St. Aubyn are very splendid. He tells me he has come home, wearied of a soldier's life, and means, for the future, to relinquish the profession of arms.'"

"'That youth a soldier!' I exclaimed, with amazement. 'He seems bound to home and gentle dreams; looks all tenderness and sensibility.'

"'You are right,' said Sebastian Leonard. 'Bruce St. Aubyn is a very gentle youth, very peaceful and very unoffending; yet has he sat round flickering watchfires at night, talking of blood, and shared the soldier's hurried meal on fields of battle. A noble race, struggling to regain their freedom, allured his soul to the wild excitement of war. You like personal adventures. I will tell you an episode in the life of Bruce St. Aubyn:—One day, about a year ago, a relative of the family called. He was about to depart to Austria, charged with an official mission of importance to the court of Vienna. From the Eternal City, Mazzini was stirring his countrymen to achieve their independence on the plains of Lombardy. In the valleys of the Magyar Kossuth was thundering as the Washington of Hungary. At the mention of the mission Bruce's energies were roused. He spoke of the cause of the Italians and the Hungarians with unusual interest. 'I know you passionately admire liberty,' said the friend of the family; 'and I know,' he added, with a smile, 'how useless it would be for me to ask you to come with me.' 'To the land of the despot?' said Bruce, with quivering lip. Then his eye glistened. 'I will accompany you to the South of Europe,' said he, 'and join either Mazzini or Kossuth.' The project took possession of his mind. His parents, who thought him a calm, inert youth, were surprised. He accompanied his friend. During his journey he made up his mind to join the Hungarians. Once, while discussing, with flashing eye and all the strength of an energetic character, the achievements of Kossuth, he exclaimed:—'Somewhere, in the regions of the Magyar, I hope to become a man, and redeem myself in the thoughts of my family.' He did. He was soon known among the Hungarians as a youth who would freely have given his heart's blood for their cause; a brave and dauntless warrior, hailing with pleasurable excitement the anticipated fight of the morrow, and reckless of captivity or death. So, wreathed with laurel, he was passing along the road to glory. In mid career he was checked by his brave leader being defeated by treachery. Thereupon he doffed his shako and sheathed his sword. And here he is, you perceive, in England again, ready to return to a life of roses, and rest on a pillow of down.'

"During this narrative I rested my glance, at repeated intervals, on Bruce St. Aubyn, each time with a softer glance, each time with increasing admiration. I thought him very handsome—very interesting. All the while he was talking to his sister with a half smile on his face and a quiet intentness of expression, indicating that theirs was the love that brought joy—the love of brother and sister, which, when pure and holy, is an unchecked dream of happiness, and makes kindred a blessing.

"I watched him till the family of the Milsingtons moved from before the door of the Customhouse; as they were walking across the green sward, said Sebastian Leonard to me:

"'What a queer romance could be made of us all, Anastasia. The friends belonging to the noble family now passing under the doorway of the Marine Hotel to wait there for the next railway train to London would form excellent characters. And what an exquisite love story Madeleine's and mine would be! No occasion to draw on the imagination.'

"'A tale told before, Sebastian.'

"'True. The repetition of Dr. Mackay's poem of "the Salamandrine"—the love of a dull mortal for a female spirit of fire. And with all her fire and sublimity and genius, Madeleine is the gentlest, kindest, simplest, and best of good-natured and affectionate creatures. I have loved her for two years and a half, each month with increasing affection; and,' he added, his eyes sparkling brilliantly, 'I think of our meeting again with a tenderer interest than you can imagine.'

"'You pay such a deferential respect to Madeleine, I do not at all wonder at her loving you so,' said I.

"'It is but the reciprocation of a most ardent affection,' he replied. 'My love for her is my piety. I worship her. And does she not deserve my admiration? What worth! What an affectionate heart, and what intellectual superiority! No one knows how I love her—no one can know the dreadful feelings I should endure if —But, pshaw! Is it not folly to think that we shall ever cease to love each other?'

"I rose.

"'Let us leave this,' I said.

"The well-kept promenade had now lapsed into quiet solitude. We left it; on arriving on the lawn before the hotel, Sebastian Leonard and I mutually separated, both refraining from walking much in public on account of the remarks which might be made by people of the world.

"Sebastian Leonard proceeded towards the pavilion; I, tempted by the beautiful fine day and the fresh sea breeze, towards the beach; reaching which, I pursued my walk along the shining white sands that glittered at my feet in the sunbeams, ever and anon gazing on the calm beauty of the sea, and listening to the hollow murmuring of the waves. In this manner I walked on with loitering steps, with a silent tongue, but a thoughtful mind."

CHAPTER XV.

A TEMPEST OF COMMOTION DISQUIETING THE CALMS OF COMPOSURE.

"My griefs not only pain me
As a lingering disease,
But, finding no redress, ferment and rage
Not less than wounds unmedicable
Rankle, fester, and gangrene
To black mortification.
Thoughts, my tormentors, armed with deadly stings,
Mangle my apprehension's tenderest parts;
Exasperate, exulcerate, and raise
Dim inflammation, which no cooling herb
Or medicinal liquor can assuage,
Nor breath of vernal air from sunny Alp."

MILTON.—*Samson Agonistes.*

Anastasia paused for a moment, and then resumed writing her diary:—

"The morning, with its fresh tints, had worn away; the glowing heat of noonday had faded, and a glorious afternoon sun shone down on Folkestone and its neighbourhood.

"Still was I wandering on the shingles of the beach, still inhaling the invigorating breezes of the ocean.

"Suddenly interrupted by slippery and weed-covered rocks, I left the deep and deserted sands of the sea-shore, and, ascending the beautiful heights that overhung the beach, found myself in a large field, the luxuriant grass of which seemed to be seldom trodden. Beneath the open sky I made my way over an easily accessible, though rarely-traversed path, that wound in a serpentine course over the green hills and through the undulating pastures, the sun sporting through the branches of the lofty trees, gleaming on their silver trunks, and striking with enlivening beams on the ground that was clothed with the brightest verdure.

"Charmed with the aspect of nature, and enjoying my walk, I had descended to the bottom of a hill, and was ascending the opposite side, when I came all on a sudden face to face with the young man whom I had seen and admired so much a few hours back on the quay.

"It was, indeed, Bruce St. Aubyn. He stopped immediately, and looked at me, and I could tell that his blood was running hot and then cold, as for several seconds he stood rooted to the spot, as incapable of moving as if his feet had incorporated with the sward. He was also unable to take his eyes off me, on whom he gazed in silence and admiration. The smile with which I met his wrapt and wondering gaze evidently caused his heart to become agitated by intense emotion, and to beat quickly, for his cheek and brow, burning, as if heated by fire, were flushed with deep crimson.

"Without tarrying, I walked on leisurely. Turning round I beheld Bruce St. Aubyn looking after me. What his feelings were I can well imagine. As for me, my breast heaved, the rapid palpitation of my heart told me that, though not given to loving at first sight, I had, notwithstanding, become desperately enamoured of that beautiful youth with the tresses of flaxen hue, and the languishing eyes that glowed with the soul of love.

"Reaching the pavilion, I retired to my room, where, seating myself near the open window, and looking on the sea, I thought of Bruce St. Aubyn, and of what I had heard from Sebastian Leonard of his amiable qualities."

Here Anastasia said to herself:—

"Well, true; I admire exceedingly that young man whom I met the day before yesterday on the cliffs at Folkestone; from his look and manner I can tell he admires me to an inexpressible degree. How his eyes beamed with delight, and his whole frame trembled as he gazed at me! Well, yes; I admire him, too: admire him intensely, and yet certainly not so intensely as he admires me. What's to be done, then? Why, I, who have charmed so many, have nought to do but to charm him. I must act so as to make him receive—ha! ha!—what Sebastian Leonard would call in his grandiloquent strain 'the foul dross of my exacting passion' in exchange for 'the pure gold,' as he would say, 'of Selina Elphinstone's steadfast love.' Ah! well-a-day! I must not torture Bruce St. Aubyn—no. Nor will I trifle with his feelings. I must, notwithstanding, twine his feelings around me, and make his soul tremble and give way at every beck and nod of mine. I must prove to him the vast power I can obtain over the heart of man. Yes, I must do that—for that is always a triumph for a woman."

Here Anastasia again laughed, and then continued gravely:—

"If what Sebastian tells me of this youth is true, the affection of a heart like his is a precious and costly thing. Never, then, must he give to any one but myself his devotion and affections. He SHALL be mine."

A tranquil smile of proud satisfaction passed over her beautiful features.

"How shall I begin to set about my purpose?" she resumed. "Ha! Sebastian told me that he was to have come to town with Bruce St. Aubyn early yesterday morning. They must then have arrived in London. I shall write to Sebastian to bring Bruce St. Aubyn to me this day, and shall make to Sebastian a full and unreserved disclosure of my whole feelings. He can then have no excuse for not complying with my desire."

She took from a drawer in the glass-case a sheet of letter paper, which she immediately commenced covering with writing.

"Dear Sebastian," she wrote, "when I saw you at Folkestone the day before yesterday, I told you that my intention was to go that afternoon by the rail as far as Paddock-wood, and take the train again to Maidstone; then drive across the country to Milsington, where Madeleine Esther is staying, and go to town with her early on the morrow. I further told you that I had taken a house in Arlington-street, where I hoped to see you frequently, and where I do depend upon seeing you often. In return you told me what your plans were—to come to town early on the morrow morning with the youth whom I saw you conversing with on the quay. Do you know that I have been considering with myself some time about the look of innocence heh as? Such a look of innocence for a youth of nineteen! And how shy he seems! Poor fellow! It's a very fortunate thing that he was born rich, for he certainly never would have made his way in the world if he had been born poor. But do you know, Sebastian, I admire that young man exceedingly, and would form his acquaintance. There is not a hair of my head I would not have, as it were, a golden net wherewith to catch that unsuspecting young fellow. I would have him hang on me as if his life depended on a thread. I would have him no more forsake my presence than the day can forsake the presence of the sun. With insinuating manner I will lay myself out for him; and I would have this lure—wind about him with the subtlety of a river, which, seeming to run only on its course, searches as it flows onwards to find out the easiest parts of entering into a bank, and, while insidiously making its way into it, glides so slily by, it scarcely touches it. These young men have not a will and faculties of choice to do or not to do. But I can do or not do this or that. If I could not, and knew not why I acted—no more than this sheet of paper—nor how I worked, nor what, I'd stop and change my course, and pull to pieces the frame of all my thoughts. I think I see you smile, and hear you say—'What *you* can do *all* cannot,' and then add: 'Yours is the master spirit that loves to ride on the rough breakers of the sea of life—a ship that loves to have her sails filled with a raging hurricane till the masts creak and the yards tremble, and the hull heels over till the keel is in the air and the scuppers are under water.' Oh! Sebastian! It is passionate desires I aim at now; and, to assuage my burning fires, I care not if I corrupt the soul of youth. At the sight of this young Bruce St. Aubyn, I am like Diana when she first saw the boy Endymion: from his eyes I take undying fire. Were I indeed Diana, I would do as she did with her boy. I would convey my sweet youth softly in a sleep, his temples bound with poppy, to the heights of Latmos, and, while night gilded the mountain top with light, stoop to kiss my sweetest. I think I I hear you again say—'Fie! Anastasia! Far from you should be these hot flashes, bred from wanton heat.' But, tut! Sebastian! I have no more forgotten than yourself what love and loving mean. With as smooth tongue would I pour as golden words into the ears of this youth as you send to the soft ears of the tender maiden you love,—'dear,' 'lovely,' 'darling' Madeleine, by whose side Venus herself would have no charms for you. From your account of Bruce St. Aubyn his mind is cast in the purest mould. I have seen him; and his person is fair—fair, indeed! fairer than the morning! So erect! straighter then the straightest pine on a Norwegian steep. So white! whiter than new milk! And his hair! its long, soft tresses *must* be more beautiful than could have been the fabulous Apollo's hanging locks! Sebastian, you must introduce him to me without delay. Let him not depart from London to join his parents in Nottinghamshire without first seeing me. Devise some means of detaining him with you. Let him accompany you to Arlington-street this day. Let me see him this afternoon, or, at the latest, to-morrow; or, if that is impossible, without fail the day after. I speak to you with earnestness, and I am sure you will gratify my desire."

Having finished this fervent letter, Anastasia sat silent for a few moments, meditating with much inward satisfaction upon the entire absence of difficulties in the execution of her new scheme. A mirror opposite suggested a glance in it at herself. As she beheld her regularly chiselled features, and her clear and bright complexion, her eyes sparkled, as if she derived a world of happiness from observing how lovely she was, and a delighted smile strayed around her roseate lips. Then she pictured to herself Bruce St. Aubyn prostrate at her feet, dazzling her with his homage and his admiration, and his murmurs of love, which would act like an opiate on her heart.

The daylight breaking through the shutters, though they were closed, and through the curtains, howbeit that they were drawn and folded across each other, reminded her of the hour. It was time for her to lie down and rest.

But she remembered what had occurred at the hotel in the Haymarket.

"The remainder of the diary to-morrow," she said, hurriedly shutting up her journal. "And now a letter to Lord Mirfield—then to bed."

Gathering up her manuscript volume—and a very bulky book it made—she laid it apparently with great care and secresy in a drawer of the ebony framed glass case, and turned the key upon it.

But she did not take the key out of the lock.

Perhaps in the excitement of the moment she forgot to do so.

Certain it is that she left the key in the lock, and began writing to Lord Mirfield, and this was the contents of her letter to the Viscount:—

"My dear Lord Viscount,—I am not a sylph: by which I mean that I am not a winged being who, if she had a mind to it, could fly away from you. Rather than having wings, I am loaded with chains—even the fetters of love which bind me to you. Since we parted in the Haymarket I have been wondering what crime I could have committed to have induced you to fly from me—fly without any forewarning, hint, or communication. Since then I have been wakeful, while you have been sleeping.

"At intervals I have fancied your voice has

been making appeals to me; and if I have not ventured to respond to them, it is because that, in order to be responsive to your appeals, it is necessary to have as fine a heart as yours. My heart, alas! only loves: in that consists its whole and sole beauty. Viscount, I am desirous of knowing more of you—of resuming the intercourse that was so abruptly broken off between us; and I know no better or more agreeable way of continuing our pleasant chat of yesterday than by beginning it again where we left it off—in the hotel in the Haymarket—and at the same mysterious hour—let me say, the midnight hour! and let the day be the present one—this Tuesday.

"Whether you go or stay, I, at the midnight hour, shall be there, in the dress I wore at the masked ball.

"Believe me,

"My dear Lord Viscount,

"With more affection than you can imagine,

"ANASTASIA, BARONESS LEONE."

When she had sealed this letter, and also the other one which she had addressed to Sebastian Leonard, she pulled a bell to summon into her presence her little servant, who occupied the room immediately under her bedchamber.

The bell could be heard tinkling for some time with a silver tone, giving warning to Pekra that he was wanted by his mistress.

Anastasia began to undress.

CHAPTER XVI.

PLUNGED INTO THE PHASES OF DESPAIRING THOUGHT.

"Love, like a weight, thrown in by force, prevails;
But honour weighs more in unshaken scales."
SIR FRANCIS FANE.
Love in the Dark; or, The Man of Business.

A quarter of an hour elapsed; still no one appeared in answer to the bell. Anastasia seemed to understand her attendant; for she exhibited no impatience at the delay, nor did she repeat her summons.

In a few minutes more she had divested herself of her clothes, and was lying in bed. A red light then gleamed into the dusk apartment from under the door, and the next second the dwarf came in.

Pekra stood stock still; he stood as quiet as a mouse. Then, like a faithful spaniel, he looked about with a glance of uneasiness and curiosity for his mistress, and seemed surprised at not seeing her.

He heard a voice from behind the bed curtains calling out to him:

"Pekra! step this way."

In accordance with his common custom, Pekra made no reply, but did as he was bid. When he had stepped close up to the bedside, he stopped there—stopped abruptly, and fixed his eyes long and ardently on the beautiful features of his mistress. He trembled, for he became excited excessively on seeing her robed in snowy white gear, lying in bed.

Negligently lay Anastasia on the gracefully-adorned bed. The tapestry fell around in rich drapery of silk and silver. Highly-wrought carvings were on the chimney-piece: a tint was thrown, like a roseate bloom, by the rising but excluded sun upon the marble table, and the basin and the vessels of ablution. Reclining in a luxurious posture, Anastasia afforded the dwarf a momentary glimpse of her unveiled bosom: the pillow, as she did so, rose at either side her head, and seemed, like a dimpled cheek, hilarious in gallantry that it supported such a world of loveliness: her breasts heaved, as though a revolution shook Elysium; and, as Jove can grasp the earth in a glance, Pekra saw all that was passing in those palpitating globes through their very translucence. Her white arm sparkled with a golden bracelet, which shone like the sunset streaming on the snowy peak of an Alpine glacier. Her tresses wandered from their fastenings, as though they were anxious to shelter, beneath their silky trellis, the loved one of their mistress. The feelings of Pekra sprung up like hothouse plants—shot up instantaneously like the the gourd of Jonah, beneath the influences of this glowing atmosphere, the prevailing character of which was voluptuousness. And there was abundance of softness in the expression of the countenance of Anastasia, as she said:

"Pekra, you are a malicious little demon. I thought your discretion as great as your devotion; but your conduct a few hours ago has proved that is not the case. It is easy enough to say you love me. But if you will only take the trouble to look into your heart you will find that's a falsehood. Love is a word easily uttered. We believe it is as necessary to us as the air we breathe. We all understand it according to our own fashion and our own fancy; and each of us pretends that he is animated by that divine breath which makes us live. Up to this time, I have seen and read of many cases of love—am uncertain still as to its existence—have formed a vague sort of an idea of the feeling—but, such as I understand and perceive it to be, I do not find it in you. I do not believe you love me as you profess."

"Put me to the test," said Pekra, hotly, "and see the stuff of which my heart is made. I have all my life been looking around me," he continued, hurriedly, and with a quivering in his mouth and in his voice which showed the great excitement he was labouring under, "seeking to love, but have found no resting-place for my soul. I have met with none but cold and inanimate beings, without that warmth of spirit that comes to us from above, and by which our poor, feeble human nature gets a touch of heaven. I know not how I am made; but love with me is such a great and sacred thing, that it strikes me it ought never to be associated with anything relating to humanity."

"In that case," said Anastasia—and there was a certain slyness in her look that almost provoked a smile—"I do not think I shall gain possession of your's now; for what I want you to do for me appertains only to the materialistic; and what I want you to do for me must be kept

THE SCENE AT FOLKESTONE.

from the knowledge of all. May I, Pekra, depend on you?"

"You may."

"Firmly?"

"Firmly."

"Cast your eyes towards that glass case, Pekra."

As he was told, Pekra cast his eyes towards the glass case; the object that principally attracted his vision was the glittering silver key in the gilt-bound lock.

"What do you see?"

No. V.

"Two letters."

"Take them."

"Well"——

"And deliver them to the persons to whom they are addressed."

"Is that all?"

"It is."

"It shall be done."

Pekra took the letters in silence; laying firm hold of them in his clenched hand, he prepared to leave the chamber. How his eyes rested on Anastasia with a singular look!—with a fixedness, as if he wished never to remove them! A quick ear at that moment might have heard him muttering to himself in low, almost inaudible tones:

"Oh! good God! If I could! Oh! good God! If I could!"

Muttering thus to himself he retired, with his usual slow deliberation, from the room.

It was not till he got to his chamber that he examined the letters. On looking at the superscription of one of them, and seeing that it was addressed to Viscount Mirfield, he staggered back and opened his eyes quite wide—so wide, they seemed as if they were all but starting out of his head; for the first feeling aroused in his bosom was astonishment; then that feeling was succeeded by rage; and, finally, by curiosity.

He did not hesitate about opening the letter.

The sight of its contents roused all the excessive excitability of his fiery temperament.

With difficulty he restrained himself from tearing the letter to pieces.

Then he opened the missive addressed to Sebastian Leonard.

As his eyes strayed over the words, it was quite curious to observe the furious fits of passion into which he flew. Every now and then he stamped his foot, and burst into some such exclamations as—

"Give me these letters to deliver! ME!! What mad confidence! What inconceivable innocence! I am astonished!—amazed! 'Tis worse than audacity. 'Tis folly! insanity! Viscount Mirfield! Bruce St. Aubyn! Traitors to my peace of mind—traitors! They must be shut out from the presence of Anastasia. If they cannot be kept away from her, they must be swept from the earth."

Then, giving vent to a violent gesture, he trembled immediately afterwards with consternation and terror at his own words, or rather at the horrid deeds they prefigured.

Swarms of fretful reflections as grievously annoyed him as the plague of flies, which, tormenting the Egyptians of old, whizzed about their faces, and would not be flapped away, nor would cease for a moment from attacking and stinging them.

Pekra, however, had not yet come to the end of the letter addressed to Sebastian Leonard.

When he came to the part where Anastasia compared herself to Diana and Bruce St. Aubyn to Endymion, the warmth of the sentiment—the fiery passion the passage breathed—struck to his heart like the sharp dart of death. In the sudden amazement of his spirit, the blood like a mountain torrent rushed back swiftly and vitally to his heart; a film came over his eyes; pallor suffused his face; his knees gave away under him: a chill crept like ice over his whole frame; he swooned: he fell to the ground: there he lay in great agony, but like to an inanimate corpse. After he was revived and had come to memory again, he sobbed, he wept; with pitiful shrieks he filled the whole mansion: his hair he tore and pulled to pieces.

"This shall never be," he exclaimed, passionately. "I shall account myself mad if I deliver this letter, and above all *this*," he added, shaking in his hand the letter addressed to Sebastian Leonard. "'Twould be like stabbing myself—taking away my own dear life. If this Bruce St. Aubyn ever come to this house and steal the affection of my mistress, I'll steep my soul in crime—I'll have vengeance. Oh! good God! Vengeance!—Vengeance!"

And in his stormy lamentation he threw himself on his knees, and, with his eyes upraised and his hands clasped, cried to God for vengeance.

For many minutes agonies racked the soul of the unfortunate little man, after which his vehement anguish was followed by a mellowed grief, and his strong intelligence and common sense returned to him.

"'Twould be useless," he then said, "to intercept these letters. Anastasia sees Sebastian Leonard almost daily; she would therefore soon know I had withheld the letter she had addressed to him. As to Viscount Mirfield, why, to be sure, I might easily enough withhold his letter; and neither he nor my mistress would ever, in all likelihood, be the wiser for it. But let me consider. It would be more prudent, and, certainly, it would be more honest, to deliver both letters. I shall find the means in due time to baffle Anastasia in all her wicked plans—ay, wicked—very, very wicked."

As he spoke he turned suddenly white.

He remembered, how, when he was just now in the chamber of Anastasia, he had seen a key in the glass case. He knew that his mistress kept a diary, and locked it up safely in that case. He was also aware of the nature of her diary.

"If Bruce St. Aubyn," he thought, "could only become aware of the real career of Anastasia, how he would abhor, abjure, despise her!"

No language can describe the malicious leer that flashed over his whole sallow countenance, from his eyes to his lips, as this thought came to him.

He left his apartment, and crawled back to Anastasia's room.

Anastasia was asleep.

Guided by the rays of sunlight that broke through the crevices of the closed shutters, he abstracted the key from the glass case, and, with a grin of triumph, left the room.

CHAPTER XVII.

THE WOLF LYING IN WAIT TO PREY UPON THE LAMB.

"A pure ingenuous elegance of soul,
A delicate refinement, known to few,
Perplexed his breast, and urged him to retire."
THOMSON.—*The Seasons.*

It was well that Pekra resolved to deliver the letters, especially that addressed to Sebastian Leonard, for he would have gained nothing by withholding that. It was only her over-excitement and excess of passion that had caused Anastasia to write to Sebastian Leonard that morning; on Sunday at Folkestone she had spoken to him on the subject; expressed her warmth of admiration of Bruce St. Aubyn, and solicited on the spot an introduction to him.

"That is scarcely possible at present," said Sebastian Leonard, hesitatingly. "He has this moment left the hotel, and will, doubtless, immediately on his return, depart to London with his parents."

"He must not do so," said Anastasia, speaking with earnestness; and then she said what she had repeated in her letter. "Devise some means of detaining him with you. Let him accompany you to London, and let me see him to-morrow or the day after."

Sebastian Leonard looked full in the face of Anastasia, with an expression which seemed to say—"What is your intention with him?" Anastasia met his gaze with a steady look, and said, with much emphasis:

"You will comply with my desire, Sebastian?"

"I will."

It was clear from this answer and from his subsequent manner that Sebastian Leonard was not in the power of refusing to comply with any of the desires of Anastasia. Evidently fretted, he rose, and walked towards the window, where, with his hands behind his back, he remained looking out, apparently absorbed less in the scenery than in thought. So he remained, lost in reverie, till Anastasia had finished her repast. By diplomacy he succeeded in detaining Bruce St. Aubyn with him at Folkestone.

It was yet an early hour of Tuesday morning, with the sun just risen, gliding majestically up the steep of a clear sky lined with silvery clouds, when the train in which they were seated was scurrying through the sylvan scenes of Kent. The toils in the field had just commenced; but all around still breathed peace; the woods were silent, and scarcely a sound had begun to be heard in the dwellings of man. The vapour from the racing train crept with the morning smokes slow along the dewy meads, where cattle lay quietly ruminating, their breath floating round them in a vapoury veil.

If the reader, as the ancients feigned of their flighty and rollicking god, Jupiter, could have seen all over the world at the same time as easily as the unfaithful husband of Juno from the snowy peak of Olympus or Ida, he would, at the very moment when Pekra, in possession of the silver key, was retiring from the chamber of Anastasia, have beheld the up train from Dover to London, in one of the first-class carriages of which sat Sebastian Leonard and Bruce St. Aubyn, just dashing under the Merstham Tunnel with a fiery speed. He would have seen those two young men alone, and in the midst of a lively conversation, Sebastian Leonard, with the dignity and easy sitting of a Turk, conversing with his wonted courtesy and cool collectedness, his talk like a forest of Scotch firs, a dark mass against which brighter colours formed an admirable contrast. The conversation, which turned on unimportant subjects, was, indeed, delightfully animated; they were both in a free and hilarious mood; so the intellectual fountain, unrestrained, bubbled over in its fulness and flowed onwards in a stream of an agreeable variety of matter, that finally centred on Anastasia. Nothing more was requisite to make Bruce St. Aubyn a good-natured listener; and a lambent light played in his eyes as he listened to Sebastian Leonard cleverly and rapidly dashing off some very remarkable traits in the character of the Baroness Leone.

"I could tell you a thousand veritable stories about Anastasia," said Sebastian Leonard; "but they are so extraordinary, I do not believe you or anybody else would believe one of them. She has no more dread of the Prince of Evil and his power than had Cuvier. You know the story?"

"No," replied Bruce St. Aubyn.

"Well, the Baron once saw in his sleep Satan advancing towards him in the popular representation of horns and hoofs. 'I have come to eat you,' said the Devil. 'Eat *me!*' exclaimed the naturalist; and eyeing his Satanic Majesty's horns and hoofs, he added, 'Graminivorous! Needn't be afraid of him.'"

"That Baroness Leone seems to be a marvel of a woman."

"Quite as much so as Madeleine Esther, to whom I am so fond of talking euphuistic nonsense."

"And, from all the accounts you give me, she is a most accomplished sinner"—

"And sins with a divine grace that pleases the nicest man of the world. Lord Chesterfield, resuscitated, would be enchanted with her."

"But what a contrast between her and Mademoiselle Esther."

"Madeleine Esther startles the world with the exhibitions of her prodigious genius; Anastasia scares it with the stupendous results of her evil misdoings."

"They have both mighty souls."

"But Anastasia's never bursts its clay prison, while Madeleine's is ever soaring aloft to brighter scenes."

Sebastian Leonard mused for a moment, and then observed:

"Anastasia is a queen of beauty, and with charms as fatal as the La Cava. We are most in danger of an evil, St. Aubyn, when the remedy depends not upon our ourselves, so much as upon others."

"What mean you, Leonard?"

"That the Baroness Leone charms like a basilisk; and that it is no more easy task to escape from the smiles of such a Syren than from the impetuosity of a hurricane."

"But I have held out for years against the charms of coquettish women," observed the young man, throwing back his head and arranging his shirt collar, with a conceited air of confidence in his powers of self command.

"Troy preserved itself during the hostilities of a war of ten years," said Sebastian Leonard, "and yet yielded in one night."

"I must tell you very gravely," said Bruce St. Aubyn, "that I am engaged to be married, and have made a solemn resolution never to marry any one but Selina Elphinstone. Never for a moment do I think of giving to any one but her my devotion and affections."

"A generous resolution, which I trust it may be in your power to keep. But the heart of a young man is not a rock. Women are the billows and tempests by which it is beaten; and it is shivered to atoms when all the mass of feminine fascination is launched at it. I warn you, then, against Anastasia. She may overwhelm you like a deluge. Did you ever read the most eloquent and learned of the Latin fathers, St. Jerome?"

"I never read works on faith and doctrine," replied Bruce St. Aubyn.

"You will find neither the one nor the other in St. Jerome, whom you may read alone for the sake of the history. Well, the old father tells a story of a young man who lay on a bed of flowers exposed to the infamous pursuits of a shameless beauty who had lured him from the paths of virtue. On that bed of roses he suffered more pain than if he had lain on a bed of thorns. Under the hand of a hangman he would have suffered less than in the foul embraces and the profane assaults of that corrupt courtesan."

"It was a novel kind of martyrdom," said Bruce St. Aubyn, smiling.

"It was," replied Sebastian Leonard, with imperturbable gravity. "Others endure martyrdom in tortures. He endured it, you perceive, amid enjoyments; and he showed more impatience in the endurance of pleasure than others in the sufferings of pain. May that young man, St. Aubyn, never be your prototype! May your senses never be satiated with enjoyment while your mind is filled with affliction!"

With a tranquil air he turned and looked out of the railway carriage window at the flowery sweeping meads of Kent. Bruce St. Aubyn stared at him with a frigid, stony look. His heartstrings were overstrained by a shock. An image of darkness had suddenly sunk into his soul. Why did his heart beat quick? Why did his blood run cold at the recital of that story of St. Jerome?—why mount provokingly to his cheek at the solemn adjuration of his friend? Why did he feel that his voice would have trembled with emotion if he had essayed to reply to Sebastian Leonard? He cared not for Anastasia, Baroness Leone; and yet—ay, yes—*yet* the very sight of her had caused every pulse to vibrate and tingle with a feeling annoying and painful, and, sooth to say, pleasing, nevertheless, from its mysterious origin. Why should he feel thus? Was it because he felt that the presence of the woman he saw on the heights at Folkestone on Sunday had for him an undefinable, omnipotent charm? Was it because he knew that he was desirous of seeking and enjoying her society?

He leant his arm against the window-sill. His eye wandered on the breezy lanscape and rested on a dark spot—the obscuration of the sunlight by a cloud. It was only a shadow. Yes, it was merely a shadow. It prefigured his life, notwithstanding.

A thrill passed through his frame. He knew not wherefore, but sick at heart and faint, he fell back in his seat, pale and trembling.

A black mass flashed across the vision.

Sebastian Leonard rose and looked out of the window. They were passing by a number of railway carriages. They had arrived at the station.

In a few seconds more they were in one of Sebastian Leonard's elegant travelling carriages, to which were harnessed a couple of spirited animals of fiery eagerness and wild appearance that would have rendered their services dangerous had they not been driven by a coachman as expert as a Neapolitan or Russian.

Entering the territory of the Lord Mayor, the carriage rolled, with an occasional stoppage, through dingy streets enclosed by vast piles of grimy brick buildings; a dull muffled noise kept the air in continual vibration; everything was astir in the populous city; vehicles of all description moved on leisurely in regular and multitudinous columns, from the light whisking cabriolet that picked its way in and out, to the weighty wagon pursuing its journey lazily, and laden to the height of first-floor windows with bags of cotton or sacks of corn. Battalions of people going through their evolutions of progression in close order, in dizzy rapidity, were twining, twisting, and passing in and out, their movements looking like mechanism, diligence and attention to business seeming to mark their operations; all was hurry in that unbroken thread of bustling traffickers, from the staid merchant, the orderly tradesman, and the dapper clerk to human toilers of lower degree, the factory operative with gigantic limbs and fingers of iron; the sailor lad with ribbons in his hat and a mass of blue shirt of coarse integument bursting out above his light trousers, and Vulcan's journeyman, absent for a moment from the red terrors of liquid metal.

Through these thronged and busy thoroughfares the carriage pursued its way, now slowly, now quickly.

On they rolled, deafened by the mighty whirl of this complicated Babylon, surrounded by every possible variety of passion and thought, embosomed in smoke—predominant element—sublime canopy that shrouds this city of the world, this vast and ever-growing city, consecrated by countless historical associations, where humanity has illustrated all that it ever has been, all that it is or can be, where the mightiest and the weakest, the richest and the poorest, the lord of learning and the slave of ignorance, idiotcy that is scorned and intellect that a world reveres, meet and jostle together, and struggle and exert themselves in the great battle of life; where the genius of the land finds its truest home, where commerce and civilisation achieve their noblest triumphs, where art and science build their grandest temples, where poetry pens its sublimest sentiments and oratory speaks its most persuasive tones.

They came to Charing-cross. There, seemingly as light as a Russian drosky, the carriage sped along, passing freely, with fewer carts and conveyances going to and fro in a favoured quarter that wore an appearance of grandeur and opulence. They traversed the length of a broad street, carefully paved, then twisted round a spacious square, then dashed by a public edifice; by a theatre; a bazaar; a crowded club; rich-looking shops; the finest buildings; hotels; lastly, stately mansions—a rich assemblage of houses.

"Where are we being driven to?" inquired Bruce St. Aubyn.

"We are now in Arlington-street," said Sebastian Leonard." I am going to Anastasia's. Will you not come with me to the Baroness Leone's? I will introduce you to her."

Bruce St. Aubyn exhibited a most perceptible lack of easiness of manner.

"I will honour the Baroness Leone with libations," he said, hesitatingly and timidly," but will no more enter her house than a Pagan criminal would have trod the floor of a temple of Tisiphone in ancient Achaia."

"Because you will be at once deprived of the use of reason?"

"Just so. Tell me, Leonard. Who were the victims of Tisiphone?"

"Generally lambs and turtle doves."

"Enough. I had rather not accompany you to your friend's. Besides," he added, with more decision in his tone, "I am no companion for such a very clever woman as the Baroness Leone."

"You have been affording me the greatest delight for hours."

"Remember, I met with one whose tastes are similar to my own."

"I am afraid, from all I have said to you of Anastasia, you stand in needless awe of the Baroness Leone. But, as I have warned you against her wayward fancies, you are proof against her wicked inveiglements. She can do nothing that may affect your happiness through life. Come, let me induce you to be presented to her. It is true, she is a physical type of an Eastern climate—fierce and sensual. But you will gain by her acquaintance. You will find much that is poetical and beautiful in her feasts and ceremonies."

"I must look for liberal entertainment in my father's hall."

"You are resolved, then, to go at once to Silchester?"

"Without delay, to that very quaint and picturesque town."

"Stay. Here we are at Anastasia's door."

CHAPTER XVIII.

A PEARL OF A LAWYER WHO DOES NO HARM TO HIS CLIENTS, EXCEPT WHEN MONEY IS CONCERNED.

> "Here, you a muckworm of the town might see
> At his dull desk, amid his ledgers stall'd,
> Most like to carcass perch'd on gallows' tree.
> 'A penny saved is a penny got:'
> Firm to this scoundrel maxim keepeth he."
>
> THOMSON.—*The Castle of Indolence.*

Anastasia was not at home. It released Bruce St. Aubyn from further importunity; and Sebastian Leonard, though he did not express, felt pleasure at the circumstance: it relieved him, if not entirely, at least for the moment, from the responsibility of his promise to Anastasia.

Indeed, Anastasia, notwithstanding the earliness of the hour, had left her home for some time. At the moment when Sebastian Leonard and Bruce St. Aubyn drove up to the mahogany portal of her mansion in Arlington-street, she was closeted with Mr. Bother, in that room in the lawyer's chambers in Old-square, Lincoln's-inn, where we first introduced her to the reader at the commencement of this history. She had gone to obtain from the solicitor certain documents relating to that portion of the Milsington property which was now in the possession of that great enemy she was so relentlessly persecuting, Viscount Mirfield.

She had been closeted with Bother a long time; and had already got from him a certificate of the late Earl of Milsington's death; a letter written by one of the witnesses; and she was at present attempting the most difficult part of the business—to get the will.

"We now come," she said, "to that melancholy part of the business—the will."

"Which you insist was made subsequent to that of 1839," fell stutteringly from the pale lips of the all but dumbfoundered Bother, so astounded and alarmed was he at the course that was being taken by the Baroness Leone.

"I know, Mr. Bother, that of this nefarious matter you are perfectly innocent, being a perfectly honest man."

"Really, Baroness, I do not believe that such a will was ever made."

"Oh! not to your knowledge. But if I prove what I assert"——

"Then I will give you any information about my client that may be useful to you."

"Say, now, I accuse Lord Mirfield alone of the wicked crime of withholding the last will and testament of the Earl of Milsington. The accusation can be made without injury to you."

"It would not hurt a hair of my head," said Bother; "at least," he added, correcting himself, "if everything was properly investigated."

"Oh! Mr. Bother, I know that you are quite innocent."

"Madam, I have nothing to conceal."

"You *have* nothing to conceal. Your defence is your facts."

"Yes, Madam. My defence is my facts. My innocence is my letters, my accounts, my attendance-books."

"You will, then, reveal everything to me?"

"I have nothing to reveal."

"In that case," said Anastasia, rising and speaking as quietly as possible, "there is no use my prolonging this interview. I cannot force you to open your lips. I must, then, place you before the Lord Mayor for examination."

Bother trembled from head to foot.

Anastasia turned to leave the room.

"You will ruin me," said Bother, hastening after her.

"I cannot help that," said Anastasia, turning round; and returning, she seated herself again, and went on:—"If I do not ruin you, I shall ruin myself; and, believe me, I have not the generosity to be capable of such a sacrifice. I am more of a real woman, I perceive, than you are a true man; for, I am thankful to say, I retain the primitive faculties of our common progenitors—the traces left of the stones from which we all took our being. You know the history?—the stones, which, thrown by Deucalion and Pyrrha, assumed the forms of men and women?"

"Is it possible, Madam," exclaimed Bother, impatient almost to anger, "that you are jesting at this serious moment?"

"Jesting!" exclaimed Anastasia.

"Jesting, Madam. Or why, in the name of patience, allude to the nonsensical fable of a silly poet?"

"Fable, or no fable," said Anastasia, with a provoking seriousness, "I am so clearly convinced that that is the origin of the human race, that I should not hesitate to dispute the penetration of any who entertained a doubt of it. We are all millstones of the hardest kind," she continued, "grinding with unremitting force. Our hearts are all flints. Yes, Mr. Bother, believe me that, in the shape of human hearts, flints are just as plentiful nowadays as they were, in the shape of unhewn stones, on the banks of the Cephisus in the days of Deucalion and Pyrrha. We are all alike in nature: we differ only in quality. Shall I say that the simple are sandstones, and the shrewd flints? Rub the sandstone, and it wears away and is reduced to a powder. So it is with the silly when they come in contact with the cunning—the foolish with the wise. If you would only view Lord Mirfield as a sandstone, yourself as a flint, you would make him the victim of your designs, the easy prey of your passions."

Bother, with a softened countenance, drew his chair nearer to Anastasia. That she would knit him closer to her by a bond of seeming sympathy by the speech she had just made was what Anastasia had anticipated. Bother expected some precious proposition. It came in due time. But Anastasia had to play with him a little longer, as a cat plays with a mouse before swallowing it.

"I cannot believe you are so hard-hearted as you would make me believe," said Bother, in his most insinuating tones. "If you attempt to prosecute me, I shall shoot myself."

"That is a promise easily uttered," said Anastasia quickly, and added smartly, "but not so pleasant to act upon."

"Well, then, you must prosecute me," said Bother, fondling Anastasia, but with no better success than the donkey in the fable, which, for leaping on his master's lap, only got doubly thrashed. "I have nothing to reveal."

"You are really in great error in acting thus, Mr. Bother," said Anastasia. "A circumstance which much influences your mind is the benefit you think you gain by being the lawyer of Lord Mirfield. You shall lose nothing by losing a client of titles and privileges, and such a very wealthy and highly respectable client. I will indemnify you for all losses by——. Stay."

She stretched forth her hand, and drew nearer to her an inkstand, and, taking a sheet of note paper, commenced writing.

Just then the door was opened by a young clerk, who came rushing into the room for some purpose or other, unceremoniously interrupting Bother and the Baroness Leone.

"What brings you here, sir?" said the lawyer, turning sharply round upon the boy, and speaking to him as fiercely as if he would have liked to have snapped off his head. "Have I not told you never to interrupt me when any one is with me? Get out of the room instantly, and never again presume to enter when I am engaged."

The boy slunk out of the room.

Anastasia by this time had finished writing.

She showed the paper to Bother.

It was a draft on those eminent bankers, Messrs. Copperas and Tinfoil, for the large sum of Two Thousand Pounds.

Bother turned pale, then red.

Two Thousand Pounds!

That was the proper bait for him, as horseflesh is the proper bait for a crocodile or an alligator, or, when pork is scarce, for a shark.

Anastasia perfectly well knew from the character of Bother that a bribe was the strongest argument she could use.

"Will you now tell me," she said, "that you have nothing to reveal?—that such a document as Lord Milsington's will of 1841 is not in existence, and has not been suppressed?"

"I will give you the information in a day or two."

"It must be given now, or not at all. If the crisis must come, let it come at once."

"I should be breaking a confidence that should be inviolate. Lord Mirfield has been my client for years"——

"And I offer you two thousand pounds, if you will give me information about the will of 1841. Oh! why this silly hesitation, Mr. Bother, when I can put you in the way of thriving, if you will only make up your mind to ruin Viscount Mirfield?"

Bother looked at her half doubtingly, half believingly, half courageously, half timidly.

"You speak to me," he said, "as if you thought I had no feeling and no morality."

"Of course," was the cool reply of Anastasia. "I know that nobody indulges in feeling who practises the art and mystery of your business, nor hesitates about pushing aside morality, like refuse, when the question is about living and letting live. What has the living of Lord Mirfield to do with your living?"

"Very true," said Bother.

"Nobleman as Viscount Mirfield is," resumed Anastasia, "you are stronger than he; and it is our nature, as it is the nature of all animals, for the strong to prey on the weak. You, then, know your course. How do great capitalists act? Would they ever prosper unless they devoured every day some man of small means? How could they accumulate their millions unless they swallowed men like alligators, and trampled them out of existence like hippopotamuses? It is by overthrowing petty traders by dozens, and grinding down to starvation handicraftsmen, artizans, and mechanics that manufacturers and the Dinornises and Dodos of commerce amass all their substance."

Bother laughed.

Anastasia went on:—

"As long as these rich people commit their sins in the dark, and conform to the prejudices of the world, they will be respected, for civilised communities always have the greatest regard for those who possess the means of maintaining and increasing civilisation. Those who have a superfluity of moral and religious feelings never get on in the world. They are the grumblers at society. Let them struggle, strive, puff, swell themselves as they may, still they remain like the labouring frog in the fable, and solely on account of their clemency—their benevolence, which will not let them benefit themselves to the injury of a fellow-creature. If, then, you would emulate the great ones of the world in their puffed up grandeur and prosperity, you must be as unfeeling as those same big bullocks of humanity."

Again Bother laughed. He was getting delighted with Anastasia.

She drew her chair nearer to him. The time was come for her to burst into a fulminating blaze of lightning, ruining and devastating. She saw success in every line of Bother's visible features. *Had he sooner understood her, it would have come sooner?* Exactly. She was just the client for his practice.

"You have this will in your possession, Mr. Bother," she said abruptly and in a tone of decision. This mystery is of no good. I know all about it."

"You seem to know all about this business," said Bother, relenting and smiling.

"Oh!" said Anastasia, laughing," you are naturally timid at the position in which you will place yourself by making this confession. But what have you to confer that I do not already know? He is guilty—you are guilty. There, do not deny it. Do you not see that no difficulty can arise if I can go into the matter with Lord Mirfield? And I shall see him again this evening. Come, give me the will, and I give you this cheque for two thousand pounds." And she held up the cheque tantalisingly before the eyes of that mortal man versed in the art of litigation. "The will in my possession will afford me an opportunity of gaining an easy conquest over Lord Mirfield. The error"—and Anastasia laid a great stress on the noun—"will be soon corrected. Depend upon it, you will hear no more of the matter. Come, the will! You have it in one of those strong boxes. The will! And this £2,000 is yours!"

And again the cheque was held up; and how big and beautiful to the eyes of grasping Bother looked the three large cyphers denominative of thousands.

Bother rose, and walked towards the wall where there were several tin cases; but stopped, as he was about to take down one of them and remove some keys from his pocket, and turned round. Anastasia was still holding up the cheque.

"Why hesitate?" she said, smiling, and enjoying the restlessness of Bother, who was like a hungry jackass snifting a bundle of sweet hay. "This is yours," she continued merrily; "and the secret is yours," she added gravely. "There is no cause for alarm. I will say the will was stolen. Can you mistrust me?" she proceeded, as Bother still paused. "Bother, ought you not to mistrust me if you do not give me the will; for in that case I must pass through the usual routine—prefer a charge of withholding the last will and testament of Lord Milsington, and you will lose this," and she shook the tempting cheque.

The nature of Bother could withstand it no longer. He opened a tin box, and handed Anastasia Lord Milsington's will of 1841. How eagerly Anastasia thrust it into her bosom, and how willingly she gave Bother the cheque!

Immediately after, the Baroness Leone took leave of the lawyer. As she did so, Bother remained standing with his hands in his pockets at the door of his room for a second or two, his eyes revolving in a very singular manner, like a turkey that has just swallowed a stone by mistake—he was in such a queer state of mind. He was pleased, he was displeased, he felt excessive anxiety, believing that he had committed a grave error in trusting Anastasia, for she might prove false to him; and he experienced very unpleasant sensations as the thought flashed across his mind that he might be suddenly placed under examination before the Lord Mayor for being mixed up in a fraudulent transaction. But then he could not conceive why Anastasia should take any steps to his prejudice—consoled himself with the large remuneration he had received, and the belief that he was all safe—re-entered his room; caught a sight of the check for £2,000 on the firm of Copperas and Tinfoil; fingered it; smiled; then began whistling, "The light of other days;" but, as soon as he had settled himself in his chair, silenced his music, and became engrossed with the multifarious concerns in his office.

CHAPTER XIX.

A STRANGE SEIZURE MADE UPON THE SPIRIT.

"Let come what will, I mean to bear it out,
And either live with glorious victory,
Or die with fame, renowned for chivalry.
He is not worthy of the honey comb,
That shuns the hive because the bees have stings.
That likes me best that is not got with ease,
That thousand dangers do accompany."
SHAKSPEARE (?).—*Locrine.*

When Anastasia left the presence of Bother, Viscount Mirfield, who had passed a sleepless night, and was sitting at a late breakfast, received the letter of the Baroness Leone.

His joy will be imagined when the reader is apprised that ever since he had fled from the presence of the Baroness he had never ceased for an instant to yearn with fresh hope towards her.

There is an instance on record of a young man who was so infatuated with a lovely woman, that, though he was aware she was plotting to poison him; though he would, on his return home after leaving her company, be seized with violent spasms and retchings, and though he was heard on several occasions to proclaim his belief that she was endeavouring to take his life, he could not, nevertheless, resist the temptation of repeating his visits to her, and even drinking what she offered him. This is what chemists call a powerful instance of elective affinity; they would furthermore inform you, reader, that some substances in natural philosophy have a peculiar attraction for others. In the animal economy this peculiar attraction is observable in man, young and old, in his relation with woman.

Now, with respect to Viscount Mirfield, when he had effected his escape from Anastasia, the feeling suddenly arose within him of regret that he had left her society, and of a strong desire to be restored to her company; and so great was the affection which filled his heart for her, that, in order to be with her again, he was ready with a dogged courage for any sacrifice—even, if need be, the loss of life.

He could not reconcile it to himself that she meditated evil against him.

He could think only of her quiet, energetic manner of acting; of her gentle and soothing words; and he felt that everything she did and said was something directed towards his innermost thoughts; and those he dared not reveal.

Instinctively and perpetually his thoughts reverted to Anastasia during the whole of that night. He saw in imagination her roguish smile; he heard in fancy her tender speeches; and the more he dwelt on her smiles and speeches, the more repeatedly he said to himself: "How foolish I was to leave her!" Such was the unfailing burden of his thoughts each time they reverted to Anastasia.

The period of affection is, indeed, one of deep and simple faith; and when that emotion is at work, confidence is in such strict accordance with it that the heart retains a certain freshness in its willing captivity.

Never once, during the whole of that slumberless night, did the image of Anastasia cease to awaken tender yearnings and ardent feelings in the bosom of Viscount Mirfield. Everything connected with her was to him like an enlivening but evanescent gleam of sunshine. Her presence was a joy—a treasure. Her absence made him like one of those heavy sleepers in the fairy tale who were turned to stone; and the magic wand that could alone resuscitate him was the glorious image of the lady herself in the fulness of life.

We have seen how at the dinner party and at Vauxhall Gardens the Viscount was charmed with Anastasia, and how he had used all his politeness to lavish it on her.

Strange ideas now floated through his mind: *she* really appeared from the terms in which she couched her letter, to woo *him*—to be entangled in the same net of passion.

"My being a bachelor," he mused, "does not preclude the possibility, I presume, of my feeling somewhat warm on the subject of love. The time, I fear, has passed by when I can look forward with joy to the blessings of wedded life: that, like many other things else in the world, has been with me an entire dream—a mere myth. But, surely, it is not my destiny to be unhappy; though I had fancied my heart had long been closed to feminine charms, I find by the occurrences of last night it is not proof against natural graces and artless manners. I am smitten—there is no denying it—with this handsome Spanish Baroness. And now she sends me this letter!

"Hm!

"I shall take it easy with her. Time—which performs such a variety of miracles—will, surely, bring forth something most extraordinary between us. She asks me to meet her to-night. I shall, certainly, keep the engagement.

"But what could that deuce of a little mannikin have meant by frightening me so last night? When he told me the Baroness had an emerald ring on her finger filled with a deadly poison which she meant to administer to me, I felt an uncommonly unpleasant sensation come over me. She poison!—I was struck with awe!—and in my fright I could only remember her as at times she had appeared to me during the night—as if chiselled in marble—with her face stern and calm—not a muscle in motion—the eye steady—the voice quiet—determination written in legible characters in every one of her features, which seemed so cold, unimpassioned, and apparently callous.—I did not feel safe at her side. Ugh! My knees shook—my hand trembled—perspiration poured from me—great drops of agony burst out on my forehead.

"But what could that deuce of a little mannikin have meant? He never could have been right in his conjecture! What! the Baroness Leone poison me! It's quite absurd! and yet the disclosure of that horrid little wretch shook me a great deal—it brought on excessive anxiety, and leaves me, even up to this moment, in a very weak state. But now that I have received this letter I am all right again—though I feel as if I had just recovered from a brain fever.

"And so this little mannikin tells me the Baroness Leone means to poison me," he continued, thinking more deeply. "Let me consider. I have seen as much cruelty and heartlessness as most men. I have seen desperate struggles—hand to hand encounters—men eager for vengeance, fighting like hungry wolves—cutting their way along blood-stained decks—the dying even attempting to destroy the lives of their enemies by hewing at them with all their remaining strength as they passed by; but I won't believe a woman such a demon as to carry on a work of destruction with smiles on her lips and a light in her eye, and, while whispering love, turning about and, teeming with infernal ferocity, finishing a man and sending him to another and unknown world. Tush, I'll never believe it."

And again the Viscount read the letter of Anastasia, this time weighing every word.

CHAPTER XX.

A SOUL BY ASSAULTS DRIVEN AS A VESSEL BY THE WINDS.

"With that smooth forehead, whose appearance charms,
And reason of each whole some doubt disarms;
Which to the lowest depths of guilt descends,
By vilest means pursues the vilest ends,
Wears friendship's mask for purposes of spite,
Fawns in the day, and murders in the night."

CHURCHILL.—*The Rosciad.*

While these thoughts were passing through the mind of Viscount Mirfield, Anastasia, rolling

THE LADY OF TITLE AND THE MAN OF LAW—ANASTASIA OBTAINS THE WILL.

through the streets in her gaily-appointed equipage, was musing over the position in which, now that she was in possession of the will of the late Earl of Milsington, she was placed with respect to the man over whom she meditated a conquest.

She! Anastasia! Meditating a conquest! Anastasia! With all the amazing powers of one of those women who go as far beyond your ordinary men in the qualifying and intensifying apparatus, as the German language goes far beyond the English! Anastasia! so subtle and so circumspect! as crafty and cautious as a well-trained, oily-tongued, old diplomatist of fifty years' practice in circumventing, shuffling, lying, and deceiving. The victory promised to be easy. But to get at the catastrophe, Anastasia was resolved to go to work in a roundabout way—as Tony Lumpkin says, in a "circumbendibus."

The reader will see how, all in due time.

Meanwhile, her thoughts reverted pleasantly enough to Bruce St. Aubyn.

As she was thinking of that handsome youth, he, with his young imagination turning to the cradle and home of his fathers, saw, with no small joy, the rumbling vehicle drive off from the mahogany portal of the awful mansion in Arlington-street, and himself excused from paying court, like Solomon, to a Queen of Sheba; and so anxious was he to avoid every temptation to danger, that he continued declining even to go with Sebastian Leonard to his house in South Audley-street. His sole wish was to arrive at the Great Western Railway Station in time to catch the express train, and briskly step, at an early hour of the afternoon, into the hall at Silchester, without any accident having occurred to break his bones or damp his spirits.

"I have to quarrel with you, St. Aubyn," said Sebastian Leonard to him.

"With me?"

"Yes."

"Wherefore?"

"That you make yourself such a stranger—never will come to see me. And yet you know you cannot be more welcome to any house than mine."

"I am aware of that."

"Why will you be such a stranger, then? I sit at home whole days without company, and should rejoice in society which I like so much as yours. I know, too, that you are lonely at times; have but little companionship. Why should we not then supply each other's wants by keeping each other's society? Come—I *will* have your company."

"You must excuse me. I must be off to Silchester."

"I will not part with you, at any rate, till after dinner," continued Sebastian Leonard, and, catching hold of his friend by the arm, he went on playfully, "I swear you shall stay to dinner. I shall have no others—only you and myself. You know your company."

"Some other time."

"No; now."

"I must go to Silchester."

"Where is the necessity? You must *not* go. I'll keep you while I have you. I am at a great loss to know what pleasure you can take in being always at home. Were I you, I should be ever at some friend's house; and having no one to be accountable to for your movements—never to find fault with you if you go or stay—who can live merrier, or more at his ease and comfort. Come"—and here the carriage drove up before the door of his house—"we will go in doors, and play at chess or draughts till dinner-time. Say, now, I should entreat you to stay a day or two, or a week, with me, or even a month, would you deny such a request? Speak freely."

"I should show a want of politeness."

"Stay, then, a week with me. We will have whole days of mirth together."

Here they entered the house of Sebastian Leonard.

Sebastian Leonard was a man of very fastidious taste, and liked his furniture, linen, wardrobe, china, books, prints, and, in a word, every article of comfort, luxury, and amusement to be all arranged in their proper places before he entered his house, and, as his servants had expected him this morning at the very hour he arrived, nothing was in confusion in South Audley-street.

The first thing that was placed in his hands was the letter of Anastasia, which had only arrived a few minutes before.

Every feature presented signs of anxiety, sagacity, and meditation.

The form and features of Sebastian Leonard hurt the eye at first sight. There was something disagreeable, harsh, and ambiguous in his exterior, taken together—something different from what the ancient Greek, the Artist, and the Man of Taste would call "handsome;" but it was owing to the very circumstance of his being a man of a very strongly-marked character, full of energy, and who exerted his powers out of the common road. Lavater would have renounced the science of physiognomy, had he, after noting only his mouth, eyes, and forehead, failed to pronounce his countenance that of a man endowed by nature with some extraordinary talent of immediately penetrating and seizing everything.

He remembered the promise he had made to Anastasia that he would introduce Bruce St. Aubyn to her, and he resolved to keep his word.

"What's to be done?" he thought.

And he walked about the room in silence, stopping almost every other minute, and crossing his arms, and fixing his eyes on the ground and speaking low to himself, and answering in the same tone.

"St. Aubyn refuses even to enter her home," he resumed. "I must devise some scheme to entice him into it. How? how? Under pretence of getting him to come with me to some bachelor friend's? Yes. Thus I might introduce him into the house by the garden entrance from the Green Park. Good! He would not know the mansion from the back; he would not detect even its situation. And then—why, then—I leave the rest to Anastasia and fate. Whether this silly youth wish it or not, he *must* have a mistress, with a good fifty thousand a year and upwards. Tut! Anastasia has her winks, her nods, treadings on the toes, pinching the fingers, smiles, sighs, becks, grins, ogles, and other tricks that win the hearts of youths. No other woman can sooner get among us men than she. Why, all the rest of the sex are fools compared to her and what she can do."

Well, as to the matter of that, few of the sex have other means of employing their time but in folly. They give themselves up to dissipation: they have a passion for everything they see: whim after whim succeeds each other with rapidity in their minds, keeping them in a state of perpetual excitement. Now it is a ring, or a bracelet, or a necklace about which they are mad: now it is a poodle, or a parrot, or a monkey that gives them delight. At other times they seriously occupy their quick intelligences about a porcelain vase, or a china teacup, or, more trivial still, the colour of a ribbon, the shape of a bonnet, or the make of a shoe. Their minds are always filled with some fresh subject for meditation; they have not a moment of relaxation, and thus you will often hear them in the midst of habitual leisure, complaining they have not a moment to themselves. Poor souls! True enough. They pass their lives in excitedly and actively doing but nothings.

Now, there was this difference between Anastasia and the generality of her sex. They passed their lives in doing nothings—the natural consequence of their exclusion from industrial and historic careers; Anastasia made a great career for herself, and passed her life in doing everything that she ought not to do.

Having finished his meditations, Sebastian Leonard left the room, not in search of his youthful friend, but of writing materials in his library, in order that he might indite a letter to Anastasia, and inform her, in answer to her request, that he would bring Bruce St. Aubyn to her house in the course of the afternoon.

He found no reluctance on the part of Bruce St. Aubyn to take a walk with him.

They were already on their way to the Green Park, while, lolling in her luxurious carriage with all the self-indulgence of a solitary traveller, Anastasia was speeding from Old-square, Lincoln's-inn, to Piccadilly. Along the whole way she continued exercising her vigorous mental, and truly womanly faculties, amid her numberless other schemes, in thoughts of Bruce St. Aubyn; and she was still musing over the passion that chance had excited in her capricious bosom, while her elegant chariot, with its equally elegant footman on the splashboard behind, in shoes as shining as the "clypei" of Pyrgopolinices in Plautus's play of "Miles Gloriosus," and stockings as white as the cap of the village "schoolmistress" of the poet Shenstone, was rolling swiftly and smoothly along the capacious and crowded thoroughfare, which led by an abrupt turn to the door of her magnificent mansion.

Her eyes sparkled again when, immediately she alighted in her hall, the porter placed in her hands the letter of Sebastian Leonard.

"It is well," she said, after she had read it. Then she resolved that nothing should be wanting on her part to enhance her charms, and effect a swift and decisive triumph over the soul of Bruce St. Aubyn.

In a short time, with grace in her carriage, she was making her way about the saloons and corridors of her superb home, with motions as beautiful and easy as those of a colubrine snake moving among the interlacing branches of a tree, than which I can imagine nothing more gracefully easy, and more truly beautiful; and these inexpressibly graceful motions were rendered still more elegant and easy from her lithe, snake-like limbs being wholly free and unimpeded in thin loose garniture—a white and green gown embroidered with flowers, that made her look like the personification of May as painted by the Ancients. Her lovely feminine countenance, soft from its tenderness and sweet from the delicacy of its features, received an additional hue of tenderness and expression of beauty from the deep vermilion petals of the rose intermingled with the light green leaves of the eglantine that ornamented her lustrous blue-black hair.

The sun was shining with golden splendour half way down the western steep of heaven, and all was calm and quiet in the Green Park, which, that afternoon, from the infrequency of its visitors, no less than from its essentially pastoral nature, was of remarkable solitude, when Sebastian Leonard and Bruce St. Aubyn reached the garden enclosure to Anastasia's mansion. They traversed a smooth gravel walk that wound round shrubs and flower beds; passed under a low door, made a few steps, and suddenly entered an elegant vestibule supported by pilasters, where some men servants in rich liveries were in attendance. One of them showed Sebastian Leonard and his young friend up a broad staircase, and opened the folding doors to a large saloon filled with pictures. Here they stopped, and allowed themselves to be announced.

Presently a door opposite the entrance opened, and a lady appeared hastily.

Bruce St. Aubyn started, and turned deadly pale.

He even staggered back, as if wonderfully taken by surprise.

The lady was, of course, Anastasia.

Immediately and with joy she extended her hand to Sebastian Leonard; and, on being introduced to Bruce St. Aubyn, she came forward to him with a friendly air, and pressed his hand warmly.

Then she invited him to follow her as she retraced her steps.

"Go in," said Sebastian Leonard to him in tones so low as not to be overheard by their hostess. "Go in. She has waited for you almost with anxiety. Ah! St. Aubyn! how much I envy you! She has, indeed, accomplished it," he thought, as he beheld Bruce St. Aubyn precede him, a hot crimson rushing to his cheeks, the evidence of a sentiment which he fancied lay concealed within the deepest recesses of his young friend's heart.

The room in which Bruce St. Aubyn now found himself was spacious and furnished in excellent taste. He seated himself, at the invitation of Anastasia, by her side at a window, in the midst of a forest of foreign plants.

He had time to observe Anastasia.

She appeared to him taller and more graceful than she seemed to be when he met her on the heights at Folkestone on Sunday, She was neither slender nor otherwise; with a face rather long than round; with sweet feminine features, a clear complexion without bloom, and a countenance peculiarly interesting from its soft melancholy.

The chaste lustre of the white muslin in which she was attired contrasted beautifully with the dark green leaves of the camelia with which it was ornamented.

He was struck more than by the fairness of her complexion by the spirituality of her face, and the kind greeting that looked forth from two large black eyes. And though he admired her form for its lofty charms, he thought what made her so beautiful was the higher attraction of graceful manners she possessed.

After they had been conversing for half an hour and more, Bruce St. Aubyn, all on a sudden, missed the voice of Sebastian Leonard, who had all along been sauntering carelessly up and down the room, now and then edging in an observation.

Bruce St. Aubyn looked round for him, and was surprised to find he had gone.

When he looked round again to Anastasia, he was surprised to see the expression of excessive satisfaction with which her large black eyes were resting on his handsome face.

She was then breathing under the same roof as that young man whose estrangement from her since she had first seen him had been such a cruel punishment to her. She was alone with him; she was seeing him sitting by her side; she was hearing the tones of his voice; she was following with her eyes every motion of his which was so full of grace; she was listening to his gentle words; and if she could only make him her slave, there would every day be a continuance of this happiness; and there would be an increase of this happiness every day. No more sad uncertainties; no more painful suspense; no more absence that weighs so heavily on the heart that beats with love.

All on a sudden she trembled. It was from fear lest a fiendish foe of her repose should sweep away, with a brush of his wings, the enchanted palace which her fancy had built, in a mood of its caprice, in the mists of the future.

Her beautiful head drooped towards the shoulder of Bruce St. Aubyn.

She remained silent and pensive.

Who could say what was the subject of her thoughts?

As for Bruce St. Aubyn he turned quite white.

CHAPTER XXI.

REALISING THE DEAREST WISHES OF THE HEART.

> "Love is for the free.
> I am not dazzled by this splendid roof:
> Whate'er thy power, and great it seems to be—
> Heads bow, knees bend, eyes watch around a throne,
> And hands obey—our hearts are still our own."
> BYRON.—*Don Juan.*

"Are you ill, Bruce?" inquired Anastasia, looking up, and seeing the altered expression of the youth's countenance. And then in an indolent and luxurious posture she reclined on an embroidered sofa, displaying the symmetry of a fine ankle, a rickly embroidered silk stocking, a neat little foot, and a pretty shoe of black chamois leather.

"Ill? No. Why do you ask?"

"I thought your words do not drop now from your tongue so smoothly; nor does there seem the quietness in your look I saw just now."

"You are mistaken."

"Am I, dear boy?"

And she stroked his hair with the perfumed palm of her soft hand.

He had never been treated with such familiarity by a lovely young woman after so brief an acquaintance.

He felt ashamed.

He hung down his head.

She tapped him on both his cheeks with her white hand: a crimson flush mounted to his brow.

She kissed him: he received it with averted head.

She drew his face round to hers, and pressed her lips on both his. He looked disturbed: he was perplexed.

"Can you not pry into my deeds, Bruce? Do you not discover my wish? Speak some comfort to me. Had I a sin I would hide from the world, would you not aid my desires."

She afforded him a momentary glimpse of her unveiled bosom.

Bruce St. Aubyn, blushing, raised her hand and kissed it.

"If you tempt me," said Anastasia, assuming modesty, but casting at him a hot, lascivious, encouraging glance, "I shall embrace sin as it were a friend, and run to meet it."

"*I* tempt you!" exclaimed Bruce St. Aubyn, with a startled look. "Oh dear, no!"

"If you urge me," pursued Anastasia, "you must swear to keep my honour safe."

"Bless me!" exclaimed Bruce St. Aubyn, amazed; "I would never think of urging you."

"If you knew how it fared with me," still continued Anastasia, "you would not tempt me."

"I will not tempt you, I assure you," said Bruce St. Aubyn, consolingly.

"This does not become us, Bruce. Shall I send for some music? and we will dance."

"Dance!"

"Yes; a Schottische, a polka, a waltz, a Cracovienne—anything."

"I cannot do any of these dances."

"Then let us be merry somehow. Why do you think I smile?"

"I cannot tell."

"Because we are alone."

"Because we are alone!"

"Yes."

"Why are you pleased because we are alone?"

"Why? You make me burst into a fit of laughing," said Anastasia, suiting the action to the word. "What think you is to be done when people are alone?"

"Mama tells me we should pray."

"As your mama tells you, that, certainly, is one way of passing the time. But shall I teach you another way?"

And drawing him close to her, she said, with a melting softness:

"Come and kiss me."

"Kiss you?"

"Yes. Be not ashamed."

"I cannot."

"Why not?"

"I love another."

"What is her name?"

"Selina Elphinstone."

"I know that you do not truly love Selina Elphinstone. Hush!"—and she put her hand over his mouth to prevent him speaking—"if you gainsay it, you lie. You wink and marry with your father's eyes. But keep your own wide open. Let them be your guide in choosing everything. Now, Bruce"—and she folded her arm round his waist—"if a man have a free will, where should he use it more than in loving? All creatures have their liberty in that. Even the bond slave has his freedom there."

"But"——

"I know what you would say. The tongue of slander has pronounced me loathsome—say, even, the tongue of truth has done so. But am I injured in your eyes? To you I appear fair. Do I not, sweet Bruce? In me you have the thing you like."

The wantonness of her look transfixed his soul and kindled amorous flames.

"Your tones," he said, "are like the softest strains of the most delicious music: they send delight to my ears; they ravish my soul."

"You are enamoured of me?"

"Away!"

"No, no. You mean, stay. Come! I *will* have a kiss. What! Refuse me! Nay, if you strive thus, you shall forfeit five for the denial."

"Leave me!"

"What means my love? Can I displease you? Are you not rather pleased? Were you not but now disturbed? And was it not with love for me? I'll wager all I possess to one sweet kiss, this is some new device to make me still more fond and loving. Oh! you men have tricks to make poor women die for you."

"What! Die for me! Begone!"

"Where shall I go? I prithee, let me stay, and speak more kindly to me. Why do you frown? At whom?"

"At you."

"At me! Oh! why at me? If I have done amiss, let my punishment be this, and this." And she kissed him again and again. "Pray, smile on me, if but for a second. If you frown, I shall die. Pray, smile—smile on me. Bestow one smile—one little, little smile."

"Pray, pardon me. I must go to see"——

"See what? See whom?"

"I want to look for Sebastian Leonard."

"Can you be so unkind as to leave me thus?—and for Sebastian Leonard? And when you know I love you?"

"Nay, I must not care how much you love me."

"Sweet Bruce, come and sit on my lap."

The reader may suppose that up to this point Anastasia had been indulging in only a little harmless amusement—that Bruce St. Aubyn was free and unshackled. He was now a poor slave and victim. Anastasia had forged chains; and, having fastened them upon him, they were dragging him down to perdition.

She had stolen upon him wile by wile, smile by smile, till he found himself quite beguiled. He saw and knew she was fond, and he was loath she should meet with a refusal that he should treat her kindly. He gave her his hand, and she repeated:

"Come, gentle Bruce, sit on my lap. I have no husband, darling boy, and will marry you. We will leave this paltry land, and sail from here to the lovely Asiatic Isles, where I will be the Golden Fleece, and you my Jason. There painted carpets overlie meadows that vie with emerald in their herbage and are bright with golden flowers; there the vineyards of Bacchus overspread soil that in less favoured climes is bare and herbless. There woods and forests grow in goodly green. I'll be Love's Queen and you Adonis. The meads, the orchards, and the primrose lanes, instead of sedge and reed, bearing blooming canes and flowering shrubs. I in those groves will live with you, and be your love."

And again she kissed him.

And he kissed her—kissed her coral lips in rhapsodical delight, muttering:

> "Rubies unparagon'd,
> How dearly they do't."

What an eye she cast on him! It twinkled like a star.

"Come, my dear love," she said, "let us go into another room together. There, we shall be still more secure from interruption."

And she led, or rather dragged Bruce St. Aubyn, almost by main force, into another apartment—even her own private chamber.

* * * * * *

The clock had chimed the half-hour after eleven, when Anastasia's voice was heard calling out, as she hurried from her bedroom:

"I must leave you alone, Bruce, for an hour; but be not too impatient for my return. After my business is done, I will be back in a twinkle."

And she ran hurriedly down the soft carpeted marble staircase of her palatial home.

CHAPTER XXII.

THE STINGS OF REALITY SEEM SHARPENED.

> "But victory not always is entailed:
> The wise their conduct lose: the strong their force:
> 'Tis Heaven alone the fate of empire weighs;
> Whose power, resistless by all human force,
> Derides our prudence, and our shallow foresight;
> By interposing the minutest accidents,
> Unthought of, unforeseen by man's dim eyes,
> Tears from the victor what he thought secure,
> And turns the fate of battles."
>
> HIGGONS.—*The Generous Conqueror.*

In passing by Pekra's room, Anastasia stopped—stopped abruptly; and she remained standing, keeping her eye fixed on the door, with all the appearance of a person seriously alarmed.

Suddenly a smile danced in her eyes, as the sunbeam dances on the waves of the sea, and vanished in a moment.

Still her air and manner indicated speechless agitation. A hundred times quicker than wont beat her heart.

She listened: she heard no sound.

She peeped through the keyhole: she saw her dwarf lying down; he was on his bed, but not sleeping: wide awake, he was evidently listening intently to every sound about the house that reached him in his solitude.

"My honest fellow, Pekra, and I," thought Anastasia, "shall one of these days be better acquainted, perhaps." Here she put her hand on the key. "But I must at present watch over the wretched little hunchback. He is of the rough and meddlesome-matty set; and takes too much on himself. Left at liberty, he will, to a certainty, follow and thwart me in my business this night as he did yesternight. He knows not what he does: I know, though, how to behave."

As she spoke, she turned the key, locking and double locking the door. Anastasia did this not quietly and timidly, but courageously and stoutly—some people would say, violently. The result was, it distinctly reached the ears of Pekra, and roused his attention. Immediately after a sound was heard within his apartment as of something falling heavily on the floor: it might have been Pekra, who, in a violent fit of rage on hearing himself locked in his chamber at such a critical juncture, had rolled off his bed. Anastasia put the key in her pocket, and, without any expression in her countenance—not even exultation—continued her way hurriedly down the stairs.

Pekra rushed to the door: he tried it to see if it was really locked, and, finding that it was, he gnashed his teeth and clenched his hands, stamped his feet with violence, and tore his hair from rage.

"Balked!" he vociferated shrieking, "Balked! 'Tis she! She has done it! And she has gone! And now she will do it! And nobody will prevent her! Curses! Ten thousand curses!" he continued, tugging furiously at the door, as if he would wrench off its handle; and he never ceased to swear and to pull at the door till his strength was fairly exhausted. Then he dropped on the floor, and there remained resting on his haunches, with his eyes fixed steadily on the panels. Thus, like a gentlemen of a thoughtful disposition and fond of solitude, he kept quiet, feeling that it was sensible and becoming to a man, as he could not break out of his chamber, to bear his incarceration with patience.

"But what's to become of the young gentleman up stairs?" he thought, still conducting himself frantically. "Oh! that I had liberty! He should know all. Yes—yes—he should know all, if I could only get to him."

And he covered his face with his hands, and shook his head dolefully—distrustfully.

"He should know how far one mortal can be beneath another. His nature should revolt. The sweet theories of humanity should fall from the mists of his mind. He should shrink from her—shrink with an aversion that he could neither conquer nor conceal. He should see her fallen—fallen!—abandoned!—wicked! Find her loathsome—unendurable. What's to be done? What's to be done?"

And without once leaving his position, and scarcely without once leaving off his meditations, Pekra remained till hour after hour passed.

The pale morning broke upon him still pursuing his excited meditations. Poor, maddened, wretched Pekra!

And on Bruce St. Aubyn also broke the pale morning.

Daylight dawned and found him sleepless.

Wherefore?

For some time after Anastasia left, he had remained waiting patiently for her return, anticipating that she would be back, as she had promised, in an hour or so. But as time wore away he got weary.

He heard the clock strike one.

Thereupon, to revive his drooping spirits, he walked about the room. After awhile he passed through a door that was ajar, and entered another apartment, which was the first of a fine suite of rooms.

Suddenly, by the light of the wax taper which he carried in his right hand, he beheld himself surrounded by rich treasures, the sight of which utterly confounded and amazed him. Several minutes passed, witnessing him still standing in one position, with his hands uplifted, his eyes staring, and his mouth open—the very image of wonder and stupefaction.

What, then, were these rich treasures which had so astounded him?

They had the look of articles belonging to a chief of a band of brigands!

Bruce St. Aubyn asked himself the question—

"Was Anastasia, then, the wife or widow of such a character?"

There were satin-wood cabinets filled with silver vessels and chalices magnificently chased; vases of every shape and cups from all countries set with precious stones; arms of an inappreciable price; garments embroidered with gold and pearls; there they lay on shelves in heaps as if thrown there carelessly; yet the least costly of them could not have been made under the large sum of five or six hundred pounds. The lids were half open of coffers that were filled with gold pieces; these precious coins exposed thus showed they were at the mercy of the first dishonest person who came into the room, or of any pilfering servant; this clearly indicated they were but a very trifling part of the riches beneath that strange roof.

Bruce St. Aubyn was particularly amazed at a fine collection of weapons that hung in a kind of an armoury. What a collection it was! There was the most complete set of poniards, Milan and Toledo blades, as supple as canes and as pointed as needles; *misericordes*, short, solid blades, used much in the middle ages in private duels to finish a man when wounded; others, the tips of which were touched with such subtle poisons that but to be scratched by them in the finger must have resulted in instantaneous and inevitable death; others, again—Venetian inventions—with glass blades that broke in the wound.

After the amazed youth had sufficiently contemplated this fearful arsenal of deadly weapons, he retraced his steps, tremblingly, to Anastasia's chamber—bewildered, pale as a ghost, and wondering if he was in the home of a murderess—or what.

The chair into which he dropped was that in which Anastasia had sat while writing her letters to Viscount Mirfield and Sebastian Leonard.

The arm of Bruce St. Aubyn rested on the drawer of the glass case which contained the diary of Anastasia, and which had been left unlocked by Pekra.

"I have much to accuse myself of," said the youth. "I have done wrong in ever entering this house. Who is this woman in possession of so many deadly daggers? She will ruin—humiliate me. A woman, doubtless, with cooled friends and triumphant enemies—a woman of a stained name. I am involved in a dangerous game—a game of chance: bad play may sometimes succeed in such games, and skill fail; but such results are only accidental and temporary chances. How shall I hope to escape the fixed principles of action of this fearful woman?"

Just then he turned. His eye caught sight—only just a glimpse—of the inner part of the drawer. It was but partially closed.

He caught hold of the handle instantly, and pulled sharply. The drawer gave way; it came open.

The first object that met his vision was a book. It was Anastasia's diary. It was marked in large printed letters—

"The Diary of My Life."

Bruce St. Aubyn clutched hold of it with the rapidity and eagerness of a diver clutching hold of a precious pearl in the deep bosom of the ocean beneath the purple waves of the Persian Gulf.

He opened it. Leaf after leaf was covered with close manuscript writing in the hand of Anastasia.

"Ah! ha!" exclaimed Bruce St. Aubyn, exultingly. "Now shall I know all about her."

He placed his elbows on the cabinet; resting his head on both his hands, he was the next moment blind and deaf to everything about him, he was so absorbed in reading with intense and breathless interest the diary of the Baroness Leone.

CHAPTER XXIII.

FEELING THE STRENGTH GROW AS THE MIND SETTLES INTO CALMNESS.

"When to its second childhood life declines,
A dim and troubled power doth memory hold.
But soon the light of young remembrance shines
Renew'd, and influences of dormant love
Waken'd within, with quick'ning influence move."
Southey.—*The Memory of Childhood.*

Meantime Anastasia lost not a moment in making her way to the Haymarket; she proceeded to it through the less frequented streets. Soon she became confounded with the crowd; everybody hurried by her without taking the slightest notice; some, however, smiled; it was those who mistook her for a foreigner—they believed a Spanish woman on her travels, who had newly come to the metropolis, and had not yet settled down to the ways of London people; her head was exposed; she wore no bonnet—only a large black lace veil, with which, by drawing it in front of her face, she completely hid her features. Thus she walked deliberately, and with her usual haughty independence, along the public pavement. No one who passed by her ever for a moment suspected that he was passing by a lady of title.

On reaching Moppy's Hotel she felt wonderfully relieved on hearing that Viscount Mirfield was there; he had arrived for some time, and was waiting up stairs in a private room for a female friend.

That moment was almost insupportable to Anastasia, from the great joy it gave her.

Viscount Mirfield was up stairs certainly, dreaming of palaces and equipages, and lovely susceptible foreign Baronesses leaning on his arm, fond and happy; he never for a moment suspected the racking situation in which he would soon be placed—ay, a situation more racking than that of Prometheus, when, bound in adamantine chains to the irremovable granite rock, he writhed under the beaks of the vultures and of the other meaner birds of prey that picked at his vitals.

When Anastasia entered the room into the presence of the Viscount, she had laid aside the black lace veil, which, like the mantilla of a Spanish senora, had depended gracefully from her superb head, and removed from her smooth, sloping shoulders a thin shawl, of rare value, manufactured from the silky hair of the precious goats that browse in the valley of Cashmere. She was very beautiful thus. Her jet-black hair, arranged in two thick clusters, in the violent contrast of its hue, brought into stronger relief, and rendered still more brilliant, the bloom of her complexion. Her form slender and flexible, now freed from an ungraceful covering, appeared in all its charms. Her small, beautifully-arched foot scarcely touched the floor. Her whole figure wore an air of blended power and grace. The Viscount gazed upon her in wonder. Still he was averse to keep within the bounds of a passion purely passive, and, approaching her with a free and easy air, he was about to clasp her round the waist, when she drew back in haste, measuring him and exclaiming—

"Why do you think I come here?"

"Why?" replied the Viscount, stepping back surprised; "to crown my joys and make me master of my best desires."

"But is not love most ridiculous in the old?"

"And yet it is the old who are most lavish of their caresses."

"No," observed Anastasia, significantly; "it is those who intend to deceive, and have already done so. Are you then so much in love?" she added in the most insinuating manner, seeing that he was touched by everything she did, or said, or looked.

"Not reasonably, as a man ought, but miserably."

"Over head and ears, Viscount?" said Anastasia, now for the first time taking a seat.

"I am pretty much in that condition, indeed."

"I must then release you from it," said Anastasia gaily, and taking the Viscount's hand in both her own; "for though I should have blushed at my want of modesty some few years back, yet frequent residences in Paris and Vienna have cured me of that unfashionable weakness; and to convince you that I have a fellow feeling of your distress, and that I am nearly allied to you in misfortunes, you must know — " and she paused abruptly and hung her head on one side as if somewhat embarrassed—

"What?"

"That I am in love, too," fell from her lips in faint tones.

"Indeed!"

"Miserably in love?" and she sighed.

"With whom?" asked the Viscount, anxiously.

"Surely you can guess," replied Anastasia, twiddling with his fingers, and keeping her head averted and her looks fixed on the ground.

"No, indeed, I cannot."

"Oh! never tell me," she said, shaking herself from side to side with a pretty pertness of manner; "you, who are neither too young nor too simple, know things and see differences—you do not require to be told whom a lady is in love with," and she placed her hand on his shoulder, and looked softly into his face.

The Viscount smiled, and said nothing.

She went on:

"In case you may guess wrong, then, I must confess with shame and passion that, since my eyes beheld you, you have been the king of my affections. If there can be violence in love, then do I feel that tyranny; and, though I upbraided the expressions of your love a short time back, believe me that every word you spoke was music to my ear."

"Oh! Anastasia!"

"If you tempt me, Mirfield, I must yield!"

"What happiness!"

"And hear me," said Anastasia, breaking forth into the language of compliment and rapture; "to requite my husband, who, when he first saw me loved me, and, without respect of dowry, married me, and advanced me to the high position he held, and then left me the means whereby I obtained those titles I now possess, I vowed a solemn vow, as long as he lived, to be constant to him, and, after he was dead, never to love another. I have done so; nor is there in the world a man could make me break that vow but you, Viscount—oh! but you. Do I love you now?" added the arrant coquette in the smoothest tones and with the softest airs of female blandishment.

Enchanted with her soothings, more especially as she was handsome—

"Beyond imagination!" exclaimed Lord Mirfield.

"True, I do, beyond imagination," continued Anastasia; "and if no pledge of love can prove the truth of my words but loss of my best joys—here, here, Mirfield, be satisfied"—and she reclined gently on his bosom and placed her arm round his neck, and, thus embracing him, went on in a low voice with an assumed coyness: "Take me. Do what you will. 'Tis in your choice."

"But you have not yet even granted me a kiss!" said Lord Mirfield, astonished at her manner.

Anastasia rose from her chair, and, sitting on his knees, "Take it," she said, "here!" and she kissed him. "And this too!" and she kissed him again. "Or what your heart can wish. I am all yours!"

The Viscount, believing implicitly in the sincerity of the artful creature, demonstrated a weakness superlatively contemptible. He, good and easy-spirited, and unsuspecting, unfolded her bosom. She, laughing in her sleeve at his simplicity, and, mastering passion, availed herself of his being put off his guard by his profane and wanton appetite, to lead him, as a Jack o'Lantern leads a simple lout of a boor a difficult and devious dance through quagmires and thickets.

The thunder is adored by those whom it dashes to pieces.

Anastasia conducted the Viscount scrupulously along the path she wished him to follow, without allowing him to see the conclusion he was about to arrive at. Not more cautious am I in preventing you, my courteous reader, from penetrating too soon the secret of the catastrophe on which my interest depends.

The heart of Anastasia was like a snowball; her affection cold; but she wearied the Viscount with doating kisses.

CHAPTER XXIV.

A SEA OF TROUBLE AND MIST.

"Before mine eyes pass all incongruous things,
Huge, horrible, and strange, on which I stare,
As idiots do upon this changeful world,
With nor surprise nor speculation."
JOANNA BAILLIE.—*Orra.*

That the mental condition of Anastasia, Baroness Leone, was all along one of gratification or pleasure was evident from her physical expression, the external modification of her countenance being a calm, unruffled smile—a soft, loving smile that it was a charm to see.

Viscount Mirfield was the first to speak.

"You are still as great a rake, I see, Anastasia, as when I first launched on this ocean of London."

"We then knew each other well, Viscount"—

"For two months, Anastasia"—

"But all of a sudden, Mirfield, you took a freak—a very prudent one—of retiring from the country. I followed your example. You went to India—I—no matter. We meet again"—

"And I gain the old ascendancy over your disposition"—

"But for it you will have to forfeit all your fortune," said Anastasia archly, and shaking her finger at him.

"All!" exclaimed the Viscount, laughing. "The devil!" he added.

"Yes, there's the devil in it," observed Anastasia, with the utmost gravity. "Your business here is to comfort me, and take some course for settling my estate. You are in debt to me."

"I!"

"And I strangely fear you will not pay me."

"If I do not, you will then seek revenge?"

"Far be it from my thoughts to seek revenge," said Anastasia calmly. "You cannot reach what I intend to act," she added still more quickly and mysteriously. "Flax soon kindles," she went on, "and is soon out again; but gold heats slowly, and remains hot long. But, as I tell you, you are in debt to me. As thus: You are a great English lord, I—though bearing an Italian title—a poor adventuress. Do you not think, now, I look for a reward?"

"You surprise me!" exclaimed the Viscount, sliding back his chair from the suddenness of his

ANASTASIA FORGETS HER WOMANHOOD, AND BRUCE ST. AUBYN HIS ENGAGEMENT.

surprise, and staring hard at Anastasia with a look of amazement. "You, the fine great lady, stately! advanced in the world! But," he continued more quietly, recovering from his astonishment, "as you have asked, and I would comply, how shall I reward the service you have done me?"

"Milsington and the Berkshire estates are Mr. Sebastian Leonard's by the will of the late Earl of Milsington, and mine by transference. Shall your solicitor send me the papers to-morrow?"

At this unexpected appeal Viscount Mirfield was so suddenly taken aback that he sprang from his chair with excitement.

Without saying a word he stood, for several seconds, staring hard at Anastasia.

"How came the estates Mr. Sebastian Leonard's?" inquired Viscount Mirfield.

"By a will made by the Earl of Milsington in 1841," replied Anastasia.

"The Earl made no will subsequent to that of 1839," fell stutteringly from the pale lips of the all but dumbfoundered Viscount.

"Oh! not to your knowledge, certainly," said

Anastasia; "but here are documents which, I think, will render you less incredulous," she continued calmly. And drawing forth from her bosom a roll of papers, she added: "Here is a copy of the will which I received but this morning from your lawyer, Mr. Bother."

"Perhaps you will give me some information about this matter. It may be useful to me," said the Viscount, with a faint endeavour at a smile.

"I think that only reasonable," said Anastasia calmly. "I will then enter into some details, as briefly as possible, not to occupy too large a portion of your valuable time."

"Oh! my time is quite at your disposal, Baroness."

Anastasia, after a bow, went on quietly, as follows:—

"In the autumn of 1841 Lord Milsington, on his way to England, was detained at Montmorency by a severe illness, when, believing his end approaching, he made a will, which turned out to be his last will. In it he bequeathed the greater portion of his property to a Mr. Sebastian Leonard, who had been a ward and an adopted son of his. The witnesses to this will were a French gentleman, M. Tournon, a friend of the Earl's, and Saunders, your valet. The executors appointed were two gentlemen of the name of Villiers. Well, Viscount, in spite of the doctors Lord Milsington recovered, brought this will with him to England, and deposited it in the hands of his lawyer."

The Viscount turned pale, and his lip slightly quivered. Anastasia, without seeming to notice his confusion, went on:—

"This was in the early part of 1842. In the latter part of that year Lord Milsington returned to Italy, and his arrival in that country was shortly followed by two very important events that never came to his knowledge;—*your* ruin, by gambling and dissipation, and the death of the French gentleman who had been a witness to the will made at Montmorency. Almost immediately after this double event, for some cause, doubtless, well known to yourself, your valet, Saunders, suddenly left for America, where he is still living in very comfortable circumstances, thanks to the generosity of his *noble* master." [A great stress on the adjective.]

"All that you are now telling me," said the Viscount, "is exceedingly strange, and as new as it is strange!"

"And as true as it is both new and strange; and what is still stranger," continued Anastasia, looking searchingly at the Viscount as she spoke, "the property in question is mine, and I must be placed in possession of it."

"Yours, Baroness!"

"Mine, Viscount; and I expect to be placed in possession of it through the professional instrumentality of your lawyers."

"Your property, Baroness!"

"Why this iteration, Viscount—I say *my* property. But you seem amazed. I will briefly tell you how it became mine. When, during my last visit to England in the summer of 1846, I had gained, from various sources, the whole information about Lord Milsington's last will, I lost no time in seeking out the rightful owner of the property. I found him. I should rather say, by diligent inquiries, I ascertained that, ignorant of his good fortune, this Mr. Sebastian Leonard was residing in Rome in great retirement and in very poor circumstances, pursuing the career of an obscure, but most talented and very ill-paid artist. I was the means of his receiving a communication. One day, on returning home from walking in the gardens on the Pincian hill attached to the Villa Medici, he found a letter lying for him, signed 'Edward Villiers,' the substance of which was—but stay—I have it in my pocket, and will read it to you."

Searching in her pocket, Anastasia brought forth a letter, somewhat soiled and creased, which she opened, and read from, as follows:—

"To Sebastian Leonard, Esq.

"Sir,—Severely rebuked by my conscience, that, having been one of the executors of the late Earl of Milsington's will, I should have allowed a great injustice to be hitherto done to you, though tardily repairing the wrong, I can no longer conceal the fact that, under the will of the late Earl of Milsington, you are entitled to a princely fortune of £13,000 a year"—

The Viscount here rose from his chair hurriedly and excitedly, but so noiselessly as not to attract the notice of Anastasia, and, with open mouth and eyes of surprise, listened breathlessly.

The Baroness read on:—

"His lordship bequeathed to you his estate in Kent, Milsington Priory, the rent-roll of which is valued at £5,000 per annum; all his landed property in Berkshire and money in the funds, amounting yearly to about £8,000. More I cannot reveal in a letter, but if you will come to London, and see me or my brother Charles, the other executor, the cause of this conduct will be explained, and the property recovered at present in the possession of Viscount Mirfield."

"Signed," said Anastasia, looking up from the paper, "'Edward Villiers,' and dated the 27th of April, 1847."

"So far back!" exclaimed the Viscount with a sneering smile and expression of countenance, "and Mr. Sebastian Leonard not now in possession of this property!"

"He is not."

"What! Has he not then seen this Mr. Edward Villiers?"

"Never."

"Nor his brother?"

"Nor Mr. Charles Villiers?"

"And the property"—

"Is still kept by you, Lord Mirfield."

"This, then," continued Anastasia quietly, "is the position in which Mr. Sebastian Leonard is placed. He is the heir, the owner, in fact, of this fortune, which, up to the present moment, has been kept from him by many and serious impediments. But before to-morrow night he will have been enabled to obtain ——. But I am anticipating myself, and will go back to a few small circumstances.

"When I had exerted myself to meet Mr. Sebastian Leonard; had succeeded; and, for a consideration—I will say, a very handsome consideration—had induced him to transfer to me the landed and funded property bequeathed to him by Lord Milsington, I then made up my mind that it should be you, Viscount, *you*, who should be the means of procuring me the large amount of money and lands I claim under the will of the late Lord Milsington in the name of Mr. Sebastian Leonard; and to which property I need not do more than what I have said to show you that I have a real title."

"It is not in my power," said the Viscount, with a peculiar play of the features, as if he was amused by what Anastasia was saying, "to comply with your desires, for really, Baroness, I know nothing of all this curious business. Nor am I worthy the implicit reliance you seem to have placed in me."

"Doubtless," observed Anastasia in a strange voice, and with a still stranger manner.

"When Lord Milsington," continued the Viscount, "died in 1845, the will proved at Doctors' Commons was the last will. The very last will, Baroness—the will made at Rome in 1839."

"The will in which you were left heir to all the Earl's property?"

"Exactly."

"I must, notwithstanding, engage you," said Anastasia, lifting up her eyebrows, "to get back for me all that property!"

"Baroness!"

"So I say, Viscount, get back all that property for me."

"What means can I adopt?" asked the Viscount, in an almost jocose tone.

"I care not," replied Anastasia quietly, "let them be ever so crafty or ever so iniquitous; or take all your precautions with subtlety; but the property I must have?"

"It is not to be done," said the Viscount blandly.

"It *must* be done," said Anastasia determinedly, "or it will fall to my lot to accuse you of concealing a will, and your lawyers of a guilty knowledge of the crime."

"Me, Madam!"

"You, sir."

"Of which concealment I know nothing."

"It will, however, go very hard with you, Viscount, to prove your innocence before a judge and jury. Listen. We are alone. Almost simultaneously with the death of M. Tournon, and the emigration to America of Saunders, each of your lawyers, of your three lawyers, Bother, Squeeze, and Crush, who, till then, had been living upon a few hundreds a year, purchased—without any ostensible increase of their business—a villa—it is true a small one—where each commenced living, and continues to live still, in the style of a man who possesses at least a thousand or two a year. With these facts before a judge and a jury, will any one doubt their complicity with you in this monstrous fraud? They will say, you bribed them."

"Bribed them, Madam!"

"Don't excite yourself, Viscount. You will be convicted—will be a ruined, broken-hearted, despised man; have your position lost, your prospects withered, and for what? Because you most unmercifully and most unrighteously withhold from me my rights? Now it would be all remedied, and everything would go on smoothly, if you would but put me in the way of getting my own. But stay—perhaps you think, Viscount, that if you give up to me my heritage, you will give up the affluence in which you now live—renounce the enjoyments which make up your power. But you shall *not* be penniless. Oh, no! I will not be so inexorable as that. I have a power over you almost without limits; but I will not be inexorable," repeated Anastasia. "A means is left by which you may escape ruin —by which you may retain the whole of your fortune."

"Name it. What is it? Tell me what I am to do, and I will do it instantly," said the Viscount, excitedly, quickly, his eyes lighting up with hope and joy, as he grasped Anastasia eagerly by the arm.

"That you instantly sit down," said Anastasia, quietly, "and on this paper write briefly that it is your last will and testament, and that you leave me the sole heir of all your property."

The Viscount laughed.

"You are merry," he said.

"Never so serious in my life," replied Anastasia.

"But of what avail will be such a document," said the Viscount, "when there will be no witnesses."

"I will find them," said Anastasia.

"Well, if it is your wish, I will comply; but the document, mind you, will not be legal," said the Viscount, smiling, and, taking a pen from the hand of the Baroness, he wrote at her dictation.

"And now," said he, when he had finished; "it must, of course, be dated. This is May, 1850, and the day?—"

"Oh, you must not date so," said Anastasia, quickly. "Date it anyhow; date it the 23rd of April, 1848."

"Anything to please you," said the Viscount again smiling, and, having signed and dated according to the wish of Anastasia, he threw down the pen.

Anastasia kissed him.

She placed the document carefully in her bosom, and, seating herself by his side, said,

"We will now have some wine."

CHAPTER XXV.

EVIL IN A PALPABLE SHAPE.

"Deck an ape
In tissue, and the beauty of the robe
Adds but the greater scorn unto the beast;
The poison shows worst in a golden cup;
Dark night seems darker by the lightning flash;
Lilies that fester smell far worse than weeds;
And every glory that inclines to sin,
The shame is treble by the opposite."
CROWE.—*The Ambitious Statesman.*

From delicate thin glasses, wreathed with vine leaves, from which flowed ruby wine of exhilaration, the Baroness and the Viscount drank with a Bacchanalian excess, at times tasting cakes so delicious they should have offered sacrifice to Fornax, and sitting before a mirror, the frame of which was covered with such a superabundant expanse of dazzling gold leaf, that it might almost be imagined to rival the fine gilding of the temple built to Fortune by Sylla at Præneste.

With their minds rounded and enlarged and mollified by travel, the Baroness and the Viscount conversed as people should converse who ride in equipages to dinner parties, dress in silk stockings, and drink champagne and Rhenish wines, Anastasia talking scandal and the Viscount greedily devouring everything that blackened character, like the Marquis de Custine listening to defamatory anecdotes of Russia in general and Peter the Great in particular.

At times the Viscount gazed with fixed eyes, as in a kind of dream, upon the beauty of Anastasia, or stooping with low brow to pore upon her words, and listen to the music of her tongue, that was like hearing Apollo's lute of silver sound.

At length the Viscount was half besotted by too copious libations from the ever-replenished cup.

Then it was that the Baroness Leone poured out for him a glass of a perfectly-perfumed and high-class claret got from the most admirably bearing vine bushes of Medoc, drinking which, with gay and bright associations of the picturesque and varied vineyards of Bordeaux, was like drinking poetry.

The Viscount was raising the sparkling crystal to his lips, when Anastasia caught his arm, and, stopping him, drew his attention to a picture on the opposite wall. The Viscount turned to look. The subject of the picture was the great-minded Edmund Burke, at Beaconsfield, with a chirping grasshopper in his hand, wondering at the works of the creation in the contemplation of the strength and activity of that curiously constructed insect.

While the Viscount's back was turned to her, Anastasia raised her hand quickly towards his glass; as she did so a close observer might have seen the large emerald ring of great value and beauty which Pekra had given her the day before, and which she wore on the third finger of her right hand, fly open with a spring, and from the cavity of the setting, at a shake of her hand, a light powder fell into the glass.

With an unagitated countenance, fiendishly expressive of malicious triumph and exultation, Anastasia watched the Viscount raise the glass to his lips.

The Viscount, ignorant that Anastasia was administering a deadly drug, with a refinement of revenge only to be equalled among the comely women of Batavia, swallowed the contents of the glass. Immediately his blood was corrupted, the poison being of such a deadly nature that its effects were instantaneous. The close atmosphere of the apartment appeared to be stifling him; he could not escape from his seat; his hands seemed glued to his chair; he felt an internal shock, followed by a freezing coldness; he would have spoken, but his voice was lost; inflammation instantaneously produced in his throat compelled him to keep his mouth open; he had an inclination to vomit; feebleness and sharp pains were in his limbs; an entire prostration of strength succeeded the highest degree of manly vigour and activity. With all these physical diseases suddenly affecting his frame, he was assailed by an universal horrible torture; his bones seemed to be exfoliating and withering like a tree, which, struck at the root, dies away, shedding its bark; his entrails burst the vessels in which they were deposited. With an inconceivable pang at his heart he perished in a moment, falling heavily to the ground, with a hideous shriek, a frightful piercing cry, that resembled, as much as anything, the yell of a Prince of the Pottawattamies, when he yells his death howl.

Up sprang Anastasia. One glance of undying hatred she threw on the prostrate form before her.

"It has settled his business," she exclaimed joyously. "My vengeance is complete."

And then—

Did she rush from the apartment?

Did she flee the house?

No—she dashed on the carpet a small empty vial, and, screaming, rang the bell violently, and continued pulling at the rope until the door was thrust open.

Four men entered hurriedly.

The four men entered alarmed.

They were Moppy, the landlord, and three of his waiters, Tom, Dick, and Harry.

Immediately on both her knees fell Anastasia by the side of the body, and, wringing her hands and bursting into tears, exclaimed in agonising accents—

"Look here!—look here!"

"Great God!" exclaimed the landlord.

It was the only exclamation of Mr. Moppy.

CHAPTER XXVI.

ACTUAL EXPERIENCE OVERRUNS CALCULATION.

"The way to govern men is by their passions;
Catch but the ruling foibles of their hearts,
And all their boasted virtues shrink before you."
HANNAH MORE.—*Percy.*

The landlord of the hotel was stricken with awe at the sight of Lord Mirfield's corpse.

The spectacle was hideous.

Already were the features livid, the lips black, the abdomen inflated, the limbs emaciated and covered with violet spots, and a mephitic exhalation proceeded from the body which nothing could have dispelled, neither perfumes nor aromatic substances.

"Harry," said Moppy, turning round with blanched lips to the waiter so named, and addressing him in trembling tones, "run immediately to Suffolk-street, and without delay bring back with you Dr. Dosem. And do you, Madam, come this way with me," and he touched Anastasia on the shoulder.

"Oh!" she exclaimed with a nervous wildness, and as if she had not heard his observation. "You cannot read my sorrow in my tears; you may behold me weep; but cannot tell what is in my heart. If you would know all that the earth contains, you must know all that is in the centre. I cannot explain now the whole of the matter that caused him to do this. Oh!" she added frantically, and catching hold of Moppy by the skirt of his coat, "forgive me—grant me pardon—I am out of my wits. Startling events, that sharpen the minds of many, make me a fool."

"Pray stand up, Ma'am," said Moppy, compassionately;" and do not take on thus. Consider; and speak by and bye. For the present, say nothing; do not. Pray, have comfort."

Here a Government official in blue armour, with steel-heeled boots, with an iron-bound hat, a stand-up collar, and a buttoned-up coat entered the room. It was Policeman X 1. As Policeman X 1 was advancing across the room, Anastasia sprang from her knees and ran forward to meet the public protector.

"Oh! I am glad you are come," she exclaimed almost joyously. "Leave not a bit of this sad business unturned."

X 1 looked at her—as policemen always do on such occasions—suspiciously and searchingly. Anastasia turned away her eyes to cast another look at the corpse. Then, covering her face with her handkerchief, she burst into another fit of tears—another paroxysm of grief. "Oh! this will ring in the ears of the world," she exclaimed more frantically than before. "He did it quickly and did it rashly. His first thought was—— Think, Sir," she continued, breaking off abruptly, and rushing up to Moppy, "think what he has done."

"'Tis better not to think of it," said Moppy, mildly, consolingly. "Those who precipitately make their own selves the horrible agents of their deaths, deserve pity at the hands of their survivors. We should afford them silence and a grave."

"Alas! what were it best to do?" exclaimed Anastasia, seemingly agonised.

"Let us go away from this," said Moppy, making a movement as if he were about to retire, and beckoning to Anastasia to follow his example.

"I'm not bound to believe as much as you," here said the hitherto silent policeman, stepping up to the landlord and addressing him. Then, turning round to Anastasia, and looking hard at her, he said, with an unceremonious and orthodox official bluntness: "Who *are* you? *What's* your name?"

"What's my name!" repeated the Baroness, drawing herself up in a stately manner, and speaking proudly.

"Name! yes, name," replied X 1 roughly. "Why, you have a name, havn't you? Where do you come from? What's your business here?"

"These are questions I have not been used to," said Anastasia, casting a scornful look at the constable, and then moved forward a step as if she were about to retire.

But the policeman, mindful of the public good, stretched forth his hand, and laying hold of her by her shoulder detained her, saying:

"May be so; but they are questions no honest person would be afraid to answer, I think. So, if you can give me no better account of yourself, I shall make bold to take you along with me."

"With you! What authority have you to"——

"The Queen's authority, if I must give you an account. And I will let no suspected person pass out of this room that cannot give a better account of herself than you have done, I promise you."

"Very well, since I find that you have the Queen's authority, I will give you a better account of myself, if you will hear it."

"It's more than you deserve; but let's hear what you can say for yourself."

"I came with Viscount Mirfield to have some supper here about an hour ago."

"And have you never been here before with him?"

"Oh! yes. I was here with him last night, after we had been spending the evening together. We had been to the masked ball at Vauxhall Gardens"—

"Just so," said the policeman, scanning Anastasia from head to foot.

"And here," resumed Anastasia, "to make a long story short—after a vain endeavour to gain my affections, in a fever of transport he committed suicide." And raising her handkerchief to her eyes, under the pretence of being deeply affected, she commenced to shed tears.

"If I thought I might believe this now," said X 1 relenting.

"I'm not used to lie, man," said Anastasia removing the handkerchief from her eyes and frowning fiercely.

"It's a likely story, indeed," said the policeman, grinning.

"Be that as it will, I speak truth now," said Anastasia firmly; "and to convince you of it, if you will attend me to my house in Arlington-street, here is something for your trouble"—and she placed her hand in her pocket and drawing forth a purse took from it two sovereigns which she laid in the hand of the astounded policeman, continuing to say, "and if that is not sufficient I will satisfy you in the morning to your utmost desire that I am the Baroness Leone."

"Ay, now," said the policeman in a respectful tone, touching the rim of his hat and bowing as he placed the money in his pocket, "I am convinced that your story is true, and that you are a much better lady than I took you to be at first; but, baroness, I beg your pardon.

"Nay, I am not angry," said Anastasia, mildly. Then looking about her confusedly: "But what am I to do?" she added.

"You may do what you please, baroness. You are welcome to go or stay, baroness—just as you please, baroness. But if your ladyship is resolved upon going to Arlington-street, I will conduct your ladyship thither."

"I will dispense with your services," said Anastasia. "I will go by myself."

"Come along, then, baroness," said Moppy, bowing almost to the ground, and opening the door with great civility.

"Come along, then," said Anastasia.

And they all left the room, the policeman locking the door and putting the key into his pocket.

CHAPTER XXVII.

LET LOOSE FROM THE FOLD.

"A lady guardianless,
Left to the push of all allurement; and
The strongest incitements to immodesty;
To have her bounds incensed with wanton sweets,
Her veins fill'd high with heating delicates;
Soft rest, sweet music, amorous masquerings,
Lascivious banquets, sin itself gilt o'er;
Strong phantasy tricking up strange delights,
Presenting it dressed pleasingly to sense,
Sense leading it unto the soul, confirmed
With potent example, impudent custom,
Enticed by that great bawd Opportunity;
Thus being prepared, clap to her easy car
Youth in good clothes, well-shaped, rich,
Fair spoken, promising ripe ardent blood,
Fair, witty, flattering: Ulysses absent!
O Ithacan! the chastest Penelope cannot hold out.
MARSTON.—*The Malcontent.*

"Perish my jealousies! Die my fears! Vanish all the baneful passions into empty air that have so long tormented me. There is now no remorse, and there *can* be no suspicion! A fact of which I alone am conscious can never be discovered, or the cause that produced it. I am above all perturbations; nor is it in the power of fate again to make me wretched."

These were the thoughts that with the wild rapidity of a hurricane rushed through the mind of Anastasia as she dashed into the street.

Heated and panting she raised her head to breathe freer. Delicacy and warmth were in the tepid morning May air. Clouds torn into mystic shapes hovered in the uppermost regions. In the East a luminous reflection was momentarily receiving greater brilliancy. Day was breaking. Yet across the street lay a line of deep shadow not dispelled by the pale blue lights of the vision-like lamps. Breadth, beauty, sweetness, was in the simplicity of the leading lines of the houses and the power of the heaped-up masses of high-topped masonry. Over all was an undisturbed tone of repose.

What a contrast to the soul of Anastasia as she walked quickly and excitedly along the comparatively deserted Haymarket, where there were scarcely any living people and no rolling vehicle!

She was like one in a mesmeric stupor—in the Stygian abyss of the Southern Pole—as if she had left the earthly sphere and was a baloon traveller, experiencing all the horrid sensations that atmospheric changes produce on the human frame. She felt as if she was actually dead—stupified into all the awful realities of her dreadful situation. It was a wonder her sensations did not affect her sanity. She felt her arms, her legs, her head—to be sure she *felt*. All was highly wrought. Her brain burned: her blood boiled: her pulse beat at least a hundred in the minute. She could not tone down her excitement which was beyond measure: strange to say, instead of toning it down she wished to increase it: she sought to be still more excited yet.

Just then a man appeared in sight.

He was young, wore hair on his upper lip, and looked as confident as any man alive that he could, like an ancient Roman, run off with any Sabine of the sex he pleased. His look—a faithful picture of the individual—breathed nothing but sensuality: from it serious projects and meditations were banished; everything suggested the thoughtlessness of early youth. He had a large Roman nose, as smooth and broad as a goose's bill. Anastasia thought that she had never seen a man who could sooner captivate her thoughts since she had been a widow. The young man looked as strong as Samson who carried away on his shoulders the gates of Gaza, or as Big Ben of Westminster who has a voice so loud you can hear him as far as Hampstead; in fact, the young man looked as if he had strength enough to stop a windmill going, or to ascend into a steeple and stay the church bell ringing.

A strange desire entered the capricious bosom of that coquette full of trick and *finesse*, and upon neither whose solidity or vivacity of friendship any dependence could be placed.

The young man looked at her as he passed.

She smiled, that he might see she was pleased with him.

But the young man continued on his way, and would have proceeded quietly on his road homeward had she neglected to stop him. She thought of her handkerchief, and let it fall.

"May I entreat a favour of you?" she said, stopping and looking after him.

"Whatever lies in my power," said the young man, stopping too. "What favour is it?"

"To stoop and take up my handkerchief," said Anastasia.

The young man smiled, and saying,

"Your desire is performed," stooped, and, picking up the handkerchief, presented it to Anastasia.

"Receive my heartiest thanks," said Anastasia.

"Pray do not mention them," replied the young man.

And as Anastasia walked on, the young man now walked with her, she, with a simpering politeness, thanking him, and he, with proper civility, declining to accept thanks for so trivial a matter. He walked on with her, his fluttering heart assailed and conquered. The Sun, when he rises in the morning, does not spread his rays more dazzlingly than Anastasia shot lascivious glances from her eyes.

"Sir, I thank you again for your great favour," said Anastasia, for perhaps the sixth time.

But the young man continued walking by her side, and would not leave her.

That young man did not "abhor," as John Bunyan declared of himself, "the common salutation of women;" nor was it with him as with the inspired tinker, "a rare thing to see him carry it pleasantly towards a woman." He was by no means shy of the sex; nor could it be said of him that he knew not whether such a thing as a woman was under the cope of heaven, but by her petticoats, or by common fame, her husband or her children. He delighted in the comely sight of the Daughters of Eve; and loved nothing so much as touching a woman's hand. He sometimes let the ill-favoured go; but he never missed the civility of kissing the handsome.

"The man's in love," thought Anastasia; the flames which she had ignited in the young man's bosom burning very strongly in her own.

"I have heard," said the young man, "you are both rich and beautiful."

It was a singular speech the young man made at haphazard, and it was thus Anastasia replied: "One you can judge for yourself, the other you must take either on conjecture or hearsay. In the eyes of those who love me I am both." Then pausing, and looking hard at the young man, she said to him anxiously, "Yet, surely you have not taken off my mask. You do not know me?"

"Truly, I do not," replied the young man truthfully enough; and continued, "Yet, if you will take off your mask, I will take off mine."

"There is no necessity of such a revelation at present," said Anastasia. "Should we meet hereafter, and often, you may know."

"And if it depend on myself we shall, for you are, indeed, most beautiful."

"You flatter."

"Why do you say I flatter?"

"Why! you do! All men flatter when they *woo women;*" and Anastasia laid a great and significant stress on the last two words.

"Who looks at the skies," exclaimed the young man, gaily and eloquently, "and does not praise their superb azure, or at the fleecy vapours that float through them and not admire their graceful forms? Who views a well-cut diamond, and is not struck by the beauty of the stone? If these deserve to be called excellent and magnificent, what word is there for you who have more loveliness and grandeur than the tongue of man can ascribe to you?"

"That is pretty poetry and good fiction, as becomes poetry. But I must leave you."

"Leave me first some comfort," said the young man, taking her hand, which she allowed to remain passively in his.

"What would you do?" she inquired, smiling.

"What I fear you will not let me have."

"You do not know my bounty. What is it?"

"No more than a modest kiss."

"Ah! if I give you one."

"Well."

"Will you, on that condition, promise not to ask for another?"

"I cannot promise."

"Then it seems you take a delight in begging, though you get nothing. Well, one kiss will not hurt my lip. And yet I shall have given you more than my modesty should have permitted, or than you will commend me for in your sober moods."

"Not so. You may be somewhat wild, but so am I."

"We cannot stay to talk thus in the public street," said Anastasia, the heart of a tigress in her. "We may be seen. Should you wish what you desire of me"—she paused, passion proclaiming itself in the glancing of her eye, speaking from her nostrils, betraying itself in her mouth, whispering its existence in the very tones of her voice.

Struggling in a great quagmire of unconquerable, inevitable, and hopeless woe, Anastasia jumped at the gratification of passion as at something most delicious, even though it might be in its bitterest and most deadly phase. At this moment she was swallowed up by blind, selfish, paramount passion: she saw possession in view, and, when it was gone, a return of pain; yet she welcomed it fiercely as a temporary oblivion, a transient solution of agony, a momentary escape from all absorbing remorse and every baleful feeling in her recollection.

"It is a horribly delicious feeling," she thought; "bale swept away from its boundaries by bliss. What is to be compared to its ecstacy? Not a whole existence."

As she mused thus, that woman of unatoned faults and uncontrollable passions caught sight of a public vehicle for hire. It was a hack-cab, driving slowly down the Haymarket in the middle of the street.

She hailed the driver.

The man pulled up immediately by the curbstone.

The young man got into the vehicle.

Anastasia followed him.

Verily, she was a fit being to inhabit the abodes of the Mormons along the borders of the Salt Lake, or to be harnessed as a goat to draw the chariot of Venus, or to be a lubricious Mœnad Bacchanal to keep converse with Pan and his Satyrs.

The male stranger, in the full vigour and energy of early manhood, drove off in the company of that living wickedness—that woman who, though a lovely fabric of human existence, was a being more ignoble than the meanest created organism which boasts the principle of life—ay, than the meanest animalcule in a drop of water. But no, no; that cannot be said with propriety and truth of such a living lump of soaring sin—such a breathing impersonation of daring deeds and bold corruption. No; that lovely fabric of feminine humanity, more terrible than a Ghaut murderer, was as fallen and malignant as the Apocalyptic Dragon, Satan bruised, the old Serpent or Herod, that fox.

In a short time she—that daughter of Abaddon and Apollyon, the God and Prince of this world—was, in the presence of that young man, as David was when he danced before the Ark, or Simon Peter when Jesus came to him at the Lake of Tiberias.

Ay?

Ay.

And she would have done it in a CHURCH! for she was as sacrilegious as Asa when he took away the treasures of the Temple, or Ahaz when he mutilated its furniture.

CHAPTER XXVIII.

SCORPIONS BREAKING LOOSE TO BITE AND TORMENT.

> "From scorching flames to chilling frosts they run;
> Then from their frosts to fires return again,
> And only prove variety of pain."
>
> ROWE.—*Tamerlane.*

"Now shall I know all about this woman—this Anastasia," exclaimed Bruce St. Aubyn, as he opened the diary of the Baroness Leone, and began reading the narrative of her life as recorded by herself. The first passage that arrested his attention was headed—"THE FIRST GREAT EVENT OF MY LIFE." After relating a variety of circumstances in her earlier life which Bruce St. Aubyn did not read, Anastasia proceeded with her narrative thus:

"There was nothing now to detain me any longer in England, so I willingly accepted the protection of a gay Spanish West India planter, named Clemente, old enough to be my grandfather, whom I met accidentally at a place of public amusement in London, and who, falling in love with me, made me, almost on the spot, the proposal which I accepted of going with him to the West Indies.

"For nearly a year I lived happily enough with him at his villa, situated on the eastern coast of the Spanish island of Porto Rico, amid enchanting scenery—for Nature, in the West Indies always vigorous, revelled in the vicinity of that habitation in splendid luxuriance; and, the ocean being near, the deep blue billows were heard, day and night, dying away softly on the shingles of the beach with that musical and monotonous murmuring which lulls the senses asleep.

"The *Hatto*, or villa, of Senor Clemente, rose gracefully, with its pointed pinnacles and Moresque balconies, above the virgin forests: it was flanked, turret-like, with four painted kiosks, decked all over with climbing plants which ascended above the gables to the very roof, thin green leaves and tendrils trailing along the walls and wreathing the parapets and window frames like the festoons of an embroidery. The hatto was backed by a brilliant screen of flowers—crowned by a dark diadem of exuberant foliage; for behind it stretched, covering the top of a whole hill, a grove of orange and citron trees, papaws and banians—beautiful trees, gemmed with golden fruit and starred with purple blossoms. The subtle perfume of that energetic vegetation; the sight of a copper-coloured sky, fringed at the horizon by roseate lines; that living poesy which catches the glance and captivates the soul;—all this made me—an European—surmise the enjoyment of Creole life—that life which passes in as sweet a sleep as the slumber of an infant lightly rocked in a cradle. Under that beautiful heaven life alone is enchantment: it is a dream of faëry, whose realms seem opening to the view on earth: the lukewarm ocean woos you to a tepid bath: there is bliss in the very air.

"In such a magnificent clime and amid such superb scenery a year elapsed in uninterrupted happiness. Then suddenly Senor Clemente died, leaving me the whole of his estate, but exacting a promise on his death-bed that I would marry his nephew, Don José; the condition being that if I did not fulfil that contract within a year after his death, I was to forfeit the estate, and it was to go to his nephew.

"Senor Clemente conceived the idea of our marriage, from his nephew being also entitled to certain lands and houses: avarice and selfishness were his predominant passions—they are frequently the only passions of an old man. He thought that by throwing mine and his nephew's gold into the same balance his selfish match-making must produce a long and unalterable happiness for both, and that not a cloud of sorrow would shade our days in our exceedingly well-assorted union. Ignorant as he was of the human heart, he thought that money—gold—mere base metal could serve as a tie to bind together two souls of different affections, and establish a perfect harmony between a couple in whom there was no homogeneity in sentiments.

"Ten months had passed after the death of Senor Clemente when Don José, for the first time, spoke to me on the subject of his uncle's desire. I pretended as if I did not understand him—from the strongest of all reasons—there was only one person in the world whom I loved.

"That person was a slave on my own estate, who fulfilled the duties of a fisherman. He was a Mustee negro, as white as myself—nay, whiter. He was an extremely fine-looking young man, with a well-developed and powerful form that combined the amplitude and weight of Ajax with the brawn and elasticity of Hector. He reminded me of the description historians give of that magnificent Lothario, Augustus, Elector of Saxony—he who exchanged the voluptuous and brilliant gaiety of his own court for the barren honour of the throne of Poland, and who, in his kingly capacity, was a mere anvil for the sledge hammers of those giants in action, the statesman Czar, Peter the Great, and the gladiator King, Charles XII. of Sweden. The Elector of Saxony was not more strong, nor of more superhuman and almost fabulous strength and personal beauty than was Eusebio, as this negro was named. Like Homer's Agamemnon, Eusebio had 'the eyes and head of Jupiter, the waist of Mars, and the chest of Neptune.' With his vast and shadowy proportions, he seemed furthermore like an ancient hero of Scandinavian Sagas, one of the Norsemen whose vocation was to fight and conquer. He had all the appearance of being a legitimate representative of the old Sea-Kings, or rather he had the appearance of being an ancient Sea-King himself, reappearing in the nineteenth century without any definite object. He was in his first youth, twenty or twenty-one at the very most, and not *one* of the handsomest, but *the* very handsomest man I ever saw. His head, which was beautifully shaped, was nicely fitted to the strong built shoulders of his symmetrical frame; and that frame, indicating great physical powers, had been brought to maturity only by free, open air life. His lips, slightly protruding, revealed when they opened magnificent pearl-like teeth. Over his blue and soft eyes rose a large forehead that seemed to defy slavery.

"Many women would have been ashamed of this passion: not I. No human mind—especially a woman's—has an immunity from the danger of such attacks. Every woman is exposed to the chance of some powerful fascination, whatever be the texture of her mind, coarse or refined, that of an angel or that of a brute: she is exposed to it as being a woman.

THE FELL MURDER—A SCENE FROM THE PAST.

"After the outburst of this passion I found it difficult to enjoy my accustomed pleasures. I must have this new absorbing prize or nothing; and now, my resolution being thus made, there was about to be—if events worked well—a great and striking romance—ay, and as proved to be the case, it was a horrible romance.

"I might have been perfectly happy had I made up my mind to be content with Don José, and to do without Eusebio. But Eusebio was the one great object in my scheme of happiness, the absence of whom converted all my worldly comforts and success into gall and bitterness. It was perfectly easy for me to enjoy the society of my neighbours and all kinds of commonplace pleasures as long as I had not this particular craving to haunt and agitate me. But here was a tormenting want, something that created a void within, and made me feel empty and hungry so long as that gap was not filled up. The lively, the glittering prize which presented itself converted into a barren and sandy waste the whole every-day land of milk and honey. A sight had met my eye, a chord was struck, a sense was encouraged, a new and fatal discovery was made. The powers of fascination had thrown their spells over me,and a soul that was free was captive and enthralled.

"While I was under the influence of this overwhelming fascination, making no kind of attempt to resist it, but allowing it full impetus and swing—while, I say, I was in this romantic state of mind which I have described, with all the happiness of life going for nothing except I possessed that particular treasure, that charming, superb, magnificent Mustee man—I was, towards the close of a lovely night in May, walking on the balcony of the hatto, attended by my negress, when I was joined by Don José. Some observations passed between us on indifferent matters, when I asked him, as he was the manager on the estate, to let Eusebio wait in the house, as I was sure he would be a good servant.

"He started and turned pale. I could see by his manner and the sinister look of his eye that he immediately knew the man who had supplanted him in his love was Eusebio—that I preferred a negro to him!

"'Oh! to be sure,' he exclaimed with a sneer, 'I had forgotten your partiality to Eusebio, and how you think him dishonoured by doing the duties of a slave. But don't for a moment suppose I have lost my senses, and am going to find out for him some nobler and more gallant employment, such as that of filling the post of your page or equerry.'

"'And, pray, what do you mean by sneering thus, sir?' I inquired angrily.

"'I mean simply,' was his calm reply, 'that you are very imprudent to ask this favour of me; and I advise you to forget all about this wretch who occupies a great deal too much of your attention. It is by treating him with consideration that you encourage and increase the insolence natural to his race.'

"'You offend me by this speech, sir,' said I, surprised at his reproach, 'for who has been so loud in praise of Eusebio as yourself? Who has expressed so much pleasure at his docility and devotion.'

"'I praised him properly,' he replied, 'so long as he was one of your best and civilest fishermen. But now there is a change in him. He is contumacious, insolent, and audacious; this you know as well as myself.'

"'I!'

"'Yes, you! Was it not the other evening, as we were walking together under the papaw trees, and you let fall your handkerchief, that he rushed forward and picked it up at the very moment I was stooping to do so myself?'

"'And so I remember he did, though I paid no heed to it at the time; but now that you remind me of it, I ought to have been pleased with him, and have thanked him for the service he did me.'

"'Then, again, there was the day before yesterday. You wanted to be rowed about on the sea by starlight. How was it we had Eusebio rowing the canoe, when it is the duty of Estevan to be boatman?'

"'What!' I exclaimed, astonished, 'was that melancholy, silent man, who rowed us about so well, Eusebio? I did not know him again, or I should have certainly spoken to him.'

"Done José bit his lips from vexation; there was no mistaking my feelings from the plainness with which I spoke.

"'You can also tell me, perhaps,' he continued, 'who is the very gallant man who every morning ties nosegays and garlands of flowers to the balcony rails of your bed-chamber?'

"'What!' I again exclaimed, surprised, but in my surprise this time laughing, 'can it be also Eusebio who is guilty of that unpardonable crime? And to think that all along I should have fancied it was some mysterious stranger who came here expressly, and that once—when I had more romantic notions—I did you the honour of ascribing that piece of gallantry to you—to you, Don José.'

"On hearing himself thus bantered, Don José held his tongue.

"He had committed a great error. He had unconsciously strengthened in my heart thoughts already roused there, and awakened others that were yet but slumbering. I could not conceal from myself the fact that the 'poor fisherman'—as he styled Eusebio—was always closely watching me, that his looks followed me wherever I went, and that his eye grew brighter whenever he saw me.

"After musing for a second, I said to Don José:

"'We have had enough on this subject.'

"'We have,' he replied. 'And now let me call your attention to another subject which is of vital importance to us both—a matter so serious that it will not bear deferring till to-morrow.'

"'Be more explicit.'

"'I came to speak to you of our marriage. Circumstances imperiously desire you should let me know your decision at once. I await your answer.'

"As I delayed my reply I could see an unquiet expression come to the eye of Don José, but flit away like the shadow of a bird that flies across your path. Perhaps only scorn had been visible in the lines of my countenance.

"'I await your answer,' he repeated.

"'You ought to be able to guess it,' I replied. 'Although you say the matter is so serious that an answer cannot be deferred, I must, notwithstanding, beg you to wait till the morrow for my reply. Come to my chamber at sunset, and you shall have my answer.'

"'Remember, you must choose between obedience to the last wishes of Don Clemente, or sacrifice this estate.'

"'I remember all; and do not think I shall hesitate for a moment as to my course of conduct.'

"The lips of Don José trembled from emotion, and his face was covered with a livid paleness as he left my presence after hearing these words.

"Did he foresee that I was considering within myself whether I had the power to resist him? Did he know that what I resolve to do I do at any cost? I wanted to remain the absolute possessor of the estate of the late Senor Clemente. I wanted to offer a stubborn resistance to Don José. How should I thwart his will? How baffle his projects?

"I looked upon Don José as an egotistical, intolerable coxcomb, even as a coarse, brutal fellow; and as he would force his affection upon me, whether it was agreeable or not, I resolved to take an unfair advantage of him—be it ever so mean or ever so foul, I cared not.

"For the first time in my life MURDER entered my brain.

"When some fascination has worked upon me and endowed some object with an absolute supremacy, my mind is then carried off and drained into the excrescence of ONE swollen passion. I arrive at the greatest degree of strength, and believe I can then do anything I like. Nothing can deter me; nothing can soften me: I am beyond hesitation and faltering.

"I now made my negress, Margaret, acquainted with the whole circumstances of the dilemma in which I was placed. She came to my relief as I expected by recommending me to seek the assistance of Eusebio; and gave me a number of valid reasons why the fisherman held Don José in abhorrence, and was affectionately attached to me.

"'Bring him to me,' I said.

"'Rather let me take you to him,' said Margaret. 'I can lead you to a place where you can confer with him in secresy and without any chance of interruption.'

"I followed without hesitation my generous guide. After we had been walking for about three-quarters of an hour we arrived on the sea-beach, which, after exploring for some time with anxiety, Margaret brought me to the entrance of a grotto excavated by nature in a rock which stood isolated on the shore. From the innumerable stalactites that hung to its sides this grotto was of singular beauty. The rock out of which it was hollowed, incessantly lashed by the billows, had a small, worn-out base. A cascade, gushing out of a height above, poured down upon the rock like water out of a reversed urn; and when the sun, from its glistening prism, imparted the variegated hues of the rainbow to this shower of falling water, the spectacle was magically beautiful. A narrow entrance was formed by a natural fissure beneath a very low vault, and it was concealed by a curtain of green and blossoming vines, the lowest sprigs and leaves of which hung drooping and dripping in the sea.

"Immediately we entered the interior of this cave, the first object I beheld was Eusebio. He was stripped naked to his waist; with his bare muscular arms he was pulling harpoons from under dry vines at the bottom of the grotto, for he was busily occupied fishing, the rock being surrounded by submarine meadows where came to graze the best turtles in Port Rico.

"Margaret, not aware that I saw him, pointed him out to me with her finger in silence, and then retired, leaving me alone with that man in that desert cave, overlooking the roaring sea waves, and beyond the call of any human being.

"But there was nothing in this to cause me trepidation. I was alone with the man whom I loved the most of all in the world.

CHAPTER XXIX.

THE SUN THAT SHINES IN THE HEAVENS GRUDGING TO GIVE LIGHT.

> "I curse the day (and yet, I think,
> Few come within the compass of my curse)
> Wherein I do not some notorious ill,
> As kill a man, or else devise his death."
>
> SHAKSPEARE.—*Titus Andronicus.*

"While I was talking to Eusebio, and was beginning to tell him of what had taken place between Don José and myself, the atmosphere was becoming every moment heavier and more laden with clouds.

"'I know not what I feel,' I observed to the handsome slave; 'but it seems to me as if my legs were tottering under me and my eyes becoming dim.'

"'And I hear a strange ringing in my ears,' observed Eusebio, 'like what we experience in the height of a fever.' Then looking forth out of the mouth of the cavern, he added, 'We are about to be the witnesses of a terrible scene.'

"'What say you?'

"'Pluck up a stout heart, and please God we be not the victims of the earthquake coming on.'

"'An earthquake coming on!' I all but shrieked. 'Oh! let us not hope to compete with the wrath of Heaven. Let us bid each other farewell.'

"And I stretched out my arms to Eusebio. Without accepting the embrace I offered him,

"'You are in greater safety here than under the roof of your hatto, Senorita,' he replied, respectfully. 'Follow my advice. Lie down here,' and he pointed to the dry leaves and herbs at the bottom of the cave, 'and await calmly whatever fate is in store for you.'

"I now saw the imminence of our danger. Already were the ocean-billows seething and roaring, without being agitated by the slightest breath of wind. The sea began to whirl in eddies and bubble as if its bed was a burning furnace; its waves, rushing swifter than usual, were crowned with crests of foam. The clouds, seemingly piled upon one another, were descending slowly towards the earth like an opaque veil. No longer was the slightest bit of blue to be seen in the blackened sky.

"All on a sudden I recoiled with terror: the hair on my head stood on end: the mouth of the cavern where Eusebio stood had just cracked beneath his feet! Another second, and he would have rolled headlong into the yawning abyss had I not grasped him tightly and convulsively in my arms. Then I staggered as if seized by giddiness; an icy thrill shot to my heart; the next moment I fell senseless to the ground.

"When I opened my eyes again, I found that I was lying with my head in the lap of Eusebio. The sky had become as black as pitch from a heap of the densest clouds which with difficulty were traversed at long intervals by darting gleams of blood-red lightning. Every time the enflamed depths of the heaven opened and the whole vault overhead was illuminated with horrible hues, I could see the eyes of Eusebio fixed on my face with admiration and love: every line of his countenance indicated joy, delight, happiness. We heard the trees over the cavern torn up by their roots or rent in twain with a great crash: we felt the convulsions of the earth, which either heaped itself up in hillocks or yawned asunder in abysses. But we were no longer conscious of what was passing about us: we were as Dido and Æneas in the cave during the tempest. Neither awe nor horror was in our hearts; only tenderness and affection. Prostrated by love, we remained during the whole of the earthquake. As if embued with superhuman courage, we felt no fear: we quaked not at the conflicts—the ravages of nature. More than once the waves which burst the barriers of the sea came and lashed our faces; but our souls were not chilled with icy coldness: we did not heed this. The whole time was passed in speechless ecstacies that left us indifferent to everything else but ourselves. And this was going on between us all the time that the land was assuming a new form; yes; for when light shone again into the cavern and we looked forth over the earth, there was a new country round us. Here a river, turned from its course, had changed a savannah into a lake; further on, hills, shattered to pieces, had tumbled into the bed of the river, and caused the waters to be broken into cascades. The border of a forest no longer presented to the sight any other aspect than that of a line of trees, distorted and broken, with their roots calcined by the thunderbolt. Everywhere you would fancy you were gazing at the remnants of an immense brazier yet unextinguished.

"When I contemplated with amazement that picture of desolation, and reverted to the sensations of a different character which I had just experienced, I said to the young man in a low voice:

"'Do you curse the passion which inspired me?'

"'Which passion ought I to curse?' he inquired. 'That which has inspired you with such ardour for revenge?'

"'Oh! let us pray for that,' said I, ardently; 'and let me trust that you will now give me your aid.'

"Eusebio looked at me with tender emotion; then with a flashing glance, indicative of intense hatred:

"'Trust to me,' said he, 'and cease to deliver yourself up to any such feeling as alarm for the continued persecutions of Don José. To-morrow he is not alive.'

"'Let me return thanks to Providence I have sought you out, Eusebio. But are you quite sure you will escape a formidable danger?'

"'Of what peril do you speak?'

"'Of betrayal—detection—of' ——

"'You would say the gallows. But let us give way to no such terror. Thanks to Margaret, she has brought you here to this retreat, of which we three alone know the secret. Here we can remain safe and sound. Here we shall be able to brave every pursuit for days—if necessary, for years to come.'

"'Be at ease, Eusebio,' said I, consoling him in my turn; 'and forget, if it is possible, that you wear a slave's chains to remember that you are a man—that you are loved by me. Now I think more of the matter—there is no need, as you say, to tremble at the thought of peril: it is imaginary. When Don José is disposed of I will sell the estate, and we will fly together. Our home shall be under no particular clime: it shall be in all directions where the earth fails not beneath our feet, where waters murmur in our ears, and space spreads over our heads. God can find places for us to dwell in—even for such adventurers as *we* shall be—since he has found space for the bird, billows for the fish, and forests and mountains for the wild beast and the venomous serpent.'

"Eusebio and I then planned together with deliberate ingenuity how we should get rid of Don José.

"The sun was nearly setting when, after having revolved in our minds many plans, we at length hit upon an expedient, which we considered the best, as being the easiest and the most certain of accomplishing our end.

"I then left the handsome slave to return to the hatto, but not till we had arranged that he was to follow me as soon as possible. I was then to secrete him in my chamber before Don José arrived; and when he heard me give a signal, the nature of which we agreed on, he was to emerge noiselessly from his hiding hole, and dispose summarily of the doomed Spaniard.

"On returning home I gave orders that I was not to be interrupted, and that I would see nobody that evening but Don José, and retired to my chamber.

"That chamber was furnished with the seigneurial luxury which, in the Indies as in Spain, contrasts so strikingly and strangely with the miserable huts of the slaves and the peasants. There I stretched myself on a couch, the frame of which was gold and the covering crimson velvet. Mats of a marvellously fine texture covered the floor. In the centre of the room stood a small silver brasero filled with fruit of the olive tree. Venetian mirrors were inlaid in the wall, with frames of burnished silver, as admirably sculptured as the edges of the oaken doors and the plinths of the mahogany Corinthian columns. On the wainscoating and on the ceiling the chisel and the pencil of the sculptor and of the painter had depicted the whole of the fantastical incidents in the temptation of St. Antony, introducing an interminable medley of chimeras with goggle eyes; sphinxes, half human and half equine, riding on sackbuts and trumpets; little devils disguised as syrens, with the tails of cods; and smooth-skinned mice with hairy wings. A velvet-covered door at the bottom of the chamber concealed from the view a moveable partition of sweet-smelling wood, the only entrance to the *Escaparate*, a large alcove that contained a small shrine; a bed of white satin, hung with silver brocade and Spanish point-lace; and two little tables covered with branches of coral, mother-o'-pearl, gold in filigree work, bezoar fossils, and other curiosities and articles of *virtû*.

"Shut up in this chamber, I resuscitated in my mind the extraordinary occurrences of that day. As they floated before my fancy, I formed a comparison between the master and the slave; the result of my reflections was by no means favourable to Don José, but infinitely so to Eusebio, and more than ever I made up my mind that the only way of avoiding giving my hand to the former was to get rid of him, unknown to any one, that night, for from the bottom of my heart I felt only contempt and hatred for Don José.

"In the midst of these meditations time was passing; every sound in the hatto had died away one by one without my having noticed it, and the lighted *belon*, or lamp with a silver stem, suspended from a cornice of the room, was shedding only a dismal light through the silent and gloomy chamber, when all on a sudden I heard repeated thrice a gentle tap on the outside of the window, which opened down to the ground. I threw open one of the valves, and Eusebio stood before me. The next moment he was in my chamber. He was heavily armed. He had a pistol, a hunting dagger, and a sabre. He had, furthermore, had the precaution to bring with him a large bag, in which to take away the dead body!

"The time was now drawing nigh for Don José to keep his appointment with me. The sun had set; the day was over; the flowers had closed their petals; the insects were all asleep except the fire-flies, which were flitting about with their starry eyes. An enchanting landscape was every second becoming more and more indistinct: in the far distance forests and hills, with their real proportions already indiscoverable, were losing themselves rapidly in the darkness; soon the stars peeped forth; finally the broad full moon streamed her silver light over the purple sky.

"I had just concealed Eusebio in the escaparate, and given him my last instructions how to act, when I was joined by Don José whose grasping and implacable nature was well betokened by his pinched up lips, his wolfish-looking eyes, with red swollen lids, and the enormous curve of his nose, which resembled the beak of a hawk. He looked to me littler, leaner, and meaner than of wont, but strong and formidable. He had no suspicion of the sinister purpose for which he had been inveigled to my solitary chamber. He bowed smiling, and closed the door after him. I shook off the torpor which seemed to hold my faculties in bondage, and, resuming all my customary ease, I rose and said to him:

"'Seat yourself, Don José, and let us resume our conversation of this morning.'

"Don José seated himself in front of a table facing the window, with his back opposite the folding doors of the escaparate, and yet not exactly that, for he sat a little aslant. He seated himself, smiling, and in a voice softer and more insinuating in its tones than I had ever heard it, and expressive, as it seemed to me, of exultation at the fancied power he had over me, said:

"'You have made a good choice of the time and the place, for I presume that you are about to speak of our marriage, and that you will comply with the last and dearest wish of the person you are in mourning for.'

"'You ought to be able to guess how I have made up my mind,' I observed.

"'A thousand pardons, Senorita,' interrupted Don José, bowing with politeness; 'but I do not see how you can refuse my request, seeing the warmth with which I woo you. Again, I am not an old man with grey hairs and a wrinkled face. I do not bring you as a marital dowry either dishonour or poverty. More than all, I love you to such an extent as to drive me almost to distraction. What more do you require?'

"'I do not see how I can reasonably require anything more, Don José. And yet you are going to find me very difficult to please, and very romantic. I want a husband who will get me respected.'

"'And I shall be that husband, Senorita. Quickly shall punishment overtake any one who shall dare to fail in courtesy to my wife. Let the assurance of this alone be a proof of my love to you.'

"'And let what I am going to do be a proof of *my* love for *you*, Don José.'

Here I raised my handkerchief to my mouth, and coughed twice, loudly, distinctly.

"It was the signal Eusebio and I had agreed upon!

"Don José did not stir.

"There was a slight pause in our conversation.

"I listened. I knew that Eusebio was already advancing across the room towards us; the most delicate ear could not hear him open the door of the escaparate, for it was left ajar, and it made no noise in moving on its hinges, for, as I have said, it was covered with velvet; it was also equally impossible for any one to hear Eusebio creeping across the floor, for he was barefooted, and his step was always as velvety and as stealthy as a cat's. As I was listening to catch any, even the slightest sound, there was, without any previous indication, a loud report by my ear. I sprang from my chair, uttering a scream.

"Don José fell to the gronnd.

"Eusebio had discharged the pistol he had in his belt into the back part of his neck; and when Don José fell off his chair on to the ground, he was perfectly paralysed: he moved neither hand nor foot, nor any part of his body. His lids closed; his head, which was lying close to the leg of the table, was the only part of his body that did not suffer at all, though neither Eusebio nor I knew that; but that his head was clear was shown a little time after by some slight signs of life returning in his left arm, on which, after a strange shudder had passed over his whole frame, he was just helping himself up gently, when Eusebio, who was standing about a yard off from him, watching him, seeing him move, walked up to him, and with a deliberate aim fired the contents of the second barrel of the pistol into his right temple. Don José then dropped back on the floor, and the blood rushed out in a regular torrent. While he was lying thus, without speech, without sight, without strength, without motion—bleeding, torpid, seemingly lifeless, Eusebio stooped down, and bent over him so closely that Don José must have felt his breath on his neck and ear. Thus he looked, to see whether his victim was dead.

"He rose, satisfied that he was.

"Don José, however, was only pretending to be dead. The bleeding was fast bringing back life to him. Strange to say, his body only was motionless, and chilled by the icy coldness of death. His mind remained as active as that of a man stricken by lethargy. He must have heard Eusebio, after he had knelt behind him for a short time, and have got up and walked away to my side, say to me, in accents of joy—

"'So, then, here he is at last, at our mercy!'

"Fool! was Eusebio, to think he had already vanquished our enemy.

"Hearing a slight noise we turned round: it was caused by Don José getting up; there he was, to our great surprise, with the whole length of the room between us, facing us, and standing at the window with a weapon in his hand. It was a Toledo blade, which had been resting in a corner of the window in a crimson velvet scabbard.

"Feeling, as he continued bleeding, that strength had returned to him, and knowing that if he could get up on his feet he could make a fight of it, and seeing within a few inches off his hands there was a sword in a sheath, he seized it and sprang to his feet.

"As we turned round and faced him he at once rushed at Eusebio, and made a blow at him with the blade, which did not take effect. Eusebio seized it short by the middle, and, making a dash at Don José's chest, knocked him over on his back. As soon as he was on his back Eusebio got his knee on his chest, and tried to smash his head with the butt-end of his now unloaded pistol. But Don José was too quick for him: he got it in his hand. Eusebio struggled some time to get it away from him, but he found him as strong as he was, and he could not do it. So he looked round to see if there was any other weapon, or missile, or object that he could hit him with. He saw none. I, guessing his intention, and seeing in the centre of the room the silver brasero filled with olives, went up to it, took it off its stand, and presented it to him. Eusebio laid hold of it firmly in his right hand, and, giving the pistol a shake with his left, he whirled the brasero round his head to give it additional impetus, and, striking him full in the middle of the forehead, not only made a great indentation in the silver brasero, but actually broke it.

"I could hear the breaking of the bones in the skull of Don José; I could see him quiver all over. But this was not sufficient. Eusebio looked around to see if there was anything else at hand. There was nothing. Again guessing his intention, I went into my chamber, and, taking a small but heavy metal image of the Virgin off the shrine in the escaparate, I hastened back with it to Eusebio. He got hold of it, and threw it at the head of Don José with all his might. In his eagerness and excitement he missed him; then, as there was nothing else at hand, he set to work to get the mastery of the pistol, which the doomed Spaniard was holding all the time.

"At this moment, and since he had been struck on the forehead with the brasero, Don José was lying on his back close under the window. After several strong wrenches and a good struggle, Eusebio got the pistol; but as it came into his hands it made him reel and lose his balance, and he fell back. He got on his legs in an instant again. By that time Don José, in this desperate struggle for life, was rising into a sitting position, which gave Eusebio a fair full blow at his head with the heavy butt-end of the pistol, which he gave with all his might and main. This he repeated three or four times, as quick as lightning. Every time I could hear the crashing of the bones of the skull of Don Jose. He buried his head under the table to escape the blows of Eusebio, who then hit him over the back of the neck; and in order to disable his hands, so that he should not again lay hold of the pistol, he hit him over the wrists.

"Eusebio now thought that he was quite sufficiently disabled, and went to another part of the room to get his powder-flask and a bullet, and, again loading his pistol, to discharge the contents of it into the head of the Spaniard, and thus finish him. But scarcely had he gone a dozen feet before Don José, his whole head and visage streaming with blood, and his hair clotted with gore, got up and walked towards Eusebio. When he had approached him nearly face to face, Eusebio stepped back to get a full swing, and hit him again on the head with the butt end of his pistol. Don José fell forward on his face like a log of wood.

"It now seemed to be all over with him."

CHAPTER XXX.

THE HINDER PART OF THE TEMPEST.

"One by one
I have parted with those virtues of a man
Which precept doth inculcate; but one grace
Remained—the growth of nature—the true shoot
Abuse could not eradicate, and leave
The trunk and root alive—one virtue—MANHOOD:
The branch whereon doth sit disdain of threat,
Defiance of aggression, and contempt
For contumely."—SHERIDAN KNOWLES.—*The Wife.*

"So Don José fell to the ground.

"From that time neither Eusebio nor myself heard any longer even the soft murmuring of the respiration of Don José. He remained lying on the floor as motionless as a marble statue.

"'There is no danger of his ever waking again; he lies fast asleep for ever,' said Eusebio to me in a low trembling voice.

"They were the first words that had been spoken since the commencement of the fray.

"'Lower, speak lower. You will awake him,' said I, scarcely knowing what I was saying, so surprised was I at the dreadful occurrence which I had just witnessed.

"'You may speak as loud as you can raise your voice,' said Eusebio, in bold, commanding tones; 'but you will never wake him again, not for one little minute.'

"'This is the first sort of thing I have ever taken a part in,' said I, trembling. 'Oh! good God! I would not be alone with this man for a second, even though I were in the flesh and he in the spirit. No—no—I would not be alone with him face to face for a second—for only one tiny, tiny second, even though he were a harmless ghost unarmed, and I armed!'

"'What have you to fear, then?' said Eusebio to me, as boldly as if he were already my lord and master. 'Forget all that you have seen. Remember, Don José cannot hurt you now; he has gone to his long rest for ever.'

"'So much the better,' I sighed. 'But what have you not done to save me!' I added, hanging on the arm of Eusebio as if from a feeling of gratitude, and yet at the same time clinging to it as if for support.

"When I considered within myself how this murder had been perpetrated, solely to please me and at my instigation, I remained standing over the corpse without saying a word, without moving a limb; without stirring a muscle; scarcely venturing to draw my breath; almost out of my mind; nearly deprived of my senses. I looked around with a terrified glance. The dimly-lighted chamber seemed a tomb. I fancied—a sensation often experienced by prisoners in their dreams—that it was gradually closing round me, and would end by squeezing me to death. I seemed to be stifling for want of air. Hallucinations flitted before my sight; of the most horrible kind were they; more horrible than are witnessed by patients afflicted with the most violent attacks of *delirium tremens.* I thought I saw all the designs in the temptation of St. Antony coming to life, and moving towards me in menacing attitudes; the dragons appeared as if they were trying to writhe themselves round me with their sharp and corrugated tails to devour me; the Cerberuses yelped at me with their triple tongues; the image of Christ suspended by my bed in the escaparate looked down upon me with an eye of pity. A cold shudder passed over my frame like a stream of ice; this was followed by a burst of perspiration equally chilly. Suddenly I felt myself brought back, by a strange, unaccountable fascination, to gaze on the floor of my chamber, and keep my eyes fixed in a stolid contemplation on the body that now lay stretched in the cold, stiff embrace of death.

"To escape from this agonising sight, I drew the velvet curtain, pushed open the window with a convulsive hand, and dragged my tottering limbs upon the balcony, without daring to look behind me, and fancying at every step that I felt the hand of Don José laid on my shoulder.

"On the balcony I breathed again.

"The night was magnificent. Stars watched, like golden eyes, over calm and silent nature. Strong-scented perfumes embalmed the air.

"The transition was so sudden, I asked myself: 'Have I not just awoke out of a horrible dream?' This hope, which my disturbed spirit had conjured up, vanished immediately on my hearing Eusebio call to me.

"He, almost as excited and agitated as I, had been remaining for the last few seconds as motionless as a statue. Standing in a listening attitude, he had been trying to hear if any sound was in the house; there was none—nobody was stirring; and yet he was afraid that the pistol-shots might have been terrible witnesses against him; and that every instant the door would open, some one enter, seize him, and accuse him of murder. This fear was not of long duration. He was endowed with a resolute character. Instead of allowing himself to be cast down by any incident which might render the danger of his situation more complicated, he determined not to be at all romantic—not to fear shadows—not to be the dupe of his imagination, but to bear in mind the true position in which he was placed—remember that he was surrounded by realities, and triumph over the difficulties of the moment. Thus his bold, noble heart easily recovered that energy which he had displayed in his struggle with Don José.

"I said that Eusebio called me; it was to assist him in getting rid of the dead body. I advanced into the chamber with a heavy weight pressing on my heart, from fearful anticipation of what we were about to do; and I felt a thrill pass over every limb, and, in verity, my feet remained fastened to the floor, when Eusebio, throwing the large linen bag towards me, as he laid hold of the inanimate and bleeding corpse, said to me, in careless tones:

"'Undo that. Draw the string well open.'

"I stood incapable of motion; my senses left me; all command of myself was lost.

"'Come, quick!' said he. 'If they find this body here, you are lost. If we say that we killed him in self-defence, or if we make up a story about his having attempted your honour, they will ask why you did not call for succour; they will smile with incredulity at all we may have to say. Perhaps they may accuse me of being surprised by Don José in a secret intrigue with you, and assert that we killed him to rid ourselves of a witness whom we dreaded"—

"'Of a suitor whom I—and a rival whom you—dreaded, would be true,' I interrupted, for a moment gaining courage, and speaking in bold tones; then, opening the mouth of the bag wide to receive the corpse: 'Deposit it in here,' I continued, 'and let us fear nothing. My honour and my life are both in your keeping; let me think they cannot be in safer hands. Come, Eusebio, come—time presses.'

"'And time passes,' added he. 'Let us to business then.'

"With my assistance, he succeeded, before a minute more had elapsed, in depositing the corpse in the bag.

"'I must now take away this dead body,' he continued, slinging the bag over his shoulder.

"He was about to take his departure, when, laying my hand on his shoulder and detaining him, I said, in hurried and feverish accents:

"'And suppose, as you are going along with this burden, you are stopped and seized, and taken by surprise by questions, what will be your reply?'

"I stood gazing at him tremblingly; every feature of my countenance quivered from anxiety. Never shall I forget his answer; above all, the grave, sublime manner in which he spake; for Eusebio, though of a violent, was of a lofty, stern, and saturnine character. I think I never saw him smile twice during the whole period I knew him.

"'Oh! keep your mind at ease,' said he; 'rest in safety. My reply will be that I, ALONE, killed this detestable man; and that *you* had nothing whatever to do with the affair. And it will be at once credited, and readily, too; for it is universally known what hatred slaves have for their masters; aye, the whole world is aware how surely and secretly hatred ferments in the bosoms of those miserable, servile wretches whose strength, industry, and even souls and hearts are sold to domineering tyrants, who, with their cruel dispositions, are incessantly saying to them: "Be dumb! Be blind! Be submissive! And for your reward you shall share with our dogs the lashes of our whips, without sharing with them our smiles and our endearments, and the crumbs that fall from our tables!" Hatred, accompanied by revenge, consequently creeps into the bosoms of slaves like a crawling snake, and, waiting there patiently, watches for a favourable opportunity of spreading mourning through a whole family by dropping a grain of poison into the bottom of the glass out of which a master drinks, or by plunging into his heart the point of a mancheta.'

"'Hush! hush! Eusebio.'

"'I say, my reply will be that I alone killed this detestable Don José; and it will be immediately believed and readily seen how revenge placed the dagger or the pistol in my hand, because Don José had less pity for me than for one of his favourite beasts of burden, his ox, his horse, or his ass.'

"'You know the punishment reserved for you in case you confess yourself the murderer of a white man—a master—your own master?'

"'I know it well; it is a punishment less painful than a tortured heart. I shall undergo the utmost penalty of the law—the punishment of the rope or faggot—be hanged or burnt alive. But I shall die happy if I can say to myself: "Thanks to my death, the beautiful lady, Anastasia, is free, is happy, is unsuspected. This mob, hooting and groaning at me, would hoot and groan at her with hideous horror if it but knew how she took an active part in my crime, and warmly instigated me to the deed; yet now it will bow to her and make way respectfully for her to pass. One word from me, then! And those who are the foremost to respect and admire her will be the first to scorn and shun, revile and curse her. Heaven has conferred upon me a great boon to let me be the instrument of Anastasia being indebted for life, honour, respect, happiness. Such a death is to be envied: 'tis a glorious death.'

"These simple, but sublime words deeply touched my heart.

"'I will not accept this sacrifice,' said I, and clasped him by the hand. 'We will go forth together. Alike we have sinned; alike we will share the same fate: we will live or die together.'

"'Let me do my duty,' said Eusebio.

"'In my company, yes: by yourself, no. I say we will go forth together; and let us trust that, at this dark hour of the night, we may escape the eyes of all.'

"We disappeared from the chamber, passing out at the window upon the balcony. When we reached the edge, of it Eusebio stretched out his hand to assist me; together we climbed over the pentice of the house door and along the palisade and the projecting stone work; thus we got on the lawn in front of the hatto. Then, with Eusebio carrying his singular burden on his shoulder, we directed our steps swiftly towards the mangle wood hard by; the border of it we soon reached; we threaded our way through its wilderness of trees with extreme caution. We walked on with muffled steps, fearing to raise the slightest sound, lest it might reach the ears of a passer-by, and lead to our disastrous discovery. We feared, above all, falling into the hands of one of my own *serenos*, or night-watchmen, who, not only at periods of alarm, but at all times, were ordered to guard the avenues to the hatto. We made our way towards the cavern; in the forest we were traversing the mangles grew so close together, and their roots were so interlaced, that we walked over them without once touching the ground. We had been pursuing our journey thus for about an hour, when we heard in the distance the bursting of waves; then beyond the outskirts of the forest we could see the ocean shining in the moonlight, and the mangles growing so far in the sea that their branches, from dipping in its waters, were covered with heaps of oysters.

"At length we reached the cave. Eusebio disencumbered himself of the load which lay so heavy on his shoulders.

"'There was no help for the rascal ending his days but in this tragical manner,' was the singular funeral oration of Eusebio as he pushed the corpse out of the bag and dropped it in the sea. A splash—a few ripples—a slow sinking of a dark body beneath the purple waves in the moonlight—and Don José was never again heard of; perhaps, in those tropical climes, he speedily became food for famished sharks.

"After such an act as this in which Eusebio and I were mutual participators, I remained with him. We stayed together in the cave, where, by the dismal light of a torch of the locust tree that flamed and smoked in a corner, I behaved as the Countess of Shrewsbury, the mother of the Prime Minister of William III., who went to bed with her lover, the Duke of Buckingham, while he was still reeking with the blood of her husband, whom she had seen him kill in a duel, while she, dressed in the clothes of a page, stood hard by holding his horse by the bridle.

"I know not how long I might have been sleeping;—perhaps I was not asleep;—my head might have been wandering, but all on a sudden I distinctly saw Don José rise out of the sea, and, entering in at the mouth of the cavern, he approached my side in the very likeness he wore when beaten by Eusebio with the small but heavy metal image of the Virgin which I took from off the shrine in the escaparate, the blood streamed from his fractured skull, and thick gouts clotted his hair. In a hollow, unearthly voice he said to me:

"'I look upon you as the ignominious, heartless wretch who shed my blood in a cruel death. Every fresh crime you commit hereafter will raise me again from the dead, with a mangled body like this to scarify you with horror. I will follow you like a phantom, day and night. Never again will my voice reach your ears in these accents; never will I give you notice of my approach. I burn—I burn!'

"Here I could see that his whole face and head were one fiery flame. After awhile a black mask passed over his features, and he continued in the same deep, sepulchral voice:

"'Give consideration to my words: mark how exact and careful I shall be in keeping my promise. Regard yourself. Further speech is denied me in the presence of a mortal. Death is my reward. You shall see me again when doing

A STARTLING APPARITION—THE MURDERESS AND THE MURDERED.

atrocious acts. You deserve to be torn limb from limb. Look to yourself. I must not delay.'

"He gathered up his chains with composure; and now I saw what I had not observed before, that—as if the bonds were symbolic of the chains of death—his limbs were worn, and weighted with iron links. Thus shackled, he vanished from my sight at a gaze, a clanking noise accompanying his departure.

"I sprang from my recumbent position with a harrowing scream, that rang through the vaulted cavern.

"I rubbed my eyes.

"Had I been dreaming? or had I been really wide awake?

"When I looked leisurely around me, and took a deliberate survey of every object; when I saw the mouth of the cave—the sea—the moonlight—the torch burning in a corner—and recollected that these were the very adjuncts which had caught my eye of the scene I had just witnessed, seemingly in sound sleep, I could not convince myself that what I had just beheld was merely an empty vision. I viewed it as a reality. I shuddered. A cold perspiration bedewed my frame when I recalled the threat of the fearful phantom that he—such an unearthly visitant from the grave!—would from time to time torment my living sight with his inanimate and revolting presence, his skull and features one raging fire, or his head contaminated with blood mysteriously masked. And at every fresh murder I committed in my career through life, I was to see him! Why! How was this? Was I then foredoomed to be an assassin—a cold-blooded, systematic murderess? Verily, I should require the strongest nerves to gaze unmoved, not in my sleep, but in my waking moments, on such an impalpable yet hideous form. And then I was never to be made aware in what image and at what time he was coming. When I was least suspicious of his advent he was to present himself before me. Oh! how terrors would shake my soul, worse than the agonies of hell. Who could see without a shudder such an unfortunate doomed to die by an untimely death? And then, how dreadfully productive of terror are those fearful feelings of dismay with which we are all apt to regard the approach of unholy and aërial visitants from the realm of shadows!"

* * * * * * * *

* * * * * * *

Bruce St. Aubyn could read no more,

He was sick at heart.

He rose from before the journal of the Baroness Leone in such a great state of excitement that he forgot to close it, and left it wide open at the place where he had just finished reading.

He really felt ill—as if a sword had been plunged into his heart.

His whole soul was roused to horror within him, and his face assumed that livid hue, which showed the horror-stricken character of his feelings.

He rose and looked around him, horrified.

He could see the morning breaking through the crevices of the shutters.

"Why should I stay here?" he thought; "here! in the house of this most impassioned, enthralled, romantic, demoniacal, atrocious, and miserable woman! How, in what I have been reading here," he continued, laying his hand upon the diary of Anastasia—"Ah! yes—how, in what I have been reading here of her early doings, all is coarse, disgusting, brutal! How, at the bottom of the whole character and conduct of this woman lies powerful, absorbing, uncontrollable passion! Anastasia, Baroness Leone, now rises up before me in the simple form of the grossest mental disease! A perfect Colossus of romance, with a will like that of a Titan! Let me *fly!—let* me fly from her! or there will be another horrible death struggle—and under this very roof—and I the victim! And when she gets a victim into her clutches, how she despatches him! Who shall say but that she may have brought me into this mansion and into this bed-chamber of hers under the pretence of affection, and, while I am sitting in a chair, she may come behind with a pistol and shoot me? Oh! how the fate of any one must quiver in the balance held by this woman! Woe to those who, arming themselves with hopeful auguries in the midst of deceptions, seeing how she comports herself with the most capital and unparalleled courtesy, allow her to become the ascendant power, the potentate hanging on the skirts of their little circle, of their world. How, in due time, she must excite alternately their hopes and fears! This woman! with a temper as repulsive, a character as alarming, and a disposition as vindictive as the most violent, cruel, and jealous of her sex—a second Amestris, a parallel to Parysatis, a counterpart of Olympias. Why should I stay here? Why keep alive a serious alarm for my happiness, my safety? Let me fly—and fly quickly! And, to prevent the formation of any force or resolution to injure me on the part of Anastasia, let me never again come into her presence. Oh! let me fly from the home of this woman of iniquity! No procrastination! Oh! no!"

And believing that that elegant edifice, which had all the external semblance of a superb palace, was in reality a gloomy dungeon, whence few that once entered ever escaped alive, Bruce St. Aubyn, finding the means of exit from the gay abode, was, in a short time after, exchanging the free air of heaven for the tastefully-decorated rooms of that magnificent mansion.

* * * * * * * *

* * * * * * *

As brothers in misery, Bruce St. Aubyn and Pekra might have clasped each other that night. Their bonds were knitted in those hours of passion. If fear was the affliction of the one, sorrow was the suffering of the other. The heart of poor Pekra apparently had too great a pressure of sorrow for him to bear the agony of reflection, yet it seemed as if he felt it a source of alleviation in his distress to break forth at intervals into passionate exclamations against Anastasia; against her he exhibited all the unkindness and all the wickedness of his remorseless, unscrupulous nature. It would appear as if he was most unwilling to serve Anastasia, and by no means ready, for the future, to obey her.

When he found himself locked in his apartment, incapable of following his mistress, and had exhibited the rage we have already described, he burst out into disjointed ejaculations, while throwing himself into the most grotesque attitudes.

"I'll make up for this some other time," he passionately exclaimed. "I'll pursue her in all directions: I'll watch her—dog her. She shan't get out of my way; shan't take a holiday, but I'll know where she is. I'll go after her in cabs. I'll not fear her—not be cowed by her. I'll not scruple to do anything against her if she puts me out of temper—puts me out of temper as she is doing now. I'll betray her if she does."

Then, in the midst of all this frantic wildness, he would suddenly stop short and imagine he heard a noise in the house, whereupon, suddenly changing his tone, he would exclaim:

"A noise! A noise! She is coming! Yes, yes, she is coming now! She has at length returned home!"

And he would drop his head to the ground, and, leaning his ear on the floor, listen.

This he continued doing at intervals, and also repeating, with some variations, the violent speech we have given above. He took no heed of time, yet he heard the clock strike four times! At length he counted eight; after that, he relapsed into moody silence, and lay along the floor with his ear to the ground, listening, and every now and then saying in a low, nervous whisper:

"What can have become of Anastasia?"

The reader may by this time be about as anxious as the dwarf to know what had become of the Baroness Leone.

We shall then see.

CHAPTER XXXI.

ENOUGH TO MOVE A SUFFERING EVEN IN THE FURIES THEMSELVES.

"Thus to the Roman palace, as our home
And proper mansion, is Megæra come,
No stranger to these walls: not more in Hell,
Than here, do mischiefs and we Furies dwell.
Let the unenvied gods henceforth possess
Poor peasants' hearts, and rule in cottages;
Let Virtue lurk among the rural swains,
Whilst Vice in Rome's imperial palace reigns,
And rules those breasts, whom all the world obeys."
MAY.—*Prologue to Julia Agrippina.*

After the cab in which Anastasia and the young man got drove away, the Haymarket and the adjacent streets began to fill gradually; for, in London, the tide of population swells steadily for the first few hours of the day. When it is as early as that, the public thoroughfares are frequented only by people who pick up a crust for themselves—cabmen, watermen, drivers and conductors of omnibuses, labourers to sweeping machines and water-carts; scavengers, dustmen, and sweeps; street sellers and street performers; vagrants, half beggars, half thieves; and some sorts of tradesmen who go to market early in their carts, butchers, poulterers, and fishmongers; and for some hours all these persons range up and down the town, having the whole pavement and the whole street to themselves.

High up in the belfry of St. James's Church, insensible mechanism, obedient to the workman's art, was telling the hour like a thing of reason and judgment. Marvellously true it struck—one! two!—then stopped, when it had satisfied all whose ears were open as to the exact time, and, with its rotating scape-wheel, went on silently governing the motion of the hands.

A screever—that is to say, a draughtsman in coloured chalks on the pavement—who was preparing his show for the day on the flagstone (a salmon), looked up. It was the quarter of the hour after eight o'clock.

Just then a lady, turning out of Bond-street, passed a man carrying on his shoulder brooms, brushes, mats, rugs, and, in his hand, a bag of hearthstones: she passed him hurriedly, almost at a running pace.

It was Anastasia, Baroness Leone.

She made towards the Green Park.

To all appearance she was swelling with wicked triumph at the fierce sport she had made during that past night of most abhorred corruption. She carried her head proudly. A hell-like paleness was spread over her cheek. Her fiery-looking eyes threw out a meteor-like light from under the sombre shade of her sallow brow. The voices of the light-minded labourers going forth to their duties grated harshly on her ear; yet, as each man wended his way gaily to his day's toil, his singing went up sweetly to heaven. The daw, the crow, the magpie, the raven, and all things with evil voices alone would have sent out sounds grateful to her racked spirit. Murky darkness rested barrenly within her bosom; fruitless pain already pined in the now eternal night of her soul. The very fresh-blowing breeze of that delicious spring morning fell on her skin like the lazy air which you would fancy the loathsome steam of the fabled Acheron yields.

She stopped at the garden gate of the princely mansion where she lived in honour. Her hand trembled as she turned the key in the lock; the thought crossed her mind that she who was about to enter that palatial residence as its gorgeous mistress was liable at any moment to be dragged forth to public shame and handed over to the public executioner.

With an appearance of hurry she inhaled the air: in great puffs she exhaled it from her chest.

Ascending the stairs of her mansion, unseen by any of her servants:

"Oh! all you blessed saints in heaven!" she thought, "how am I tormented! A terrible tempest is in my soul! I think if I were now to lift up my eyes and see another happy I should loathe the sight and hate him. I could not but avert my vision. But who are happy?—ay, who? Why, my very friends, Madeleine Esther and Sebastian Leonard, they look forward to the enjoyment of the lawful pleasures of marriage. Apostacy and wild revolt must follow instantly upon the immediate eve of their nuptials. I can ravish from them the air they breathe. I *will.* They shall no longer interchange chaste looks and fond kisses. Why should they share joys that fill me with jealousy? They dote. They view each other every minute with endless and undiminished delight. In their unsuspecting souls they confidently hope a better fate will call them forth to live in blissful union, while I am drowned in woe at the dismal chance of the continuance of my peace of mind, my splendour, even my life."

At the last word she caught her neck with her hand: the impulse was involuntary: from head to foot she shuddered: in the fervour of her wild excitement she imagined herself already in the hand of the hateful hangman.

"I hold it as a thread of life!" she said.

And, attempting to be merry, she chuckled; but uneasy was the smile that dimpled her thin, pale cheek.

She staggered forward into her dressing-room. Her bosom heaved heavily. Into a chair she dropped, exhausted by fright and her evil fancies.

Seconds passed—many—nearly a minute; still she sat, without moving a feature, without stirring a muscle, without a thought: she was quite downcast; quite idealess. Suddenly she raised herself upright in her chair: her eyes shed glances like the returning sun: light came over her face. She clasped the taper fingers of her hand with a wrenching grasp as if she was striving with her whole might to keep all her courage within her frame.

"My spirit must not forsake me," she said, with intense energy, "or I shall be done for. I shall be in utter darkness. I would be as if the sun was to forsake the day with his glorious presence."

As she thought thus her eyes grew moist with coming tears: ere they had fully gathered, she brushed them away, exclaiming:

"Tush! I am in an overpassionate mood. This is not April weather, that we should have unexpected showers. I must not outweep the clouds. I must subdue myself, or I am not worthy to have a thought wasted upon me, for then I were no longer a reflective woman, but a vile weed."

She rose from her seat with an air of determination; she rose very quietly; with steps that fell upon the carpet as soft as velvet she ranged with her lithe frame restlessly up and down one side of the room like a caged lynx. She looked a stern picture of fierce expression; all acquainted with her character, seeing how her countenance at this moment indicated the ferocity of her heart, would have foreboded from her appearance that something terrible was in agitation; and for a long time commotions everywhere seemed to be raging in her soul's elements of darkness. A great change at length passed over her: gradually she became calm. When she was quite so she stopped; she rang the bell: she seemed to become entirely composed on hearing the tinkle of the distant bell in the basement premises.

After that, she seated herself as firm as a block of marble, and awaited patiently the arrival of her servant.

Soon the door was opened; a female domestic stood in her presence.

"What is your will, my lady?"

"My breakfast, Jaconetta," replied Anastasia in a firm, steady voice. Yet, though her voice was steady and firm, and her manner cool and collected, her heart, pierced through with anguish, palpitated fast, and her blood, from a true sense of misery, seemed to be choked and stifled in her hot veins.

When her servant brought her breakfast and removed the silver covers, she had no appetite for the rich and savoury dishes before her.

She dropped her knife and fork, and fell into meditation.

"My confidence should be at its full," she thought: "yet it is not. My rapidly palpitating heart tells me that I am in a desperate plight. Hark! What noise is that? A footstep!—A strange footstep!—Coming up the stairs!—To my chamber door, too!—Hush! hush!—It comes.—'Tis here!—No!—Hush!—'Tis nothing!—To what am I come to when I am moved thus? I! who should *not* be moved.—At every sound that rises to my ear, I start, knowing not from what quarter danger may come. I am past all courage now. And yet did I not think that I was prepared for storms and tempests, and the foulest season that ever the rage of men let forth—ay, the very wildest hurricane that ever blew from incensed society? And shall I not be bold to say I never was a coward? And yet—Yes——

"If ever I should be worth a house again I'll build it all with private passages. There shall be no common way for everybody. I'll grudge no expense. No art shall be spared. I must bar myself from the reach of men; this dreadful fear batters my reason piecemeal, and rarefies my comforts to air. I must turn my back to the world.—What!—to the world? And look at—Heaven? It must be Hell now!

"Oh! I am sorely affected by a disease," she continued, resting her head on her hand with an air of fatigue and agony. "I infer a darkness to my mind which oppresses all my comforts. Why should I think of harm? I have metal in me to withstand the shocks of twenty thousand terrors—ay, and as many deaths. Well, then; let them hang me if they will. Revenge has burst forth as swift as the lightning of heaven and cleared my heart. If they *do* kill me now, I fall satisfied. Desire of life must leave me. I will not look on hanging with horror, but view it as a calamity sent from heaven, therefore beyond the powers of human remedy; not the first, direct aim of the action, but an accidental circumstance connected with a certain deed. If I must suffer the death of a Milesian virgin, let me with impetuous ardour rush on death by the help of the halter. As the virgin Apollonia leaped into the fire which was already lit for her burning, let me, inflamed with as ardent a craving for a doom which is inevitable, break from the hands of the horrid hangman, and thrust my head into the noose prepared for my hanging."

She jumped out of her chair at this point of her soliloquy; and the next moment she was stamping violently up and down the room, each step of her foot shaking the sounding floor. To have seen her then, with such a dauntless look as she assumed, and her eyes glaring with the light of such a daring spirit, even the fearless fabled keeper of the gates of hell, the snaky tailed monster of tremendous visage, the triple-headed Cerberus, would have recoiled from before her, alarmed at her sudden gust and violence of passion.

When she had somewhat calmed her turbulent spirit she resumed her seat, and continued her meditations thus:—

"Ah! me! I must do something—Else my life will henceforth pass without mirth.—What had I best do?—Love?—Excellent!—What else should a woman do but love?—But whom shall I love?—The beautiful boy I saw at Folkestone on Sunday, Bruce"——

With a sudden change of countenance she here stopped abruptly—stopped with a bewildered look—stopped with a kind of surprise. Then she pressed her hand on her brow as if she was striving hard to collect her ideas.

Was her brain wool-gathering?

What was she thinking of?

Bruce St. Aubyn!

Why—

Yes—

During the many hours that had just passed,

her mind had been so completely filled with terrible deeds, that she had entirely forgotten that that young man had been with her the whole past afternoon. She had also even entirely forgotten that she had left him in her bed-chamber, promising soon to return to him. His absence, moreover, on her return to Arlington-street, had contributed further to make the whole circumstance slip from her memory.

As this occurrence, which it was a wonder how it had ever vanished from her recollection, now flashed in all its vivid entirety across her mind, she cast her eye slowly and searchingly round the room, examining carefully every object, as if she was in expectation of meeting in one of them with the image of the handsome youth.

When she saw he was really gone, it was positively quite curious to observe the extraordinary change which took place in her whole appearance. She who, while, a moment before, engaged in a struggling effort to recal what had happened, was grave, calm, and complete mistress of herself, was now scarcely recognisable as she sprang to her feet, a savage virago, with a furious glow in her eyes and quivering passion on her lips.

"Gone!" she exclaimed "My mansion to a hut but the day will come he would have found it more prudent to have remained here!—Provoking! That after my other enterprise succeeded so well to-day, this should fail!—Gone! Why? His departure is inexplicable. He seemed to reciprocate my love—to rejoice in my presence. Oh! there is some mystery here—something to be solved. What motive could have induced him to go from here? Yet"—

Again, as she paused suddenly, she traversed the room with her eyes. She could see nothing that afforded a clue to Bruce St. Aubyn going away from her house so unexpectedly. Terror could here be read in her looks: death could be anticipated in the destiny of Bruce St. Aubyn. She felt ashamed, disgraced, stung to the quick by his conduct.

"Shame! shame! That he should thus have left me—thus deserted me!" she thought.

Thinking thus she was still looking about the room.

All on a sudden her eye fell on the glass-case. An object there caught her sight which she had not remarked before. It made her stare: it made her look still more closely as if she doubted what she beheld. No. She was *not* mistaken. It was her diary! and *wide open!*

What's this?" she said, feeling her heart sink within her; and she advanced closer to see it better—to touch it—handle it—and, laying hold of it, convince her senses. "My diary! and open!" she continued. "How came this here? How? How?" and she put her finger to her forehead. "I kept it locked securely in this drawer—the key, too, hidden—always, *always* hidden! Did I mislay it? Where did I leave it? Where?" She could not recollect. "If I then heedlessly left it anywhere, there's none to blame but I—and I—I must forgive myself. But the greatest woe that could befal me unfortunately alighted on me when I gave the young viper this opportunity to ruin me.—I must seek him out without delay, and shut his mouth—shut it for ever. Curses! Ten thousand curses! —This is why he has fled. He has become acquainted with the foul deeds of my youth; he has fled, doubtless cursing me.—Oh! God! Oh! God! Here is Thy power and justice! that when we think ourselves most safe, straightway Thou breakest our trust in ourselves, and, frustrating our confidence, makest that which seemed to be our prop and solace, our greatest, and often our only cause of ruin.—Oh! I was a child—a very, very child.—But love makes us all children. I cried for Bruce St. Aubyn, as a child cries for a knife, and, when he gets it, hurts himself. So Heaven grants what we desire too frequently only to punish us."

She stood staring at the open diary; for in the confusion of his spirit and the alarm of his heart, as well as in his hurry to escape, Bruce St. Aubyn had not taken the precaution to put the book aside or even to shut it; and she saw that he had been reading the passages which she herself had recorded of the murder of Don José.

She raised her hands to both sides of her head as if she was about to tear her hair, and she fell to cursing—cursing horribly—cursing till she foamed at the mouth.

The secret of her life was known then to at least one!

Her life was in the hands of Bruce St. Aubyn!

"*He must not live, then!*" she shrieked.

She paused for a moment; and resumed her musing thus:

"Oh! black Fate! To what hast thou doomed him? DEATH! Never more must he see the home of his fathers—never again be sheltered by the gods of his household hearth. He must perish with my secret unrevealed. 'Tis agony to me—his dread fate! I cannot spare myself the agony—cannot spare this painful duty I owe to myself. There must be no mercy with me here. I must shut out every sense of pity."

Thus horribly communing with herself she was interrupted frivolously. She heard the moving of the handle of the door, and knew that somebody had entered and was observing her.

Considerably annoyed at being caught in the solitude of her chamber, at a moment when her features were disfigured by the play of the evil passions—when she was, in fact, in a towering rage—a weakness to be expected more in a child or schoolgirl than in a sensible, full-grown woman, she looked round sharply. From the quick, angry manner in which she turned about, it was easy to see that she was on the point of giving a good scolding to the intruder for breaking in upon her privacy so abruptly, without giving any warning of an approach; but whatever might have been the angry words she was about to deliver she suppressed, on seeing her favourite servant Jaconetta standing on the threshold of the door.

In a moment she was as sedate and mild as she had been before furious and angry.

A few words will suffice to explain why Anastasia was so frequently subjected to those wonderfully sudden changes of temper.

Hers was one of those robust and powerful organisations which Nature seems to have been particularly careful in arming with caution, out of regard to the violence and frequency of those shocks in which it is the fate of persons so endowed to be involved. Anastasia possessed at once the strength that strikes and the skill that parries. Her first impulse was always to be hot and headstrong, but then there came an immediate reaction. No sooner had she given way to any ungovernable outburst of temper than she saw the wisdom and necessity of heeding the dictates of a cool, calm, calculating spirit. Moreover, she could conceal, when she liked, fury, even of the most vehement and enraged kind, in hypocrisy—useful scabbard! which, in moments when prudence made it necessary, hid the blade of the sword without dulling its edge.

When turned to good and pure in aim, these powers are beneficial to ourselves and others, and deserve praise. When they are directed to evil, under the influence of that inexplicable fatality which seems to hold an invincible dominion over peculiar temperaments, they are productive of the most disastrous results.

"A man who knows not how to dissemble is incapable of being a ruler," was the saying of a Prince who acted himself with dissimulation. The same maxim was held by Anastasia to be applicable with as much justice to the art of vengeance as to that of ruling; and she unhesitatingly resorted to it whenever she was avenging herself on her enemies or on those who had it in their power to injure her. Convinced of the truth of this, she nurtured her vengeance, and brought it to maturity in silence; and, in order to render it efficacious and complete, she bore a calm and unmoved demeanour in the presence of everybody so as to ward off any, even the least, suspicion that she was engaged in any plan necessitating the manifestation of the passions.

On entering the presence of her mistress as unexpectedly as described, Jaconetta held in her hand a large printed broadsheet, which Anastasia, seeing to be the newspaper, stretched out her hand to receive.

It was the late edition of one of the London morning journals.

Anastasia had not been reading it for more than a minute, when it dropped from her hand and lay on the carpet at her feet.

She had read in it the tragedy of that morning in which she had acted the principal part!

The account stated :—

"There was no clue to lead to a discovery of the frightful death of Lord Mirfield:" "There was no believing he really put an end to his existence:" "The cause of his death remained wrapped in an impenetrable mystery which defied all investigation:" "He had gone to the hotel in the Haymarket at midnight, where he was shortly joined by a woman—a lady of reputed rank—in whose company he died:" "About this lady there was such a strangeness of manner as to cause suspicion to rest on her:" "What was stranger, nobody knew anything of her history:" "The case was, altogether, very strange:" "The more it was considered, the more it was involved in enigma:" "There was hope, however, that in the course of the day the mystery would be cleared up, the Coroner having determined, though at great personal inconvenience, to hold an inquest on the body that afternoon at Moppy's Hotel."

"I must strive by a walk," said Anastasia, laying her hand on her throbbing temple, "to dissipate my thoughts: they are grievously painful: they oppress me."

She looked about the room with a lack-lustre eye.

"I seem as if forsaken," she added: "as if in this house alone—all, all alone—as if remaining here neglected.—Ha! what noise was that I heard just now at the door?—Hush!—Gone!—'Twas fancy, then.—Nothing is here but solitude and silence. They are ill-boding, both of them."

She passed her hand over her brow, and murmured:

"My presaging soul is filled with ghastly fears."

At that moment the light of the sun began to shine dimly!

CHAPTER XXXII.

THE TRUE MATERIAL FIRE OF HELL.

"Dost thou imagine thou canst slide on blood,
And not be tainted with a shameful fall?
Or, like the black and melancholic yew-tree,
Dost think to root thyself in dead men's graves,
And yet to prosper?"

WEBSTER.—*The White Devil.*

The sunlight was dim, because there was a mist in the room: it was a growing mist, that gathered gradually into a little curling cloud; and the little cloud went on curling and accumulating quicker and thicker, and darker and denser, till at length it was as white and as compact as a volume of smoke issuing in a pillar-like form out of the crater of a volcano, like that of the Souffrière, in St. Vincent, in the West Indies, just previous to an eruption.

The door of the room had not been opened; and yet, if a human figure was not in that bedchamber keeping Anastasia company, there was, at any rate, a human head.

YES.

There! There!

At the top of the cloud!

Ugh! What a head!

How disfigured!—wounded! bleeding! What a mummy-looking, monstrous visage! The nose crushed—the lip slashed—the jaw broken—the head and face one swollen and blood-covered pulp of flesh.

The clotted locks stood on end; the lips moved, but breathed no articulate sound: the eyes glared, but there was no speculation in them.

At the sight, the senses of Anastasia nearly deserted her.

She knew it was a ghost—even THE GHOST OF DON JOSE!

To her the head was a terribly frightful sight.

Not the least change was visible in it; 'twas as she remembered it when Don José was alive. It seemed, moreover, exactly as it had appeared to her at the moment when Don José breathed his last in the agonies of a horrible assassination.

Yes; it was Don José's head—his stout, heavy, crushed, ill-shaped head—that was floating about the chamber, in the air, in the midst of a cloud, unsupported, without limbs attached to it.

Oh! the enigmas of the realm of Death!—How grave they are! Who can solve them?

We behold the lifeless tenement in the coffin—on the bed or the dissecting table of the surgeon—perhaps upon the wheel or the gallows—or, as sad, on the bare board of the workhouse; and, if we happen to be strong-minded, we say, "There is the end of all." The end of *what?* As little as life commences with the first motions of the embryo, so little does the end commence with the presence of visible death. Of the end as of the beginning we know little. All we know is that the powers of Nature labour silently and imperceptibly; and that creation and dissolution border so closely upon each other that, with our blunted senses, we are incapable of distinguishing them. Observe but the members of the medical faculty, how, after years of toil—years of untiring industry—they arrive at nothing which approaches to certainty! How, after long and anxious searches, aided by the knife and the microscope, when they think they have made a discovery, and prepare to give it a fitting place in the human system—lo! a new discovery appears, and all the old systems are thrown into confusion. If the brain is almost turned by pondering long on the relation of Life to Death, how is it not distracted by brooding on the relation of the Spirit to the Body? None of us fear to commune with death; many of us daily and hourly make acquaintance with its victims. Yet the disembodied spirit is a fearfully serious subject; and none are careless of its terrors when, clothed, it would seem, in the flesh, it comes to us a visitant from the aërial world.

Anastasia looked upon that head as the ancients looked upon that of the Gorgon—as of a formidable monster—to terrify. And yet she knew it was the spirit of Don José. Mighty goodness! Even as it retained his lineaments and appeared in the same lacerated and wounded condition as at the time of his dire assassination, so it retained a distortion of the features expressive of ineffable pain.

Why did it appear to Anastasia at all?

When spirits assume the likeness of their former bodily shapes, all is not right: the state of things is wrong—they come to shadow forth the Divine indignation. So it was in this instance. Whenever Anastasia committed a crime she was visited by this dreadful spirit; and in the course of her existence this spirit of Don José haunted her about as incessantly as the spirit of Cleonice haunted Pausanias.

Deeply, indeed, did Anastasia feel the unearthliness of this intrusive form. Her eyes were lit with a wild lustre that gave her countenance a look of speechless fear—such a look, that she was the very personification of horror.

"Maker of heaven and earth, preserve me," she exclaimed. "Preserve my soul, my senses. Sustain my heart. Give me strength to overcome the terror of this hour. I have taken wrong, oh! abominable steps, and am fit to be numbered only among the children of darkness, but I call from on high for courage and comfort."

Wrapt in fervent, spiritual, inward prayer, Anastasia, with clasped hands, stood in silence.

No agitated surprise passed over the lineaments of the shade—no expression of passion came from the lips of the head.

"The sight of you horrifies me," pursued Anastasia, trembling in every limb; and seeing that the ghost kept its eyes fixed upon her with a chilling and unmeaning gaze, "If this goes on," she continued, "it will cost me dear.—In God's name, speak! Say yes—say no—say something—if it be to curse me!—Speak! But if you have speech, promise never, while I live, to disclose to mortal man a word of what you know of me. Promise!"

The ghost made no promise.

"Tell me you will be silent."

The ghost spake no word.

There was a pause. Anastasia shudderingly beheld the visage become more and more hideous: she saw the frame attaching itself to the head limb by limb.

The whole figure of Don José at length, enveloped in a thin mist, stood before her in broad day, in the pale, dim sunlight.

Anastasia trembled.

Anastasia groaned.

Ghosts are afraid of fear, and will not approach the timid.

The phantom of Don José retired with majestic slowness to the further corner of the room, Anastasia all the time showing signs of horror, though she looked upon that human form as an airy thing—a vaporous body, a shadow, a dream, a disembodied spirit from the future world, the innocuous soul of Don José.

"Thou knowest me," she said. "Address me."

The ghost stood in silence, looking at her as if it recognised her, but spoke not.

"Oh! speak to me," she added, with increased fervour. "Inform me of the meaning of this—of anything that relates to you or me."

Still the ghost spoke not; with a deep sigh it glided along the floor like a shadow, and, moving with slowness, placed itself directly before Anastasia.

She, who had been standing with shrinking body and averted glance, looked up, and fixed her eye on the ghost with a sort of fascinated gaze.

A hollow voice smote on her ear, and she heard these words:

"You said you loved me and would marry me, but you wounded and slew me. When you had reft me of life, you denied to my body those funeral rites, the absence of which has ever been accounted by every people the cruellest of punishments to a fellow being; for the souls of the unburied wander one hundred years in the realms of space before they can be transported to their place of rest. For awhile I lie concealed, but ever and anon, obedient to the command of a superior will, I come on earth. I shall continue to come by night or day each time a fresh soul appears in the region of shadows sent there by your murderous hand."

These words were uttered in unearthly sounds, that did not seem to come from the shade before Anastasia; but at one time from the wall, at another from the ceiling, then anon from the floor.

Anastasia strove to speak: her tongue clove to the roof of her mouth: every organ refused to perform its function: she could neither speak nor move, advance nor retreat: she was as a statue, mute and motionless.

As Antigone preferred, before the stately palace of Labdacus or the towers of wealthy Thebes, the craggy mountain of Cythæron, so Anastasia wished, at that moment, that she were in the most inhospitable wilderness, even the ruckiest fastnesses of one of those unpeopled Asiatic or African deserts which are traversed only by rapacious, famishing, and roaring wild beasts: infinitely rather would she have been there than in that peaceful princely abode, so long as she was in the presence of that impalpable but most terrifying phantom.

What but her own impiety did she now behold? The shade brought before her that unscrupulous soul of hers in its hideous blackness;—it made her see and loathe her crimes;—it forced her to take a retrospect into an early passage, so dreary and so dreadful, of her criminal life, showing how all sense of virtue, as of light, was dead within her;—it placed before her a mirror reflecting clearly to her conscience how she lay concealed from the eye of Heaven. Oh! Memory! How she would have crushed Thee! Ay, how she could have killed Thee! that no one in after years might relate her story.

Again the hollow voice sounded in her ears:

"You have been unjust—oh! most unjust and cruel to me. Think! If I deserved death by murder, I deserved burial from mercy.—Oh! I am accursed! incapable of peace—beyond the reach of comfort. Nothing is in me but horror, grief, despair, misery.—And there is no means of rescue—no way out of this—none, oh! none."

"Leave me!" fell in faint accents from the muttering tongue of Anastasia.

A distortion of the features, expressive of pain, was visible in the face of the ghost of Don José.

"I am in pain, because I am without you. Come; be with me for ever.—Come! come!"

And the phantom beckoned to Anastasia to follow him; all the while it was advancing with its customary majestic slowness towards the open window that overlooked the Green Park.

With a gurgling sound in her throat as if she were choking Anastasia staggered forward, with her arms outstretched, her eyes seeming as if they were about to start out of their sockets, her mouth open and her chest heaving; her voice, as she endeavoured to utter something, failed to articulate a syllable; without a word, without a scream, without even an attempt at an outcry, she sank gently, as if her knees were failing under her, and her legs too weak to sustain her frame; then she dropped on the floor: in another second she was insensible.

The clock struck noon.

The ghost vanished.

Whither?

CHAPTER XXXIII.

THUNDER GONE BEYOND—DROPS REMAIN.

"Ay, but to die, and go we know not where;
To lie in cold obstruction, and to rot;
This sensible warm motion to become
A kneaded clod; and the delighted spirit
To bathe in fiery floods, or to reside
In thrilling regions of thick-ribbed ice;
To be imprisoned in the viewless winds,
And blown with restless violence round about
This pendent world; or to be worse than worst
Of those that lawless and incertain thoughts
Imagine howling!—'tis too horrible!
The weariest and most loathed worldly life
That age, ache, penury, and imprisonment
Can lay on nature, is a Paradise
To what we fear of death."
SHAKSPEARE.—*Measure for Measure.*

Anastasia was awakened from the state of paralysis into which she had fallen from—she knew not what. On opening her eyes and recovering her senses, she was surprised and alarmed to hear the floor of the room make a noise like the report of a gun! She had heard that floors sometimes make that noise, owing to the length of the boards, upon change of weather or some other cause, but she knew that that was not the case with the floor of her bed-chamber. With a pallid countenance she raised herself on her elbow, and looked timidly around with a sort of film on her eyes.

How, at that moment, that fierce and determinately savage woman—as fierce and savage as that bold beast, the rhinoceros, which destroys anything and everything that comes within its reach—looked most feeble, harmless, and even meek.

The noise with the boards being repeated, Anastasia, thinking of ghosts, and alarmed at what she had just seen, being frightened, got up and was going into the next room, when——

She heard somebody try to open the door on the landing, but, finding it fast, he went to another door, which formed a communication between Anastasia's chamber and the adjoining room, which he opened.

With a stronger sensation than can be described, Anastasia saw the door move, as it were, of its own accord, back on its hinges.

Without seeing any form, she heard that somebody had come into the room.

She perfectly knew it to be the step of Lord Mirfield. It came to her side and spake to her these words:

"Baroness Leone, I am going a long journey, and am come to bid you good bye."

Upon which she answered, in a fright:

"Who are you? Lord Mirfield? You are dead!"

In reply to this there was only a groan.

Anastasia heard nothing more. She saw nothing.

THE SWOON.

The whole time the room was all light and full of sunshine.

"Is this a dream?" she thought. "Am I perfectly awake? Are all my senses about me as ever?"

And she pinched her arms, and rubbed her eyes; still she could see nothing. And she stretched out her hand; still she could discover nothing—nothing solid.

"I am sent to you from heaven," continued the ghost, "to give you warning that when you die, in your due time, your death will be still more harrowing than mine."

The hair of Anastasia stood erect: her eyes seemed starting from their sockets.

"If it were possible for you to be returned to life again," she muttered, in faint accents, and as she spoke the words she shuddered, "I'd do the deed again."

As she uttered these words she saw a pair of eyes of flaming fire staring her in the face.

The sight of those fiery eyes sent her almost frantic with fear; her horrors increased to the degree which is the case with those flagitious persons who, having committed a murder, believe they are haunted by the ghost of the murdered one; for conscience, that busy monitor, is ever active to its own pain and disturbance.

"You are under the utmost terror on my account," continued the ghost; "but your terror cannot equal mine; nor can your agonies. Were nature to work miracles, she could not make my sufferings less. Everything adds to my misery; the black night the sun brings—the day the morning star ushers—the seas that meet the sky. And yet you will escape execution for my murder."

Anastasia, terrified as she was, caught at the words with all the eager wildness of a man who, in the pang of drowning, catches at a passing plank. "How know you?"

"I can tell things to come," was the reply. "Nothing can happen which I foresee not. It is easy for me to compass what, with mortals, are impossibilities. Listen!"

"I am all ear."

"The alarm was given, the place was searched, my body found. You were with me, and had been the only one: still, you will not be committed—not even on suspicion; nor will you be even apprehended. Were a warrant granted for searching this house of yours, no proofs of guilt would appear against you. You can only be condemned by confessing the murder yourself, and that you will never do. Undeniable witnesses will swear you are a woman of the most unblemished character; in the course of the examination it will not appear there was any manner of quarrel or grudge between us: all will believe you perfectly innocent; and, as there will be no evidence against you, either positive or circumstantial, you must be acquitted. Still you are my foul, merciless murderess; and supernatural powers will assist me from this time forth in depriving you of all peace of mind."

Anastasia glared around frantically; and, as her glance fell on nothing but the viewless air, she betrayed symptoms of violent emotion—indications of indescribable horror. To add to her terror, she could now hear the footsteps retreating—departing out of the room as invisibly as they had come into it.

The whole of this was enough completely to dethrone her reason. Excitement and alarm deprived her of strength. She tottered—she stumbled; to hold herself upright she grasped at one of the chests which stood against the wall. She laid hold of it; she overturned it; it fell on the floor, crashed into fragments, with all the valuables it contained shivered also into pieces.

A wild laugh broke from her lips, to which the articles on the walls around gave a shrill echo; the next moment she fell to the floor, reeling thither with a piercing scream!

CHAPTER XXXIV.

THE SOUL OF QUIET TRANSFORMED INTO DISTRACTED MADNESS.

> "Few heroines in the tragic page
> Felt more than thee in thy contracted stage;
> Fair, fond, and virtuous, they our pity move,
> Impelled by duty, agonised by love;
> But no Mandane, who in dread has knelt
> On the bare boards, has greater terror felt,
> Nor been by warring passions more subdued."
> CRABBE.—*Tales of the Hall.—Ruth.*

That harrowing scream of Anastasia, piercing the ears of all whom it reached, and sounding through the whole mansion, echoed in every room and vestibule, corridor and passage.

In a moment the whole of the Baroness Leone's household was in commotion. All her servants, of the female sex, hurried in pale and speechless agitation from every part of the house, towards her bed-chamber. Before her room was crowded with these domestics she had recovered her senses; 'twas but for a second. The first object on which her opening eyes alighted was the livid countenance of Viscount Mirfield. Wracked to agony by the sight, and for the moment believing that the whole remainder of her life would be miserably and horribly passed in receiving nothing but unholy visitations from ghostly images, she, like the unhappy Ino, who, when pursued, leaped down into the sea from a high and fatal cliff, flew to the window to throw herself down upon the terrace beneath, but, hitting her forehead violently against the sash, she fell back, seemingly in a swoon; if it was such, it was almost immediately converted into an hysterical fit of laughter, screams, sighs, tears, and sobs.

The foremost of her servants, rushing into her chamber, were just in time to see this furious act and its painful consequence. Without waiting to be loud in lamentations over their mistress—for they could not understand the cause of this violence on the part of the Baroness—they ran up and down the stairs, uttering such exclamations as:

"Mistress is in dangerous hysterics!"

"The doctor must be sent for immediately!"

"Restoratives must be instantly applied!"

"Why! what ails her?" was the question put by those who had not been in the chamber; and the reply was:

"She has flown at the window to throw herself out."

The shock of the sudden appearance, for the second time, of the ghost of Viscount Mirfield, had been too great for the enfeebled nerves of Anastasia. She recovered from one fainting fit only to fall into another; soon she grew so ill that her alarmed domestics sent at once for her physician. The elastic temper which had carried her through so many trials seemed at length to be crushed within her.

After the first explosion was over, the fumes of terror so far evaporated as to allow a glimmering of reason to find its way into her mind. She began to get calmer and calmer, till at length all her fears and anxieties disappeared as if by magic. The energy she exerted on the occasion was wonderful: she said nothing; but it was evident she thought a great deal, for she appeared to treat her domestics with something like suspicious reserve. As she looked round upon them in silence, she missed Pekra.

"Where is my dwarf?" she inquired.

A servant stepped forward.

"He is locked in his chamber, my lady."

Anastasia pressed her hand to her brow, and, for the first time, recollected that with her own hand she had locked Pekra in his room just previous to her going out to meet Lord Mirfield in the Haymarket. She gave the servant a key, and told her to liberate Pekra.

All her domestics then slunk away. In another second the room was as silent and deserted as before.

The doctor who had been summoned to see Anastasia, after examining her, called her servants aside to give them instructions how to treat their mistress. Without saying a word they listened to his injunctions, simply obeying through that instinct which teaches human beings to follow in the hour of need those who are willing and able to lead. They acted as he directed: they gave Anastasia the physic which he sent a few minutes after: it was an opiate: shortly after, Anastasia was fast asleep.

She could not have been asleep more than a few minutes before Pekra entered, creeping quietly into the room. His attitude was that of marked attention: at every step he stopped and listened, and peered into every nook and corner—every dark spot that might be converted into a hiding hole in the chamber. Presently he saw Anastasia on the bed.

"Ah! There she is! fast asleep!" he muttered to himself, and advanced as quietly and as creepingly as before towards the ebony-framed glass case.

When he got there he stopped, and stood for a few seconds looking cautiously at Anastasia.

"Yes! She is fast asleep," he again murmured.

He drew from his pocket a small silver key, with which he locked the case; and, leaving the key as he had found it the day before in the drawer in which Anastasia kept her diary, he seemed on the point of retiring; the opportunity had been easy for his effecting an unnoticed entry into the chamber; it presented equally great facilities for his beating an unobserved retreat; but when he had accomplished the purpose for which he had evidently come into the room, he placed himself in the middle of the floor. With strong feeling visible in every line of his countenance, he seemed by no means inclined to retrace his steps. He stopped and fixed his eyes on the figure of Anastasia—that commanding and lovely figure, which, attired in silk and satin, laces and ribbons, was reposing in the depth of slumber voluptuously on the bed; diamond and other jewelled rings glittering on the taper fingers of her snowy hands; the lower edge of her garment revealing, or rather not concealing, tiny feet; an artful and coquettish attitude, even in sleep, contriving to give, through the ample drapery, such promise and vague indications of the perfection of female proportions, that Canova, had he been alive, would, for the mere sake of copying from such a model, have made a pilgrimage to Arlington-street, just as it was said that he came all the way from Italy to London for the simple purpose of having a view of Waterloo-bridge. For several minutes Pekra remained looking upon the beautiful apparition of his slumbering mistress with eyes half dimmed by the conflict of various yet overpowering emotions. He knew she was fast asleep and did not see him; nor did he wish that she should; his conscious soul would have sunk under the ray of her glance. Conquering his violent agitation by a strong effort of vigorous will, he approached, and seated himself at the side of the bed, muttering to himself:

"That infernal Viscount! That profligate young scamp—that Bruce St. Aubyn! They both worship her; in return she idolises them, or pretends that she does. But I will thwart them yet, dependent as I am! Soft! soft! Why think of my dependence? Let me forget degradation and misery, and nurse this sentiment in silence. There is a fate in this!"

With every outward demonstration of attention Pekra planted himself beside the bed of Anastasia, with a fixed determination in his bosom not to leave his mistress till she showed signs of a return of all her former energy, and not to be surprised at anything the day might bring forth; for he had heard from some of the servants what had happened, and he half suspected he knew the cause of Anastasia's agitation and fits of violence and agony. It was a suspicion he scarcely dared whisper to his own conscience.

"This mistress of mine," he thought, "is a villanous imp of Satan—a bold, stout, valiant, stomachy woman: no intolerable wax-nosed simpleton, but a very shrewd devil—a knowing Lucifer in petticoats, as diabolical as haughty. If, now, she raves afresh, and any bad thing should come to my knowledge of her, I'll keep it all to myself—no more communicate it to the ears of others than make inquiry of its origin from her. If I get at any guilt of hers, why make it known? When her riches, her brilliancy, her fascination, her deep dark eyes, her chiselled features, her swelling form—all her matchless embodiments, fill me with intense, absorbing, frantic love for her—poor, enamoured me! for whom the obstacles are fearful in my course towards happiness."

Forgetting himself, and thinking only of his mistress:

"If she were put in a book," he thought, "she would be pronounced the most clever monstrosity that ever amused or excited a novel reader. Her acts beggar probability and nature with so bold a front, one thinks it scarcely worth while to quarrel with her. *I* do not; I never shall."

While Pekra was musing thus, Anastasia got involved in a series of short dozes that left her dwarf doubtful whether she was asleep or awake. Out of this demi-torpid condition she started up suddenly, and leaned on her elbow.

Her eyes were half out of her head, her tongue muttered broken sentences, and all but inarticulate words. What she said clearly intimated to Pekra that the chamber was haunted, at least to her senses—that she was seeing objects and hearing sounds—perhaps, awful speeches.

"I hear you," she exclaimed, with apparently scattered senses: "you are counting—counting up to two.......the number of the years I have to live? No: I'll live longer. What! not so long? Yes! 'tis my name you syllable; you throw my secret crimes in my teeth.........That my doom—my doom! say you? You pronounce it in such fearfully grim and hollow voices—ah! like the voices of demons! You laugh! 'Tis too much! You mock me! See! see! They rush away! They burst into the next room! They are gone now. I'll go, too! Yes, I'll go away from this."

The effect of the whole of this was overpowering to Pekra. He could not understand what it meant. He could make out the room quite distinctly; yet he could see nothing. No: there was nothing at all remarkable in the chamber—nothing to indicate the presence of supernatural visitors. Yet there was Anastasia uttering the laments of a tortured spirit, as she continued in broken accents:

"They rush into the next room. I'll find a free passage out now."

And she moved as if about to effect her escape, but drew back instantly as if stung by a serpent:

"I cannot—cannot. They push me back with their icy hands. Their faces are cold—their bodies rigid. 'Tis their faces!—Don José's! Viscount Mirfield's!"

The dwarf sprang to his feet at the mention of the last name. The next words whispered by Anastasia verified his worst fears.

"They are dead!—both dead and MURDERED! Ha! ha! ha!—I have had my revenge! Ha! ha! ha!—ha! ha! ha!"

And she laughed with the wildness of a maniac.

Immediately after, pale as ashes, her forehead bathed in cold perspiration, and harassed by feelings she was unable to master, she yielded to terrors which goaded her like the whips of the furies. The most indescribable fears disturbed her bosom and shook her frame, paralysing her soul.

A fearful spectacle was now before her eyes.

In at the window a singular figure had made its appearance, a loose garment hanging like a talar about its limbs, and its distorted and swollen face covered with large black patches.

A voice, addressing itself to Anastasia and heard only by her, said, in an awful, monotonous tone:

"You must let me take up my abode here: the gravedigger has too much work on hand. I must wait and take my turn when the hundredth year from this shall come."

Anastasia was almost dead from fright already, when lo! on the opposite side of the bed there arose from the floor first the head, then the body, and finally the limbs of Viscount Mirfield.

More dead than alive, Anastasia raised herself up to listen to this other phantom, who said to her:

"I have come to you to revive me a little. You can bring me something better than the poison."

"Oh! God!" sighed Anastasia.

"When you torture another to death, I will call upon you again," said the ghost of Don José—and departed as it had come, in great silence, and with equally great dignity.

The ghost of Viscount Mirfield exclaimed:

"You refuse my request—refuse even a little money that I may provide for myself something better than poison"—and vanished instantly.

At that moment Pekra caught a sound distinctly in his right ear, as if something had passed within an inch of him. The sound that fell on his ears was loud and whistling, very coarse and very hollow, something like what a man makes by whistling into the end of an empty cask; it made him feel immeasurably uncomfortable. The loud current of air which had rushed by him was like the wind on a wild night.

Immediately he had ceased hearing the whistling sound, he turned toward Anastasia.

She had fallen back upon the bed, cold and apparently lifeless. As she sank thus into a death-like stupor, Pekra sprang forward and bent over her—bent over her for awhile, then sank upon her body, uttering a wild and maniac laugh:

"She is dying, oh! God! she is dying!" he exclaimed in death-like terror. "Don't die!" he added in despairing accents. "Live, Baroness Leone: I will keep you living. No one shall harm you. Oh! God! this is a fearful day! For sins she has committed Heaven visits her with this intolerable agony. What shall I do? How will it end? Her soul is desolate. So is mine—so is the soul of poor Pekra."

And he sank back on a chair, and concealed his face in his hands.

The loving dwarf's faint-heartedness did not last long. The necessity of succouring his unhappy mistress stood clear and plain before his soul. He sprang from his seat. He would go and call the servants. But no; Anastasia might rave again, and make fresh disclosures of her secret crimes in *their* presence! He must recover her, then, unassisted by others. A sudden thought struck him. He hurried from the room. Soon he returned. He carried in his hand a small decanter of brandy. He poured some of it down the throat of his mistress. Then he seated himself near her and chafed her hands. At last he succeeded in restoring warmth to her chilled frame. The first thing she did on opening her eyes was to fix them on the face of her dwarf. A faint smile passed over her countenance.

"Pekra!" she said.

"What is it?"

"Have I not been raving?"

"Very much."

"And what have I been saying and doing?"

It was scarcely to be expected that Pekra, who was there to console his mistress in her affliction, would confide to her the truth of what had occurred, and inform her that, in the midst of her ravings, her misdeeds had come to the light.

"Nothing," he replied.

The answer seemed to give Anastasia relief.

She rose, telling Pekra to accompany her to the drawing-room.

To THE DRAWING-ROOM!

Well, after what had happened—after she had been, as if in a churchyard, wandering among the tombs for so many hours—it might be thought she was not equal to any new enterprise. But she was a woman, reader, of enormous energy.

It was scarcely questionable that a diseased excitability of the mind had generated the condition in which she had found herself. It was also equally clear that new tortures were developing in her breast, and that in her own opinion a new crisis was near at hand. Yes, Fate and her own Heart were hunting her to another crisis, even as they were ever hunting that poor worm of the earth from crisis to crisis, till it might truly be said of her life, "It was one long malady." Often did it seem to her as if any end were desirable, be it ever so speedy or ever so violent.

The ground, as she left her chamber, seemed to cling around her feet: the marble pillars soaring up in stately grandeur by her side hung over her with a dull and dizzy weight: the boards she trod awakened the fear within her that they would grimly speak forbidding echoes from human voices: she shuddered lest unbodied arms should pluck at her as she passed, and socketless pale eyes look glaringly upon her: icily, shiveringly cold she moved on with slow respired breath and lazy, lagging limbs, as if every one was gyved with its own particular weight of manacle.

But hers, as it has been said, was a valiant and resolute spirit: she would have accounted it a point of cowardice to fear an evil before it fell upon her; and, as great spirits are ever above their fortunes, she retreated into that fortress of her mind—Determination: she called up her resolution to guard her soul from timorous thoughts.

By the time she reached her drawing-room she was already relieved. She felt as if she would no longer be pursued with the vengeance of Heaven. She was prepared to bring forth new battalions to the field, to awake the drum and trumpet, and summon up the last hopes of her weakened strength.

Seeing that the faculties of his mistress were restored to her, Pekra left her alone.

As he retired, he mused:

"I cannot rest content," he thought, "till I know the full meaning of those strange exclamations that I heard fall from the lips of Anastasia in her chamber just now. She was not doing all that to mystify me—to turn me into derision. No. She was light-headed—betraying her own confidence—letting me read her heart. Has she then *really* committed murder?—poisoned Lord Mirfield? Then Heaven and Earth, the Destinies, and all the Immortal Powers have, with the iron pen of fate, written down for her—CERTAIN DEATH. Then, instead of my eyes weeping tears, my heart will weep blood for her! I am confounded quite. Not yet have I abjured all interest in her. On my soul I love her as my soul. Therefore can I not loathe her: my nature knows not how to entertain an ill opinion of her; so there comes a softness to my mind, and I forgive in her the usage of the bowl or dagger. Let me see, now; let me see. Can I think of no plan whereby I may wade no deeper in mystery as to all this?"

And he pursued his way, attentively turning over in his mind what he had best do.

Suddenly he resolved to go at once to the Haymarket, and ascertain if what he had heard from the lips of his mistress was mere ravings or realities.

CHAPTER XXXV.

LIFE'S BITTERNESS, THE HEART'S INQUIETUDE.

"Infernal guilt!
How dost thou rise in every hideous shape
Of rage and doubt, suspicion and despair,
To rend my soul. Why did I not
Repent, while yet my crimes were delible,
Ere they had struck their colours through my soul
As black as night or hell—'tis now too late.
Take me, all
Unfeeling guilt. Oh, banish, if thou canst,
This fell remorse, and every fruitless fear."

REV. DR. BROWN.—*Barbarossa.*

Pekra was the only individual in Arlington-street when he stepped into it from the hall-door of Anastasia's house.

But presently there came rumbling into the street a market gardener's wagon laden with cabbages, and under it walked a bull-dog—a surly, grim, crop-eared, brass-collared beast, as fierce as any dragon. No prudent man would have liked to tackle him. Glowering about him with his leaden eyes, he spied a small, black-nosed, stunt-tailed terrier, trotting smellingly along the pavement, and not more than two-thirds his great size. Without the slightest provocation he darted at him, and, before the little terrier had even time to bark, threw him on his back.

"Call your dog off!" angrily shouted the terrier's owner—a natty stable-boy, "seven stun six" at the heaviest in weight, and "four foot three" at the highest in stature.

"No," growled the market gardener, as ferocious as his bull-dog. "Let 'em fight it out."

"Agreed," said the stable-boy; and clapping his hands and whistling to his terrier, he shouted gaily: "Wake up there, Bobby; mind what you are about."

Bobby heard and started—started faster than steam let from a valve by an engineer.

And Pekra, though he took but little interest in dogs in general, had, notwithstanding, his curiosity so excited by the novelty of the contest, that he stopped to see the gallant fight that ensued; and it did him good (depend on that, considering the dwarf he was) to see how the "big 'un" got it.

Pekra could not drive this little incident out of his head. He thought of it and thought of it as he wended his way along the crowded Piccadilly, with people running past him like rainwater from a spout. Reeking omnibuses, crammed to the roof, went by unnoticed: noisy newsboys, brimful of animal spirits, screamed their alto voices in his ears at the corners of the streets without his hearing them. He was thinking and thinking how applicable the whole of that scene was to Anastasia and her victims, and how strikingly like her conduct was to that of the bull-dog. And then the moral! The retaliation that came when the stable-boy cried: "Wake up, Bobby, and mind what you are about." And Pekra thought, and everybody, at that stage of affairs would have certainly concurred in his opinion, that when the coroner should hold his inquest on the body of Viscount Mirfield he would "wake up, and mind what he was about," and that the "great" Anastasia would get the worst of it.

With sad steps Pekra walked along in the direction of the Haymarket—how moonily! how silently! with how wan a face! Thus he proceeded on his way, musing in the solemn solitude of his lonely walk, and lost in the memories of care, and with sorrow clinging to him like grim despair.

He was going down the shelving street of the Haymarket, when he found a considerable crowd gathered round the entrance door of Moppy's Hotel. From the animated gestures of the bystanders it was easy to perceive something unusual had occurred. Police-constables were hurrying backwards and forwards; every now and then a Superintendent of Police stepped from the house. It was from this official that Pekra ascertained the particulars of the excitement.

"What is the matter here?" he asked.

"A dreadful crime has been committed," replied the Superintendent. "Viscount Mirfield was found dead—it is supposed murdered—this morning in one of the upper rooms of the hotel."

"And the murderer?"

"Not known."

"But who was last in his company?"

As Pekra put the question all his calmness deserted him, and he burst out into a cold perspiration.

"Baroness Leone," was the curt answer.

Pekra literally staggered backwards: then he shuddered; immediately after he felt a tingling all over his frame to his fingers' ends. He was what novelists call stricken with terror. With strange agitation he turned on his heel, and pursued his way back to Arlington-street in haste.

"This event was not so unexpected by me," he mused, "that it should excite in me so much commotion. But now that I know what *has* happened, I am determined to exert myself so as to make Anastasia smile again in loveliness. If danger threatens I must shield her—even if it be at the cost of my own life; for rather would I lose my own life than she hers. Had I ten thousands lives I'd give them all to her. But now, I fear, 'tis DOOMSDAY with her."

Indeed, indeed, it seemed now, as Pekra observed, as if it was doomsday with Anastasia.

When she was left alone by her favourite dwarf, her brow, which had been dark enough before, grew black as the blackest midnight.

"Where am I?" she thought, in allusion to her mental condition. "How am I deformed! What air affords me breathing? Where shall I hide me? Where go, that no human eye may behold me thus disfigured, alarmed, dejected?"

Arranging her curling locks which hung loose on her shoulders, she approached the window, sighing:

"I am quite worn out with fatigue, and have a stupefying headache. Let me breathe the air."

With heavy-lidded eyes, and weak uplifted hands, she looked forth over the undulating meadow-like land of the Green Park.

The day was warm and delightful. The wind moved lazily through the picturesque clumps of trees, flapping its wings and fanning the fainted air, and making it a luxury to breathe the breath of life.

The mixed and busy populace were abroad, away from the busy streets and crowded thoroughfares, inhaling the invigorating breeze, and enjoying relaxation and bracing exercise in temporary seclusion from their cares and toils under the blossoming, shady trees. There was the merchant; there, too, was the busy shopkeeper, the pale mechanic, and the exhausted factory operative; there, also, was the family troop, children with their nurses, and sporting juveniles in the company of their staid seniors. All were free to walk or spend their playtime as they listed—to find every mode of recreation, amusement, and entertainment suitable to their tastes. The sight was pleasant; but, as the eyes of Anastasia wandered around the scene, there came over her face an air of gloom.

That day in spring, like a day in summer, with all its wonders and delights—delights and wonders rehearsed and sung by innumerable poets, good and bad—were stirring life and pleasure in every bosom. The thousand opened buds and the thousand flowers, breathing around their balsamed perfume; the beautiful brightness of the air; the pure azure of the heavens unstained by a cloud; the mild, warm beams of the sun; the sweet odours given forth from the earth—all fell with joy upon the hearts of those happy folks, who, talking with familiar gaiety and laughing with glee, were walking arm-in-arm beneath the clear, bright sky, on the smooth, soft grass of the Green Park. But not all the wonders and delights of that day in spring, like a day in summer, stirring life and pleasure in every bosom; nor the thousand opened buds, nor the thousand flowers, breathing around their balsamed perfume; nor the beautiful brightness of the air; nor the pure azure of the heavens unstained by a cloud; nor the mild, warm beams of the sun; nor the sweet odours given forth from the earth—could fall with joy on the heart of Anastasia. With her but a single step was wanting to lead her to madness.

It could not be said of her as was said of Sir Philip Sydney, that no ugly thought nor unhandsome meditation could find a harbour in her mind.

Even now she was musing how, like the Helena of Shakspeare, she could reverse the ordinary laws of courtship, caring little, if she could again obtain Bruce St. Aubyn, how far she violated the habitual feelings of sexual delicacy; and, in the inability of predominating over her situation, how much she suffered abatement of the full lustre of the female character. She was like a pigeon-house, smooth and round and white without, but full of holes and stink within.

"I could be frantic, mourning the departure of Bruce St. Aubyn," she thought. "Accursed fate! Why did I not devise means of detaining him during my absence by keeping him under lock and key a close prisoner in my chamber? In losing him I feel as one that has lost everything; and when he was with me it was with my heart as if it had nothing left to wish for. Take, gentle air, the secret of my heart; take it, thou gentle air, and ever after breathe more balmy sweet—I love this youth. Thou hast no eye to scan my looks, nor voice to echo me, nor ear to catch my words; yet my secret, sweet, invisible confidant, once being thine, I tell thee again, and again I tell thee, and yet again—I love Bruce St. Aubyn."

A smile passed over her lips as false as water rippling over a shallow or a quicksand.

"Were it any other who had so slighted me, I would not lose him, and let him still live!"

Thus was this thought ever present to her—MURDER!—which had become the passion, the habit, the act of her mind—its only one mode of compassing its objects and gratifying its passions. Like insanity, 'twas deaf to reason; it was hardened against the virtuous indignation of the world, and against the remorses of conscience. Strange was the tenacity with which she followed a selfish object, the fury with which she obeyed the dictates of an evil passion, the obstinacy with which she clung to a delusion.

"Would that in this rage," she continued, "I could but now forget him! But that I am to bear him in my heart appears my doom. From whom can I find comfort? From whom, except those who can give me aid? Sebastian Leonard can! He is bound in all obedience to me. And if he *can*—Why do I say *if* he can?—Why, he *must* bring Bruce St. Aubyn back again to me. I will send at once and seek him."

She was about to despatch a missive to Sebastian Leonard—had sat down—had already written the words "My dear Sebastian," when one of her gaily-liveried servants entered, without giving any warning of his approach—not even by the creaking of the hinges of the door—for the weather being hot, the door was wide open to air the room—and, as he entered, he announced at the top of his voice:

"Mr. Sebastian Leonard, my lady."

Anastasia dropped the pen immediately, and hurried forward to greet her friend.

CHAPTER XXXVI.

ALL HER GEAR OUT OF ORDER.

"But why are all my thoughts turned to despair?
Why think I now of death? Methinks my Genius
Checks this cold fear, and Fortune chiding tells me
I am ungrateful to distrust her now.
My race of life and glory is not run,
Nor Cleopatra's fortunes yet arrived
At that great height that must eternize her,
And fix her glorious name above the stars.
* * * * * * * * *
And why should I despair? Are Cupid's fires
Extinguished quite? Are all his arrows spent?
Or is this beauty that can boast the conquest
Of Julius Cæsar, and great Antony,
So wanëd now, it cannot move the temper
Of one whom youth makes fit for Cupid's conquest."
MAY.—*Cleopatra.*

Anastasia and Sebastian Leonard clasped each other by the hand.

"Dear Sebastian," said Anastasia, "your presence recals my spirit, which but now was groaning deeply. You are more to me than father, mother, brother, sister."

"You are very pleasant."

"You'll find me very serious."

"Is it a matter of joy or sorrow, pleasure or pain, hope or fear," inquired Sebastian Leonard, "that is now struggling in your heart?"

"'Tis a matter of life or death," replied Anastasia, "of liberty or confinement. Sit down here by my side, and I'll tell you all. The tie 's already severed between Bruce St. Aubyn and me."

"Already!"

"In my absence he went way without a leave-taking."

"Let us hope, not for long."

"Come, Sebastian! 'tis for you to restore him to me. If you have a notion of distraction, you can form the most correct idea of my feelings at this moment; and from my distraction I shall recover only by being alone with Bruce St. Aubyn."

"You expect a little agreeable excitement with the youth?"

"Sebastian, in the agony of my heart—at this time when severe sorrow presses me down to the very depths of woe—I do beseech, I do implore you to fetch him back to me. Even in this extremity, something whispers to me, 'Despair not! He will be with you soon again.'"

"There, there!" said Sebastian Leonard, consolingly. "Comfort yourself. Cheer up, and look not so mournfully. Before many days I will bring you together again."

"Days! 'Tis too long."

"Hours, then."

"That 's better; and I do implore you, by all the ties of friendship, to employ your utmost diligence."

"I am not used to jest time away. It shall be done with all despatch. The very moment I leave you I will begin; and even now I think I know where to find him."

"Really?"

"Verily."

"Then assist me at once in reobtaining him. Without his love I am resolved to die."

"That were a desperate act, beyond the reach of fury."

"Hear it, then; and do not doubt the truth of it. And so you know where to find him?"

"I met him on my way hither in the Burlington-arcade. After we had shaken hands and had greeted each other, we walked together from one end of the arcade to the other without exchanging a syllable."

"Singular!"

"Bruce St. Aubyn was discomposed. Consternation sat upon his brow. He told me that his friend Lord Mirfield had been found dead—in fact, murdered; and turned away his head to hide the tears that came into his eye. Then, saying that he wished to be alone, left me."

The heart of Anastasia was this day shivered to shreds.

At the mention of the name of Viscount Mirfield she felt that sickening sensation of the heart which is the prelude to insensibility. She was on the point of fainting, but rallied, though she shook in every limb, and slunk timidly from the gaze of the man who confronted her.

"What further said Bruce St. Aubyn?" inquired Anastasia faintly.

"Nothing; but that in the hotel where the body was found an inquest was at that moment being held."

This announcement came to Anastasia with the elemental crash of thunder.

The investigation that was to determine her fate was then going forward, and she was not there. She not there! when her life was in her hand; and when she knew so well how the secret of security is in a multitude of small and simple precautions, which all may use, and few will stoop to practise.

That there was truth in the statement she had no doubt, for she now remembered distinctly what she had read that morning in the newspaper, but which had hitherto escaped her memory, that an inquest on the body of Lord Mirfield was to be held that afternoon at Moppy's Hotel.

She got rid of Sebastian Leonard as soon as she could.

When she was alone a wild, solemn, preternatural cast of grief appeared to be bewildering her soul. There was a startled, terrified look in her eye. A sudden pain seemed to be goading her. As if vainly striving to free herself from herself, she paced hurriedly up and down the room; now quickly, now slowly—sometimes stopping altogether, then looking irresolute—as if she knew not what to do. She was doubting whether to go about the business or stay at home. At length she rang the bell, and ordered her carriage. She hastened from the drawing-room to her bed-chamber. She changed her dress, attiring herself in the costliest costume. That done, she ran rapidly down the stairs and flung herself into her carriage; and in a few minutes more it was rolling with her through the streets in the fashionable locality of Piccadilly, along which it rattled with a whirling speed, then, dashing down the Haymarket, drew up before the door of Moppy's Hotel.

There Anastasia got out of her equipage, and entered the hotel.

CHAPTER XXXVII.

A BREATH OF HOPE RUFFLES THE CURRENT OF MISERY.

"Whither should I fly?
I have done no harm. But I remember now
I am in this earthly world; where, to do harm,
Is often laudable; to do good, sometime,
Accounted dangerous folly. Why, then, alas!
Do I put up that womanly defence,
To say, I have done no harm?"
SHAKSPEARE.—*Macbeth.*

Some time before Anastasia reached Moppy's Hotel, Hardkick, the coroner, had arrived, preceded by Smartfire, the foreman, and about thirteen or fourteen respectable neighbours, "honest men and true," to act as jurymen in inquiring into the cause of Viscount Mirfield's death.

Waiters and others were moving in much bustle up and down the staircase, passing from one apartment to another, and treading as gently as if they were afraid of awaking the dead. When they had occasion to address each other they spoke in hushed tones. Policemen were stationed on the landings of the staircase and along the passages; the hall door was open; a landau, a chariot, and several hack-cabs were standing in the street; almost every five minutes some person—always of the male sex—walked into the house or came out of it, without asking a question.

From what had taken place the night before, the cause of all this mystery and gloom was alarming to Anastasia, who felt sensations unusual, and such as she had never experienced before. She felt as a person feels who has just been stung by that small venomous viper, the chopper-poora—that is, a great glow spread instantly over her body, accompanied by a full pulsation and a strong palpitation of the heart, besides a very singular sensation, as if a warm fluid was circulating in her veins to the very extremities of her fingers. This heat, and the palpitation of her heart, increased so much as to render her very restless. Still no appearance of restlessness was visible in her manner. She passed along gently and quickly; nothing, even to the closest and most minute inspector, being discernible in her countenance beyond a slight pallor on her cheek, and an all but imperceptible twitching of the muscles about the mouth.

Making her way hurriedly to the top, where a young waiter was standing, she said to him:

"What is the matter? Has anything serious happened?"

"Oh! no, m'm, only Mr. Hardkick, the coroner, a setting on the body of"——

Here, by this time having had a good look at the countenance of his interrogator, the waiter stopped abruptly as if his very soul was split at the sight of Anastasia. He had recognised her, having been one of those who had gone into the room the night before, after the scream of the poisoned nobleman had been heard.

Anastasia was, of course, of an extreme unwillingness to appear distressed in mind, for she could never hint to any one the true cause of her uneasiness, and she said in a very subdued manner to the waiter:

"The jury then are assembled"——

"In this room, m'm," interrupted the waiter, thrusting the door beside him wide open, and before, at a sign from Anastasia, he could close it again, she had time to see a number of decently dressed men sitting round a long mahogany table covered with green baize, and each having before him pen, ink, and paper, and in front of them, in an arm-chair, sat Hardkick, pen, ink, and paper also before *him*.

"They are going over the evidence of the surgeon," said the waiter, volunteering information.

"The surgeon!" exclaimed Anastasia, arching her brow from surprise.

"Yes, m'm; Mr. Watersedge, who came here early and made a *post-mortar* examination of the body."

This was something quite unexpected to Anas-

DEATH OF VISCOUNT MIRFIELD.

tasia, who seemed struck. Her look was one of visible anxiety.

"And," she commenced—

"And," continued the waiter, "his examination, m'm, proved a fact."

"And what was that fact?"

"That the *W*icount had come to his sudden decease by the diorama."

"The diarrhœa!" said Anastasia again surprised, and added faintly: "I thought people said it was poison."

"Yes, m'm; *pis*on, m'm—*pis*on resulting from the diorama."

Anastasia walked on towards a private room, which she entered.

Her nervous sensibility was now excessively great, her apprehension of danger causing symptoms that were really quite alarming. Her fear excited the action of her heart and arteries to such an extent as to produce incessant and universal great heat over her whole body. The stimulus was of the most powerful nature: it threatened, if it continued, to destroy life by its excess.

She was so oppressed that, to keep off a stupor, to which she had an extreme tendency, she walked briskly backwards and forwards; in the end she was left in so languid and exhausted a state, that, unable any longer to walk, she was obliged to throw herself upon a sofa and there remain. The palpitation of the heart, which had subsided, was succeeded by a most distressing oppression in breathing, that compelled her to make frequent deep inspirations; and the extraordinary sensation, as if a warm fluid was circulating through her veins, was followed by a deadly coldness of the skin and profuse perspiration, with a slow, weak pulse.

"There are fires that scorch, but don't consume the heart," thought Anastasia; "certainly not break it, for, in the midst of all the destructive heat, it goes on cherishing infinite desires and impossible hopes. How is it with me now, when I am sinking fast?—when I have a slight return of oppression in breathing at every other interval? Is it want of confidence?—When want of confidence fails with respect to the efficacy of a medicine in the cure of a disease, the patient dies. Nothing but a powerful stimulus will save me now."

Musing thus she rose from the sofa and rang the bell. She ordered brandy, of which she drank such a strong mixture with water, that it would have sent a red Indian reeling from intoxication.

Finding that the first glass agreed with her, she took a second, and a third, and a fourth, and a fifth, and a sixth. The alcohol then began to have a favourable effect; it seemed to have diffused itself over her body by the venous blood, destroying all irritability and rendering the system quite composed, all but paralytic. The nervous sensibility of Anastasia totally went. She was no longer uneasy.

Now being mistress of herself, with an admirable intrepidity, she began to act, undismayed by the difficulties and dangers with which she was beset.

"If I am wary, who can penetrate my purposes?" she thought. "What my particular projects are is a secret to every one but myself. I have no confidential agents. Let the coroner then suspect. Who cares? He has no evidence by which to impress his suspicions on others, or countervail confident assertions from me, favourable to myself."

When she had thought thus, she placed herself on a chair, and wrote a note to the coroner in characters as elegant and distinct as a Chinese Mandarin corresponding with his Emperor, and said to the waiter to whom she gave it to be delivered:

"Do not interrupt Mr. Hardkick, but at the end of the whole examination give that note to him."

And sat down, laying her watch on the table before her.

So she sat, calm and composed, though anxiously looking forward to the passing time.

CHAPTER XXXVIII.

CAST DOWN, BUT NOT DESTROYED.

"As in a theatre, the eyes of men,
After a well-graced actor leaves the stage,
Are idly bent on him that enters next,
Thinking his prattle to be tedious:
Even so, or with much more contempt, men's eyes
Did scowl on Richard; no man cried, 'God save him:'
No joyful tongue gave him his welcome home;
But dust was thrown upon his sacred head."
SHAKSPEARE.—*King Richard the Second.*

Watersedge, the surgeon, who had made the *post mortem* examination, had just finished giving his evidence at the time Anastasia handed the note to the waiter, to be delivered to the coroner. The evidence of Watersedge was conclusive as to the fact that Viscount Mirfield had come to his sudden death by poison. Other witnesses had also tendered their testimony; and to make it clear to the mental vision of the jury whether the deceased peer had poisoned himself, or been poisoned by another, the coroner addressed them in the easy, conversational manner adopted usually by men in his position.

"From the evidence of the numerous witnesses now heard," said he, "we have every reason to believe that the deceased perished between the hours of three and four o'clock this morning in one of the private rooms of this hotel, from the effects of poison. But the point not yet solved is how the poison was administered—whether by the deceased himself, or by the woman who was in his company at the time. I think the witness whom I am now going to bring before you will set your minds at rest on that score. Peter Snimpkin," continued the coroner, addressing a policeman, who was standing, keeping guard at the door, "call Thomas Swigg."

The member of the constabulary force vanished through the doorway to execute the order; in another second he returned, accompanied by a man about forty years of age, dressed in black clothes and a white neckcloth. He was invited by Peter Snimpkin to take his place at the table and be sworn as a witness. At the conclusion of this interesting ceremony, the coroner said to him:

"Your name, I think, is Thomas Swigg?"

"Thomas Swigg, sir."

"And your occupation is head waiter at this hotel?"

"Head waiter, sir."

"You were at this hotel this morning?"

"I was, sir."

"And you waited on Lord Mirfield?"

"I did, sir."

"You recollect, of course, the fatal event that happened here?"

"Yes, sir."

"Tell the court, Mr. Swigg, what came under your observation at the time."

The witness, addressing himself more to the body of the jurymen than to the coroner, then entered into the following narrative:—

"The clock might have gone three some twenty minutes this morning, and I was standing in the coffee-room, talking to Button"——

"Who is Button?" interrupted the coroner.

"One of the waiters, sir."

"Known as Button?" again said the coroner.

"No, sir," replied Swigg, "known as Harry."

"Go on, Mr. Swigg."

"Well," continued Swigg, "Button had just returned from private room, No. 6, where the nobleman and the lady was, and whom Button had just served with a fresh bottle of wine, when all of a sudden a screech, the most piercing I ever heer'd, resounded through the house, startling me and Button terrible. For a second we stood staring at each other, quite speechless from fright. 'Holloa!' says Thomson"——

"Who is Thomson?" interrupted the coroner.

"Another of the waiters, sir."

"Known as Thomson?"

"No, sir—known as Dick."

"Go on, Mr. Swigg."

"'Holloa!' says Thomson. 'Holloa!' says I. 'Crikey!' says Button. 'What's that?' says I.

'A scream,' says Thomson. 'Where from?' says Button. 'Private room, No. 6,' says Thomson. 'The nobleman must be taking an unfair advantage of the lady,' says Button. 'Sure*ly*,' says Thomson, 'he can't be a-murdering hon her.' 'What?' says I. Says Thomson: 'A murdering hon her.' "

"There is no necessity," here interposed, with his usual blandness of manner, the ever affable Hardkick; "there is no necessity, Mr. Swigg, your entering so much into details at present. It will be sufficient for the court to know what you did and said after hearing the scream that proceeded from the private room, where the deceased and the woman were."

"After these remarks had passed between us," continued the witness, "Button and me hastens away to go to private room, No. 6, to see what was the matter. Button follows close after me, and me and him was going rapidly up the stairs together, when the landlord and some other gents comes rushing after us, and we all then hurries up the stairs—gents and hall. I was the fust to open the door, and there, in the middle of the room, I see'd the body of the deceased stretched flat along the floor, and by his side a bottle of p'ison."

Here a juryman, who was trembling in every limb, sighing, and, at times, wiping with his handkerchief the cold perspiration as it gathered in big drops on his clammy forehead, came to the relief of Thomas Swigg.

"Who was in the room when you entered it?" he inquired.

"Only the party of the female sect who had accompanied his lordship to the hotel."

"Where was she?"

"Standing close to him."

"In what state of mind?"

"Halmost in high-strikes."

Here the juryman ceased his queries, which were taken up by Hardkick, who put this question to the witness:

"What observation did she make when she saw you enter the room?"

"She dropped on her knees by the side of the copse, and, exclaiming 'Look here!—Look here!' burstes into a shower of tears."

"What was the immediate impression on your mind?"

"That his lordship had p'isoned himself."

"There was nothing, then, in the conduct of the woman to make you think she had administered the deadly potion?"

"Nothink."

"Did you observe anything remarkable in her?"

"As to the matter of that, I did, and I didn't.'

"Explain yourself, Mr. Swigg."

"Well, sir, she seemed to be more affected at the fate of the Wicount than all of us, and we was all took on a deal. For a long time she couldn't be brought to think the Wicount was a copse; and she was about to be seized with the high-strikes, to which I have made delusion, when the pollisman came in."

The coroner nodded to Swigg to retire.

Peter Snimpkin then stepped forward.

"On being taken into custody," observed a juryman on the right of the coroner, "what was the conduct of the woman?"

"She was never took into custody," replied Peter Snimpkin.

"Now, sir, attend to the questions I am about to put to you," said a perky little juryman, with a large bunch of gold watch seals, with his hair standing erect over the middle of his forehead, like a cockatoo's feather, and rising from his chair as he spoke: "Answer me on your oath. Was there any embarrassment in her manner?"

"Not the slightest."

"Did she turn pale?"

"Her complexion never haltered."

"Did she tremble?"

"She was as firm as a hoak."

"She accompanied you willingly?"

"I never took her into custody."

"How was that?"

"'Cos there was no grounds for suspicion."

"On your oath, then, you think Lord Mirfield poisoned himself?"

"I'm sure on it."

"On your oath?"

"Hon my oath."

The perky little juryman resumed his seat.

"That will do," said the coroner.

Peter Snimpkin retired.

The jury were now about to come to their decision, when a young man in black—the waiter who had been talking to Anastasia about the inquest—entered the room and handed a note to the coroner. After reading it Hardkick addressed the jury as follows:—

"The note which has just been put into my hands is from the lady who was in company with Lord Mirfield this morning. She now offers herself as a voluntary witness, and is willing to answer any questions we may put to her, in order to enable us to arrive at a right verdict as to the cause of death of the noble deceased. I need not point out to you the importance of her testimony, and as she is now waiting in a room down-stairs, I will have her brought into the court at once. Peter Snimpkin," continued the coroner, addressing the policeman at the door, "call the female witness."

Peter Snimpkin left the room to go and do what he had been told.

Profound silence now prevailed throughout the whole court; every voice was hushed; every breath was suspended; every eye instinctively turned towards the door, and was kept anxiously fixed there, in eager anticipation of the momentary appearance of Anastasia.

—

CHAPTER XXXIX.

WORKING WITH HER LIFE IN HER HANDS.

"Our life, methinks, is but the same with others:
To cozen and be cozened makes the age.
The prey and feeder are that civil thing
That sager heads call body politick.
Here is the only difference: others cheat
By statute, but we do't upon no grounds,
The fraud 's the same in both: there only wants
Allowance to our way. The Commonwealth
Hath not declared herself as yet for us.
Wherefore our policy must be our charter."
CARTWRIGHT.—*The Ordinary.*

At this moment, when there was such an unexpected turn, if there was any possibility of pen and ink affording an accurate idea of the great excitement that pervaded the minds of the jury, certain it is that my poor pen and ink cannot.

A close observer could have seen the cheeks and noses of such of the jurymen as were winebibbers—cheeks and noses that vied with the hue of the poppy, turn white, while the faces of those who were pale and oleaginous assumed a carmine tint. In a few seconds the sounds of approaching steps were heard: first on the tympanum fell the steady tread of the burly Peter Snimpkin, then the lighter footfall of the more fragile frame of a delicate being, accompanied by the rustling of silk. The excitement had now reached its height. Even the stout heart of the usually callous coroner thumped violently against his ribs; and the blood seemed for a moment to be arrested in its course in the veins of some of the more excitable gentlemen of the jury. Another moment, and, under the doorway, advancing into the room with the majestic sweep of an imperial gait, was seen Anastasia, who, the reader by this time well knows, was one of the loveliest and most voluptuous creatures ever sent into this world to enthral the senses, and make captive to the bonds of female fascination all classes and degrees of men; the wise, the strong, and the virtuous; the foolish, the weak, and the bad; the hot and giddy youth, the man of mature age and sober passions, and the cold-blooded sexagenarian, infantine and doating.

As she stood, bending gracefully and respectfully to the coroner, with her white veil thrown over her blue silk bonnet, and a narrow scarf hanging negligently on her arms and shoulders, she produced an irresistible impression on the jurymen, every one of whom she subjugated with the charms of her face and figure. Her pale cheek, with its somewhat olive tint, gave her face an expression full of interest, and this interest was considerably enhanced by the depressed state of her mind, to judge from the expression of her eyes; for those eyes, superbly shaded by their long silken lashes, wandered uninterestingly over every object with a vague and vacant look.

A beautiful face being as good as a letter of recommendation, Anastasia was well received by Hardkick. He ordered a chair to be placed for her, and she prepared to give her evidence seated. After a second or so, Hardkick commenced by complimenting her in the following handsome terms:

"Madam," said he, "the honourable step you have taken in coming forward uninvited to give your evidence is a step that the jury and myself most deeply appreciate, and the more so when we take into consideration the melancholy and regretted position in which you have so recently stood."

At this speech, Anastasia, who had been hitherto keeping her eyes on the ground, raised them in the most bewitching manner; she bent forward her slim, swanlike neck in acknowledgment of the compliment; and, while a soft, sad smile passed over her graceful, chiselled lips, she fixed her eyes, which were as black as the eyes of the Angel of Darkness, and sparkling with the lustre of intelligence, full in the face of the coroner, who, just then must, surely, have been dazzled, for they shone like the stars of the night, or rather like the lights that glitter on the heads of the glow-worm and the firefly.

Hardkick felt his heart for a moment cease beating, and the blood in the veins of every man in the room boiled.

"Madam," resumed the coroner, after he had recovered from the fascination of her glance, which was greater than a basilisk's, "the jury would know the name of a lady who so obligingly comes forward to inform them as to the death of Viscount Mirfield."

"Friends and strangers know me by the name of Anastasia, Baroness Leone," fell from the lips of the witness as from a speaking automaton, so motionless she sat, and so calm and devoid of expression were her features.

"All that you know of the death of Lord Mirfield, Madam, we shall be glad to hear from you," said the coroner.

"The narrative is brief but painful," said Anastasia. "Lord Mirfield and I dined together on Monday evening at a mutual friend's, and in the evening went to Vauxhall, where we wandered about those delightful gardens, for the purpose of breathing a little the embalmed air of the summer night. The moon in all her splendour shed over us her soft light as we walked. Few words passed between us, for we had much to think of. Lord Mirfield—for now it were useless, it were foolish—it were, in fact, an act of false modesty to conceal it—Lord Mirfield LOVED ME. I was not in a position to accept his love; and he knew it; for I had repeatedly told him how I was situated; I had also told him often that I would never accede to his wishes. Apparently he never believed me; for on the evening in question he persisted in his advances. Bending over me, as I was leaning on his arm, he said in a low, but firm tone: "I wish you to know, Anastasia, I love you enough to do anything for you. To-night or to-morrow you shall be convinced of it."

A juryman sprang to his feet.

"When was that speech made?" he inquired, hurriedly.

"I have said—in the gardens at Vauxhall, as we were walking, he made that speech to me," continued Anastasia, in the same calm, monotonous tone, as if she were not at all aware of the vast importance which would be attached by the jury to the answer she had just made to that question. "It must have been between one and two o'clock," she continued; "for, shortly after —somewhere about two o'clock—we retired, I thought homewards, but no—we drove in a carriage to the Haymarket, and there we went together to a hotel, frequented almost entirely by persons who pass their lives in dissipation—in gaiety and drinking, and, sometimes, in gallantry."

Here a smile passed round the court at the astonishing freedom of speech of Anastasia. With her eyes still cast down, and without noticing the effect of her words on her audience, she went on with a cold and inconceivable apathy:

"After we had drunk some glasses of wine, and Lord Mirfield had smoked a cigar, he took me by the hand, and, looking tenderly in my face, said:—'Anastasia, you have no notion how passionately I love you, and what happiness I feel when I am in your presence. Believing that there is no other woman like yourself, I think myself the inhabitant of another world, speaking a language and feeling sensations unknown here below. When I am away from you I am like a dying man; I am insensible to the verdure of the beautiful summer and the freshness of the balmy air. When I least expect it, bitter tears flow down my cheeks; when I wish to shed them, my eyes are dry. At times a thrill passes over my whole frame. I shudder from head to foot. I love you—love you deeply, love you passionately. You are always with me, always; and here—here in my heart, where you are causing the death of me as surely as the worm the fruit which it gnaws to the core. And you do not love me—Anastasia, you do *not* love me.' I disengaged my hand from his, and, looking him steadily in the face:—'Augustus, Viscount Mirfield,' said I to him, 'what is there to save me from dishonour but love? If I loved you, many excuses might be made for me; but as I do not, what should I then be?—The vilest of women!' 'You will then,' he observed, 'make no sacrifice for me?' 'Sacrifice!' I exclaimed. 'Sacrifice! Of what?—My honour! virtue!'"

Anastasia's eyes flashed fire as she uttered these words, and her bosom rose and fell in a deeply troubled manner, as if she was overcome with indignation at the recollection of the scene.

The jury sat in breathless silence: every one of them was filled with admiration. From this point they awaited with interest the sequel of the Baroness Leone's story.

Anastasia resumed her narrative with every semblance of innocence, as follows:—

"Viscount Mirfield, wringing his hands, and speaking in tones of the most violent despair, continued:—'Anastasia, I am in a fever of transport, and will, in this room, this morning, in your sight, prefer death in its most terrible form—aye, and a million times over—to your frowns.' 'Oh, God! what do I hear?' I exclaimed. 'The words of a madman,' he replied, 'and a madman who will do what he says. Think, then, what a crime will weigh upon your conscience for the remainder of your life if'"——

As if overcome by the recollection of the scene, Anastasia, while uttering these words, threw herself back in her chair. There she sat, convulsed with grief, her face covered with both her hands: so she wept—wept till she sobbed.

Such a public exhibition of deep feeling told with wonderful effect upon the jury. But, as the reader knows, it was the most consummate piece of acting.

The admiration which the jury had felt for Anastasia on her first appearance among them had been gradually expanding, as they continued to regard her and hear her sentiments. They could well understand the feelings of Lord Mirfield. They had never before seen such exalted beauty, such sweetness in look and manner; they could not govern the direction of their eyes, nor suppress the glow which momentarily spread over them; they felt inspired by an ardour which they could not overcome, and, at every fresh gaze, found their admiration growing still more predominant.

After awhile, having recovered her composure, Anastasia, with her accustomed calmness of tone, resumed her narrative, which was listened to with unabated attention. She related how she had parted company with Viscount Mirfield in the early part of the morning of Tuesday, with the promise of again meeting him at night, with no other object, she alleged, than to allay his passion by reason and persuasion. As she proceeded, her voice grew louder, her manner warmer, her speech quicker; her pale face became flushed; her calm and quiet-looking eye shone with animation; her bosom rose and fell: she resorted to gesticulation; at times a big tear glistened in the corner of her eye: occasionally gentle tremors passed over her delicate frame.

"When I met Lord Mirfield the following night," she continued, "and again refused to listen to his vows, he again revealed his intention to me of the frightful crime he premeditated. Horror-struck, I fixed my eyes upon him, and he seemed in agony. His mind had lost its balance—all its accustomed composure: verily, it was shaken by the very tempest of passion. His bosom heaved: his eye glared: his breathing was hard and difficult. A whole hour passed thus—in a struggle with passion. His only happiness was at my feet. He knelt before me; he clasped and kissed my hand; he wept; he implored me. In vain—I would not listen to him—much less grant his request. Cruel was his position!—bitter was mine! The more indifference I displayed, the more his passion increased. How should I escape the importunities of so pertinacious a lover? Should I fly? Fly!—And hear no longer his despairing accents? Witness no longer his mad behaviour? I rose to leave. With a cry he sprang forward and held me back by my dress. 'Would you leave me?' he exclaimed. 'Wherefore not?' I replied. 'My presence is like plunging a dagger into a wound which I cannot heal—my absence may make you forget the passion which devours your soul.' 'It will but increase it,' was his answer; 'for my whole being is absorbed by it. I can—I *will* no longer endure the torments I suffer. Therefore I have condemned myself to one or the other of two destinies. My life is in your hands: it depends upon your decree. Speak, Anastasia.' But I said not a syllable in reply. I clasped my hands and fixed my eyes on the ground. Not a ray of hope was there for him.—— When I looked up, my flesh crawled, my heart stood still, the blood in my veins ran icy cold. I would have spoken, but I could not—my tongue clove to the roof of my mouth: I was as if petrified. For there he stood face to face with me, a terror-striking image of ungovernable passions; wild, grinning, raving; grasping in his hand a small phial on which was written 'Poison,' and, through his grinding and gnashing teeth, he moaned unintelligible, inarticulate sounds. Never before had I seen a human being the victim of such intense feelings. My brain reeled; a mist swam before my eyes; my legs tottered under me: feeling that I was falling, and seeking for support, I stepped backwards to lean against a chair. Perhaps he thought I meant to retire, and was about to leave the room, for, at that moment, he raised the phial to his lips, and, before I could move a limb or utter a syllable"——

Out upon the wall, seen only by Anastasia, came the figure of Lord Mirfield—the phantom that was to pursue her for ever in all the most trying moments of her life—even in those moments when she was committing fresh and great crime. Out upon the wall it stood, a hideous spectacle, as when it fell in death, with the features livid, the lips black, the abdomen inflated, and the limbs emaciated and covered with violet spots. It fixed a glassy eye on Anastasia, and beckoned to her as if to follow him.

In return Anastasia fixed a glassy stare on him; and there was heard in her throat a low, gurgling sound. She had seen the ghost at the precise moment when she was uttering the last word—"syllable"—and the few last words she had uttered were spoken in a hoarse, choking voice. Then she paused—paused as abruptly as I have represented. She rose slowly, and, standing up with her head extended, fixed her eyes before her on the nobleman's ghost with a wild, stony stare. In the direction in which she looked the jurymen looked also: they could see nothing but empty space. In this position Anastasia remained for, perhaps, upwards of a second, when the ghost of Viscount Mirfield, beckoning to her a second time to follow him, vanished through the wall like unsubstantial mist. Then intelligence, which till that moment had deserted Anastasia, seemed returning, as the spectators could observe by the smile which was beginning to curl the corners of her lips; but suddenly—unexpectedly she threw her head quickly forward, as if by the impulse of a jerk; and, uttering a long, loud, piercing shriek, fell from her chair like a stone.

CHAPTER XL.

HOLD ON PATIENTLY.—ALL WILL COME OUT WELL.

"My lord, there's great suspicion of the murder;
But no sound proof who did it. For my part,
I do not think she hath a soul so black
To act a deed so bloody: if she have,
As in cold countries husbandmen plant vines,
And with warm blood manure them: even so,
One summer she will bear unsavoury fruit,
And ere next spring wither both branch and root:
The act of blood let pass."

WEBSTER.—*The White Devil.*

As Anastasia swooned thus, the coroner and every juryman immediately sprang from their seats, and hastily gathered round her, pitying her, and offering their services to assist to recover her. Four or five of them lifted her carefully from the ground, and gently bore her, still lifeless, from the court into a room down-stairs, where she was waited upon, without delay, by the surgeon who had made the *post mortem* examination of the body of Lord Mirfield.

On the reassembling of the court, after this affecting incident, the coroner was proceeding to address the jury when a voice in the body of the court was heard saying:

"I am acquainted, Mr. Coroner, somewhat with this affair, and am at your disposal to communicate what information I am in command of to the court, if needed."

"What is your name, sir?" asked the coroner.

"My name is Thomas Bother, of the firm of Bother, Squeeze, & Crush, solicitors and attorneys, of Old-square, Lincoln's-inn-fields."

"We shall be most happy to hear what you have to communicate to us, Mr. Bother, and I must beg you to be sworn at once."

Bother was accordingly sworn. Thereupon he entered into a narrative of the conduct of the Viscount to the Baroness on the evening of the day they dined with him.

"Did you hear anything particular pass between them?" asked Hardkick.

"I heard the Viscount say to the Baroness that *his life depended on a word from her.*"

"Where did that occur, Mr. Bother?"

"On the terrace of my house, sir, just after we had all dined together on Monday."

"Did any thing further pass between them?"

"Yes; the Viscount solicited the Baroness to meet him again that evening; on her refusing to do so, he said that *then he could not answer for what he should do to himself*; and added: *if you knew the mad thoughts that are careering through my brain, you alone can save me from the sinister act I meditate.*

"You were not then astonished when you heard of the death of Lord Mirfield?"

"Far from being astonished, I fully expected it."

"What caused you to have such an expectation?"

"Not only from what occurred at my house, but also from what I afterwards saw in Vauxhall Gardens."

"The Baroness then met the Viscount again that evening?"

"I presume so; for on going to Vauxhall Gardens that night with my two partners, I saw them there; and Squeeze, on seeing them together, said that the Viscount would *tarnish a merry life with a little bloodshed.*"

"Is Mr. Squeeze here present?"

"He is, and my other partner, Mr. Crush, who remarked that the 'love-making' of the Viscount was '*a dangerous game,*' *that might end in suicide.*"

These statements were corroborated, as the reader knows well they could have been, by Squeeze and Crush. There was then an end to all further inquiry.

The coroner went over the whole evidence, and at the end of his summing up observed that it had been satisfactorily proved to them that the deceased had put a termination to his own existence; and that all that remained for them to decide was whether Lord Mirfield, when he committed the act of suicide, was in a sane or an insane state of mind.

The jury took but a short time to deliberate, and returned a verdict of "Death from Temporary Insanity."

Anastasia had in the meantime recovered from her swoon, thanks to the restoratives of the medical gentleman who had attended her. Immediately she was restored to her senses she was informed of the verdict of the jury. She said nothing, and took her departure quietly. The court was breaking up at the time she was passing with a grave step and a serious face along the hall of the hotel to gain her magnificently appointed carriage, which was waiting for her at the door. She got into it: a tall lacquey, bedizened in velvet and gold lace, put up the steps, closed the door, and touched his hat for her orders.

"Home," she said.

The finely caparisoned horses started off with her equipage at a brisk trot. She sank back in the soft silken cushions; the expression of her face suddenly changed from gravity to gaiety; a smile of triumph curled her lip; and she said, half aloud to herself:

"'Tis over! The jury have given their verdict—'Death from Temporary Insanity.' Admirable! I am revenged! I am satisfied!

CHAPTER XLI.

TAKING MORE TIME TO FORM AN OPINION THAN KING SOLOMON TO PASS HIS FAMOUS JUDGMENT.

"Madam! Tell me—
What place is this? For you have led me
Into a subtle labyrinth, where I never
Shall have fruition of my former freedom;
But, like an humble anchorite, that digs
With his own nails his grave, must live confined
To the sad maze for ever."
GLAPTHORNE.—*The Lady's Privilege.*

That woman, whose vices were the vices of strength, and in whom the highest heroism was coexistent with preternatural ferocity, rolled on in her carriage from the hotel in the Haymarket to her home in Arlington-street. Had she passed for ever and successfully the rocks and rapids of the scene of terror, which had opened out upon her most daring crime? Was the stream of her life henceforth to glide along quietly? Were the waters of her fortune, as from a new fountain, to flow on to a peaceful destiny? She hoped so. Yet in her swollen heart passions were leaping like torrents; and, as she looked before her, she beheld, even in the immediate vista, the current of her existence winding its way with expanding force and features of enlarging magnificence.

The first object that occupied her thoughts was Bruce St. Aubyn. Was he destined to contribute to her happiness, or consummate her immolation? She hoped, yet despaired, the former; for, after he had made himself acquainted with some of the most dreadful secrets of her history, the wisest step she could take seemed to her to get him out of the way by depriving him of life. As she was pondering over this terrible matter, wondering at the same time what had become of Bruce St. Aubyn, and if she should again obtain him in her power for the purposes either of lust or of self-safety, her spirit quailed, notwithstanding that her soul was firm,—notwithstanding that there was everywhere in it, at all times, power, energy, and will.

And what *had* become of Bruce St. Aubyn?

After leaving Anastasia's house, he reached home at nearly five o'clock in the morning. Even at that late hour he went to bed; but he had little sleep. The stirring drama in which he had just finished playing a principal part kept him awake: every little portion of it he recalled with that intensity of emotion which a person feels when reading a romance of absorbing interest.

Now, there are some men whose lives are crowded with adventures to such an enormous extent, and of such an alarming character, that the particulars could not be severally and circumstantially told by even the most exact and the most painstaking biographer: with such men little stress would be laid on the mere occurrence of coming in personal contact with a woman whose days had been passed with men of violence and bloodshed, or who was, perhaps, even herself a creature of crime; it would appear a commonplace enough incident, nor is it probable that the recollection of it would at all disturb their slumbers. With Bruce St. Aubyn it was different: it was a strange, a wondrous event, which took the more possession of his soul on account of its standing forth in bold relief to his hitherto dull and monotonous existence.

Though his father was alive, he had been brought up principally under the eye of his mother, who, as will be seen hereafter, was a woman of a domineering temper, and a truly masculine frame of mind—who lorded it over even the Earl of Milsington. Bruce had been brought up by his mother with all that strictness which Byron ascribes to the early education of his hero, Don Juan; and though arrived at that period of life when he should have assumed a part of manly independence, Bruce St. Aubyn still showed the most submissive deference to his mother, attending to all her wishes and commands quite as much from the force of habit as from the instinct of filial affection. The result of such an education was, that, though he was not naturally weak-minded, he was imbued (at any rate, at this early age) with a certain feminity of character which the reader must have already observed: he had been carefully kept away from a life of gaiety and enjoyment, which expands frequently into an ocean of tempestuous adventures and of stormy passions—a life which seems to be the legitimate and infallible inheritance of young men. The rigid principles inculcated by his mother found in him a docile spirit; and though at times he broke out into fits of irritability, he displayed on all occasions symptoms of profound respect. His character was marked at once by timidity, gentleness, candour, and simplicity, and yet by decision, quickness of apprehension, subtilty, and penetration: he had a certain delicacy of disposition, and a certain pride of heart, which held him aloof from the enjoyments, sometimes insipid, and sometimes brutish, to which the majority of his companions had recourse without choice, stint, or scruple. In their opinion he was a prudent fellow—a philosopher, because he shunned their enjoyments, which he thought coarse; and if he was present with his friends on such occasions, it was to study their vices for the purpose of abstaining from them, just as the young Spartan nobles of antiquity watched the drunkenness of the Helots, in order to be more attached to habits of temperance.

Partly from regard for his mother, partly out of respect for himself, somewhat from scorn of common things, but particularly from that timidity of temper which is so strongly allied to pride of disposition, Bruce St. Aubyn had up to this period passed his days in retirement and restraint: it might be said of him, that he had been *sleeping* away life; and just as water usually designated by that figure of speech has its peculiar character —is calm on the surface, but flows frequently over an immense depth—so was it with him: deprived of holding communion with others, he became self-absorbed: meditation took the place of action; as will ever be the case; for when the realm of reality is confined within narrow bounds, imagination roams undefined in its uncircumscribed empire.

On leaving Anastasia's, Bruce St. Aubyn felt the liveliest emotion of security and joy on being released from the chains of a woman so dangerous and so unworthy of love: but the image of Anastasia never ceased to appear before him as he lay in bed striving to snatch a few hours of sleep: she was seen as a serpent with forked tongue gliding slily towards him, and seeming that if slumber came she would make the sleep eternal; therefore her image frighted "Nature's soft nurse," and "sleep, gentle sleep," would not "weigh his eyelids down, and steep his senses in forgetfulness."

He arose, and walked out, caring not whither he wandered, a prey to a feverish agitation.

Chance took him to the narrow passage which leads from Saville-row to Conduit-street.

There, without any other motive than to beguile the time, and, perhaps, slightly out of curiosity, he stopped before a bonnet shop, attracted by the gay picture presented by the window: in front of it were about thirty bonnets, varying from yellow, with chocolate coloured ribbons, to sky blue, garlanded with roses: all these sorts of fabulous coverings for the ornamentation of ladies' heads were ranged with a learned symmetry in straight lines, circles, curves, and triangles, with the view evidently of taking captive the hearts of female passers-by with their dazzling intermixture of shapes and hues, the latter illustrating all the shades in the gamut of colours.

Like a grassplot upon which a thousand rival flowers blossom in emulation to one another—as if contending who shall make the best show—a green silk curtain was the ground to this fascinating picture; and its colour, somewhat dull naturally, and very much tarnished by constant use, served but to bring more boldly into relief all the brilliance that was before it. Besides the production of this artistic effect, which had been very cleverly calculated upon by the arranger of the window, this curtain had another purpose: it was to protect about half a dozen girls who sat inside the shop from being stared at by the inquisitive glances of the men who came along the passage; and, as a necessary consequence, of keeping this bevy of damsels, who, on their part, in common with the other daughters of Eve, were remarkaably inquisitive, from looking at the men who passed along outside, and of being thereby impeded in their work; but in this latter and secondary purpose the curtain, it must be confessed, answered its end but imperfectly.

A slit—more correctly speaking, a space, scarcely perceptible, was between this curtain and the window shutter. The space was either there by accident, or, which was far more likely, it had been made expressly; for almost always on such occasions will a peep-hole of some sort or other be managed by some blooming nymph, who, in her benignity, wishes to be indulgent to the youth of the opposite sex:—well, this space, or peep-hole, enabled a quick eye to see distinctly enough that part of the shop which was occupied by the bonnet-makers; and, to be brief, the looks which several of these girls, every now and then, cast furtively in this direction—which, strategetically speaking, was the weak side of the fortification—appeared to announce that, in case of attacks, a certain class of besiegers would find no difficulty in meeting with a perfectly good understanding in the very heart of this by no means inexpugnable citadel.

It was to this treacherous peep-hole that Bruce St. Aubyn applied his eye with the air of a man who does not think that peeping at women is quite so incompatible with the modesty of the male sex, as it was found to be in the case of Peeping Tom of Coventry.

Peeping, then, through this hole, Bruce St. Aubyn saw five young girls sitting behind a counter which served them as a work table. They were all busy in different ways. One was unpicking, with a great deal of art, a knot of ribbons; another, with the help of pins, was

BOBBY ELPHINSTONE LETTING THE CAT OUT OF THE BAG.

arranging a wreath of flowers; the third was sewing a lining, the fourth fastening on a loop, and the fifth binding a bonnet.

Two of these young ladies had very plain features, and very mean faces and figures. The eye of the Honourable Bruce St. Aubyn accordingly roamed over them without being arrested by their charms. This, however, was not the case with the third. He looked at her for some time, and yet with no interest. She was a brown-haired girl not quite sixteen. She seemed as lively as a kitten, though she was nearly as round as a ball. She had a saucy face, a merry eye, white teeth, and a complexion with the bloom and beauty of the peach and the redness and freshness of the cherry.

The eye of Bruce St. Aubyn next wandered to her neighbour, whom he should have looked at first; for her fellow workwomen conceded to her superiority in two points—in years and in position—yes, in position; for she presided over their labours: she was the forewoman. She was fair; tall and lean, which she considered gave her a stylish air; and had regular enough features; but whatever charm they might otherwise have had was spoilt by the expression of her countenance, which was insipid and even silly. Already she had a worn look, which is very frequently the case with light-haired women as they approach their thirtieth year. Her greatest beauty was her hair, which was flaxen, long, silky, and remarkably abundant: it fell in numberless ringlets, like so many corkscrews, even down to her shoulders.

From her the eye of Bruce St. Aubyn strayed to the fifth and last workwoman.

She was at the end of the counter, apart from her companions. It was a young girl of delicate appearance, and poorly but neatly clad in a black merino dress. She was working with her head down; and so taken up was she with her work, or, perhaps, with her thoughts, that she never once looked up; and Bruce St. Aubyn, notwithstanding the anxiety he felt to complete his inspection, began at length to despair that he would ever succeed in getting a glimpse of her face.

She remained, indeed, for such a long time without once changing her position that Bruce St. Aubyn, tired of waiting, was about to take his departure, when, to his surprise and joy, she suddenly dropped the work with which she had been exclusively occupied—she dropped it on her lap, clasping her hands together at the same time with a kind of convulsive motion, and giving vent to a suppressed sigh. Then, immediately after, she sprang up in her seat, throwing back her head as quickly as a person awaking with a start out of a dream that has startled him. Her face was, at that moment, fully lit up by the broad daylight that streamed into the shop, and that contributed, perhaps, to render its paleness more striking. That face arrested the gaze of the Earl's younger son by an instantaneous fascination.

Now was Bruce St. Aubyn as eager of observation and as full of admiration as he had hitherto been inattentive and indifferent to the charms of the other heroines of that workshop.

A forehead a little prominent—in fact, with a slight bulge—very open, and which would, possibly, have been considered too large in development, had it not been partially concealed by abundant masses of dark auburn hair, the silkiest and the softest, which were arranged over it in smooth, broad, circular bands; large hazel eyes, with pupils that looked as soft as velvet, and with the ball of such limpidity that every now and then it presented to the view that blue tint, which you will occasionally detect, and think so exquisitely beautiful in a child's eyes; a nose all but aquiline, with a curve more delicate than exact, and with pinky nostrils that in their mobility were indicative of passion; a mouth, which was indebted to its wonderfully clear and marked outlines for the power of expressing, even in silence, the most transitory emotions;—such were the principal features of a face the oval shape of which, thin and pale from perceptible indisposition, still retained its characteristic as a type of delicacy, loftiness, and refinement.

Powers the most varied, and feelings apparently the most contradictory, seemed to possess in common the privilege of giving expression and animation to this striking countenance. One after the other, and frequently at the very same moment, there were seen reflected in it as in a mirror the intelligence of the clever woman, the curiosity of the ignorant one, the merriness and liveliness of the playful wit, the chastity of the maiden, the energy of the heroine, and the innocence of the child. Nothing more was required than to watch that countenance, even in moments of indifference, when there was an end to all expression, even of the very lightest fancies, easily to see how wrath could dart lightning from that eye of fire, how love could wreathe those charming lips with smiles of fondness, and happiness crown with a beaming aureola that brow of such purity and such poetry.

At this moment melancholy of the most mournful nature gave a touching character of sad suavity to this captivating countenance.

The young girl for some time preserved the position into which she had thrown herself, with her hands clasped, her face upraised, and her eyes fixed straight before her; and, gazing thus into vacuity, she seemed to be contemplating some of those anticipatory evils which are frequently without cause created by a morbid imagination, and serve but to add ideal sorrow to the stern realities of actual misfortune.

This melancholy thoughtfulness, so strange in a girl who was hardly anything more than a child, was suddenly disturbed by the forewoman.

"Here you are, Annie Bertie," she said, "gaping about you doing nothing, and wool-gathering, I suppose, as usual." And had Bruce St. Aubyn been within ear-shot—close enough to hear the exact tones of that amiable lady's voice, he would have thought it far from good tempered. "I should say you'll get that bonnet finished to-day."

The young girl, whose name is now known—Annie Bertie—appeared for a moment to experience that amazement—that shock which we all feel when we are suddenly interrupted in a day dream. With a start she immediately recovered herself and replied to the rebuke she had just received with a look of scorching indignation; then taking up her work again, she slowly bent down her head, and resumed her work without deigning to utter a single syllable.

"Conceited thing! I have no patience with her!" observed the forewoman; while the three other bonnet-makers exchanged looks, and smiled—as women do when they have no great liking to a companion.

Nothing of this little scene was lost on Bruce St. Aubyn: the meaning he fully understood, though it had come to him all through pantomimic action.

Involuntarily he took a liking to that girl: involuntarily he felt an interest in her, not so much for her beauty as for her sadness. Hoping that she would soon raise her head again, and thus enable him to look at her a second time, he remained peeping through the hole without thinking of an engagement he had to dine that day with his future father-in-law, Sir Henry Elphinstone.

Suddenly the neighbouring clock of St. George's, Hanover-square, roused him by striking the hour.

He looked at his watch, and, finding that it was time to think of keeping his engagement with Sir Henry, he bent his steps in the direction of Grillon's Hotel, where that gentleman was staying.

As he walked onwards, he thought of the girl he had just seen. He could think of nothing else. In his ardent admiration of her he exclaimed to himself:

"How pretty she is! And yet I do not think her merely pretty. That's an epithet applicable to those doll-like women—waxen images of lilies and roses—about whom only idiots fall into raptures. But a face like that I have just seen is worth a million of those; with its extraordinary assemblage of charms, it is deserving of unbounded admiration. What intelligence! what passion! what purity! and what poetry! What heavenliness in its melancholy! and what a lightning flash of indignation! All the graces, in short, whether soft or severe, which can beautify the face of woman, are united in the countenance of this young girl............Ah! yes, young; and too sad for one so young. She seems to me as if she were Niobe, the child; Niobe, foreseeing her misfortunes, and suffering before being stricken."

Then, clasping his hands and throwing up his eyes, he exclaimed enthusiastically:

"Oh! how happy Leonardo da Vinci would have been could he have painted her, and made a companion picture to his exquisite portrait of Mona Lisa!"

CHAPTER XLII.

MAKING A GOOD TACK ON AN ADVENTUROUS CRUISE.

"How fine is the texture! how fragile the frame
Of that delicate blossom—a female's fair fame!
Like the sensitive plant, it recoils from the breath,
And shrinks from the touch, as if pregnant with death."
WASHINGTON IRVINE.

As Bruce St. Aubyn walked onwards, musing over the beautiful girl he had just seen, the image of Selina Elphinstone, to whom he was affianced, crossed his mind; immediately he thought of his approaching marriage, there rose in his bosom a strong antipathy against the race of the Elphinstones in general, and Miss Selina in particular. Were he now to show himself averse to the nuptials, and refuse to celebrate them, he would overthrow a plan which it had taken his mother three years to bring to maturity. True, he had objected to the proposal when it was first mooted to him; in the end, however, he yielded to his mother's persuasions; but now again all his old repugnance rose within him as strong as ever. He had ever considered Selina Elphinstone exceedingly plain; he had also ever thought her uncommonly silly; he knew that he could never love her; and it was while occupied in deploring his miserable fate of being united in matrimony to a plain, silly girl, whom he could never love, that he reached Grillon's—the hotel where his future father-in-law was residing during his stay in London, and where he was now awaiting his arrival, in company with our old acquaintance, Sebastian Leonard, and his son Robert, whose name, by the way, the ancient Dorians—had they known it—might have abbreviated, without much of the appearance of brevity, into what his friends usually called him —Bobby.

Now, as Bobby Elphinstone will shortly take an active part in the history a short description of him may not be unacceptable to the reader. He was about twenty-one years of age—what is commonly called an awkward "hobble de hoy." His freckled face was not improved by the colour of his hair, which was as red as carrots; and his whiskers, which were of the same hue, were beginning to grow, thinly on his cheeks and in little tufts under his chin. His round shoulders were just now painfully confined in a tight coat he was evidently wearing for the first time, his large feet were pinched in glazed boots, and his large hands encased in yellow kid gloves which, though new, were creased and soiled. These were the chief points in the personal appearance and decoration of this most characteristic individual.

His father, Sir Henry, was an iron manufacturer in the neighbourhood of Birmingham, who had made a great deal of money by lucky speculations at a time when the majority of men engaged in the same business could with difficulty maintain their establishments against the competition of rivals. From the interest he took in the general affairs of his town, he stood high in the corporation, holding in it the position of Alderman, and he had once served the office of Mayor—on which occasion he had received the honour of Knighthood. He was one of those enterprising, laborious, persevering men, who, having once made their way into the path of fortune, pursue it with a resolute step, never swerving to the right or left, never stopping and never receding. To men of his stamp, the paths into which geniuses and people of imagination stray, and the mirages that have fascination for minds of idle fancies offer temptations that are unheeded and considered despicable, while the acclivities at the foot of which the weak become disheartened, and the sloughs from which the delicate turn aside to go a longer road, present but obstacles that are impotent and easily baffled. From the moment they set forth on their career they keep their eyes fixed steadily on the object at which they aim, they walk on towards it with imperturbability, and they are not the less assured of attaining it than they care for the splashes of mire with which they are bedaubed on their progress to reach it, so long as they do arrive at it.

Alderman Sir Henry Elphinstone, at the time of Bruce St. Aubyn's arrival, was deep in conversation with Sebastian Leonard on his favorite topic—the state of the iron trade. Unlike his son, who was attired in all the colours of the rainbow, he was dressed in plain black from head to foot. He was apparently about fifty-five years of age, of a mean appearance, but of a strong constitution—one of those lean, sinewy men who seem "cut out" to live to a hundred, and to whom may be applied with equal fidelity two epithets that appear to contradict each other—*dry* and *juicy*. His complexion, originally ruddy, had for many years undergone that discolouration —or rather, had that absence of colour—which the scorching atmosphere of blast furnaces almost always produces in the long run on men with an abundance of humours—on plethoric men; and here I may glance aside for a moment to observe that though some artists have painted the Cyclops with red faces, and given even Vulcan rosy cheeks, they never could have set foot within a forge, or they would have known that such complexions are never found there. In addition to his paleness, which had an artificiality about it, from not being adapted to the character of his complexion, Sir Henry Elphinstone had by no means improved his facial beauty by an accident which he had met with in the exercise of his vocation: at the very outset of his career he had had one of his eyes scorched, and consequently blinded, by one of those red-hot scoria which fly under the blows of hammers from an iron bar glowing with white heat from a roaring furnace. Nature, by way of compensating him for this cecity in his left eye, had gifted his remaining one with an extraordinary power—it shone with the brilliancy of a star from quickness of penetration and subtlety of thought; this eye—the look of which when once seen it was difficult to forget—composed, with a constant and almost convulsive twitching of the lips, which were thin and ashen, the principal feature of a face which expressed the following rare combination of qualities—craft, suspicion, presumption, vanity, and stiffness in opinion.

The dinner, at which these four striking individuals found themselves assembled, offered no incident worthy of being related. Whatever anxiety or grave considerations were in the minds of Sebastian Leonard or Bruce St. Aubyn, Sir Henry Elphinstone or his son, were speedily dispelled by the delicate wines and viands of a perfectly unexceptionable banquet—for such was, in reality, this dinner. Before the end of the first course Sir Henry was in excellent humour, and from that time discharged his duties as Amphitryon with all the courtesy of a man of the world.

His son, Bobby, who never was an enemy to good cheer, and who had nothing to disturb his mind, not even the paying of the bill, did full justice, by the enormity of his appetite, to the larder and cellar of Grillon's. Nobody would have ever suspected, to see how he ate of every dish and drank of every wine, that he had lunched heartily at Stevens's only a few hours before. By the time the dinner was over and coffee brought, he had considerably over-eaten and over-drunk himself: in fact, he had greatly exceeded the bounds of sobriety.

By the side of this good-tempered, convivial country youth, Bruce St. Aubyn had anything but the air of a happy person: he ate little; he drank less; when he was forced to speak by a question being put to him directly, he replied but by monosyllables: he was absent; he seemed full of thought. In vain his future father-in-law tried to get him out of his moody fit by kicking his foot under the table or nudging his elbow; but every time he was kicked or nudged he started up, and had in him about the same amount and length of animation that an automaton has when it is wound up: he poured wine into his neighbour's glass, or caught hold of the first dish that was within his reach to help the contents of it; edged in a word or two whether to the purpose or not, and then relapsed into his former state—a gloomy, moody, grave, contemplative state, indicative of much unhappiness, to judge from the extreme melancholy that was visible in every line of his countenance.

At about ten o'clock Sebastian Leonard rose to take leave of Sir Henry Elphinstone; Bruce St. Aubyn followed his example, and Bobby Elphinstone, saying that he would go to his club—the Erechtheum—also took leave of his father; and the three young men left Grillon's together.

The rapid transit from the heated and close atmosphere of the room where they had been dining into the cool, open air of a spring night contributed greatly to increase the dizziness which had been produced in the brain of Bobby Elphinstone by the fumes of wines mingled with the smoke of cigars. Without being drunk—for his speech was not sufficiently thick for that, his pronunciation was only now and then indistinct—he was still in a state of very great tipsiness, perceptible enough in the giddiness which showed itself in his unsteady gait and in the lightness and highness of spirits which visibly manifested themselves in his speech and demeanour.

"Hurra! old boys," he exclaimed, placing himself in the centre and catching hold firmly and familiarly of the arms of Sebastian Leonard and Bruce St. Aubyn, and steadying himself between them: "A good job we've bid the old chap good night. Here's to Young England for ever! And now we are all by ourselves, what say you to our having a lark?"

"It struck me you swallowed all the larks at dinner," said the satirical Sebastian Leonard to whom the question was put.

"Ha! that's not bad. Just the case. I drank like a rhinoceros and ate like an elephant. The governor behaved well to us though, gave us a banquet like a Lord Mayor—a Belshazzar's Feast—and he callsh it only a quiet dinner."

"Your father would be happy to hear you praising him in this fashion," said Sebastian Leonard. "But he would say you were flattering him."

"No! 'pon my honour—no! I never flatter anybody. I only do justish to the old fellow's virtues, and am not blind to his faultsh. He's a good judge of wines and cigars—though he doeshn't smok'sh them—and of made dishes and spiritsh; but he is no judge of women—no; and I'd tell him so to his face. Now, what do you think?"

"Well, I think it's getting very late," said Sebastian Leonard, who was wishing to get rid of his companion in order that he might have a quiet chat with Bruce St. Aubyn, and induce him to renew his visit to Anastasia. He therefore added: "I think the best thing we can all do is to go home."

"You're not speaking sheriously," said Bobby Elphinstone, dropping his head lower at every word he uttered.

"I am."

"Advis'h ush to go home?"

"Yes."

"Then you surpris'h like Startle in the play. What do you think, Bruc'h?"

"Think the same, that it is time for us all to go home."

"Listen here, Bruce. Do you know what I took you for the first time I saw you?"

"No."

"A fellow like myshelf."

"And now?"

"You're a fellow whom I don't esteemsh."

"Why?"

"You eat like a tomtit—drink water—don't joke—don't smoke"—

"Yes, I do."

"I shay, you don't. I watshed you this evening throw away your cigar every time as soon as you had lighted it; and now you talksh of going home. What are you afraid of?"

"Perhaps of the perils to which our virtue is exposed by walking the streets at such an hour as this. Still, I am sorry you should have formed so bad an opinion of me."

Sebastian Leonard, seeing that there was no chance of getting rid of the drunken country youth, and having inwardly resolved to take advantage of his presence by turning the conversation into a channel which he thought would be most likely to suit his purpose, here interposed with—

"Do you object to my speaking on the subject?"

"Not at all," said both the young men at once.

"Well," continued Sebastian Leonard, addressing Bobby Elphinstone, "I think our friend here has for some time past been taking a leading part in a comedy, not exactly that of Startle to which you have just likened me, as that of Lothario or Benedict. I should say nothing if there was any amusement in the comedy, but, on the contrary, it's an uncommonly dull affair."

"I don't understandsh what you mean by Bruce taking a part in a comedy," said Bobby Elphinstone with truth.

"You know that a comedy is indicated by a series of incidents terminating in a marriage; I'll therefore make it clear by reminding you that Bruce is going to marry your sister."

"Oh! yes—to be sure—I know that—and Seeley—I always call shister Seeley—Selina 'sh too long a name—almost breaksh the jaw in pronouncing it—well, Seeley's no beauty. But what's the oddsh so long as she'sh happy? Seeley has no end of money—that'sh the reason Bruc'h is going to marry her—and when the Governor hops the twig she'll get a deal more out of the iron, and the Consolsh, and railway shar'sh, and what not—for the Governor's well up in the stirrups, as rish as a Jew, though he doesn't like to be thought so, for fear he would have to spend more than he doesh, for he wash always a money shaving man, though if you were to believe him, you would fancy every day he wash going to smash."

Hearing this coarse, but, though coarse, true version of the motive which had induced his mother to contract a matrimonial alliance between him and Selina Elphinstone, Bruce St. Aubyn could not refrain from colouring and feeling annoyed. His future brother-in-law not observing his annoyance went on:

"That's why Bruc'h is so d-dheucedly fond of my shister, and as you must know that she is prudish and a shrew, and d-dheucedly pious, he behav'sh quietly for fear of spoiling himself with her should he show his real character. Ish it not so, Bruc'h?"

"If there were not many things to be passed over in a man when he is the worse for liquor," said Bruce St. Aubyn angrily, unable any longer to curb his indignation, "I should get into a desperate quarrel with you."

"Quarrel with *me!* That *ish* fine! Quarrel with *me!* I admire your gratitude!"

"For what am I to be grateful to *you?*"

"A great deal; but I forgive you."

And Bobby Elphinstone, with that sudden emotion which people frequently display in the first stages of intoxication, was almost on the point of crying. "You'd quarrel with me," he continued, "when I have your interest more at heart than anybody in the world. I don't care about your going on playing the hypocrite with Seeley; it'sh all one to me. But I do care about —I do care about"—

"What?"

"Your treating me—oh! booh!—as if I wash likely to tell shister of all your pranks. That hurtsh my feelings: I say it'sh very—oh! booh! —very painful to my feelings."

Bobby Elphinstone spoke the few last words in a choky voice, and was about to burst into tears, when Bruce St. Aubyn exclaimed impatiently:

"What a cursed ass you are!"

"When a man'sh a shensible fellur, it'sh very hard to be taken to be an assh," said Bobby Elphinstone; "and when a man hash a liking to another, it'sh equally hard to be mhistaken. I took an immediate liking to you, Bruc'h; and when I got to London I was glad to shee you again, because I was in hopes you were going to take me about to shee all the shights of London. But I have been disappointed in you, Bruc'h—very much disappointed—very, very mush."

And Bobby Elphinstone stopped, and, letting go of the arms of his companions, stood in the middle of the pavement and shook his head from side to side in a dolorous manner.

"If you go on in this way," said Bruce St. Aubyn reprovingly, "everybody that passes will be staring at us."

"You have no confidence in me," said Bobby Elphinstone, in a more lachrymose tone of voice, as he caught hold of the arms of his companions and walked on: "fact, you shuspect me. You think me capable of doing you an injury in the eyesh of shister."

"Instead of talking and rolling about in this fashion," said Bruce St. Aubyn, "suppose you try to walk as steadily as possible to the nearest cab stand. There we'll take a Hansom, and I'll see you home, for you had better go home and go to bed."

"Go to bed!" exclaimed Sebastian Leonard. "Why, you don't think he is ill?"

"No, you don't think I'm ill?" added Bobby.

"Only a temporary illness," replied Bruce St. Aubyn, "the effects of which you will not feel to-morrow."

"I shee what it ish," observed Bobby Elphinstone; "you fancy I have taken too mush of the Guv'nor's wines." And as if to show this was not the case, he tried (but unsuccessfully) to steady himself in his voice and on his legs; and continued: "You are quite wrong, my dear fellur, I wash never more shober in my life. But that won't prevent me from shaying shister's a scold, and from opening your ey'sh to her faultsh. I like you too mush to shee you desheived."

"But why do you speak so against your sister?" asked Bruce St. Aubyn, with no little curiosity.

Bobby Elphinstone turned his head towards Bruce St. Aubyn, and spoke in his ear in a low and emphatic voice: "I have a sp—ite against her."

"You have!"

"Yes; and she has a spite against me. If you had not annoyed me just now, I should have told you all about it."

"You may as well tell it."

"First place, you don't deserve to hear it, because you have 'noyed me; second place, Seeley would be rampant if she knew I told it to any one. If she heard I had spoken about it to *you*, she'd scratch my eyes out."

"You are wronging your sister," exclaimed Sebastian Leonard. "She is not capable"——

"No," echoed Bruce St. Aubyn, "she is not capable"——

"Oh! Of what? Of scratching out my eyesh? Well, you may be saying right, and for a good reason—*I'd not let her*. As for *trying*—it wouldn't be the first time"——

What! Miss Elphinstone!" exclaimed Sebastian Leonard.

"Selina! whom I thought such a model of meekness! such an angel of gentleness!" exclaimed Bruce St. Aubyn.

"So she is, when you are present. But lor', doesn't she make up for it when you're away."

"You surprise me!" continued Bruce St. Aubyn. "Really, I can scarcely believe what you say."

"Well, if you don't like to believe me, don't. I'll give you, though, a little advic'h. When you are married, *take care of your eyesh*. That's all I've to say—keep it dark."

If up to this point Bruce St. Aubyn had thought his intended plain, silly, insipid, altogether incapable of inspiring love, still he had thought she was gifted at least with that kind, meek, gentle disposition which Nature gives as a small but solid atonement to those from whom she has withheld her best favours. The thoughtless words uttered by the son of Sir Henry Elphinstone, in his inebriety, caused Bruce St. Aubyn to see the question of his marriage in a perfectly new light. For a moment he reflected over what he had just heard, and he felt a greater aversion than ever to the match which had been made for him by his mother.

There was a moment's pause, during which Bobby Elphinstone, over whose reason there had not yet come a total eclipse, knew that he had been saying too much, and that if he made any more imprudent disclosures they would produce an impression of disgust to the marriage in the mind of his future brother-in-law.

"You must not take sheriously what I have been shaying," he resumed, trying to repair his error. "Sheeley's at bottom a good girl, and I can foreshee you will be happy with her."

"Do you include the eyes of our friend in your foresight?" asked Sebastian Leonard, rejoiced at the turn the conversation had taken, and wishing it to be kept up in the same strain.

"Don't make mattersh worsh," was the reproving remark of Bobby Elphinstone, in a tipsy voice, and with a more indistinct pronunciation than ever. "Bruc'h must shee I wash only joking. Beshid'sh, brothers and shisters sheldom praise eash other."

"But what is that grudge you bear your sister?" asked Sebastian Leonard, desirous of bringing the conversation back to the point from which it started.

"Nothing so very partic'lar. I'll tell Bruc'h all about it shome day."

"Why not now?" said Sebastian Leonard.

"Ay, why not now?" said Bruce St. Aubyn, desirous of obtaining a full explanation.

"It'sh getting late," said Bobby Elphinstone, in a splendid fit of discretion. "I think we had better follow the advis'h you gave us just now, Bruc'h, of going home."

"Let us do nothing of the sort," said Sebastian Leonard.

"I feel my stomach out of order," said Bobby Elphinstone; "and I do believe the wine I have been drinking hash got into my head."

"You will get rid of your dizziness by keeping in the open air," said Sebastian Leonard. "What do you say to a stroll up Regent-street?"

"I had rather follow the advis'h just given me by Bruc'h, and go to bed."

"What! Before eleven o'clock!" exclaimed Sebastian Leonard. "You ought to be ashamed of such a thought. You! A young man from the country come to see life in London! You! fond of gaiety and pretty faces! Fie!—For shame!"

"But I feel so bad!" whined Bobby Elphinstone.

Bruce St. Aubyn said nothing. He was considering within himself how to act towards his future brother-in-law. Desirous as he had been a few minutes back to get rid of him, he was now quite as anxious to detain him; from him alone could he ascertain what it was so much to his interest to know, whether there were as many moral as physical defects in Selina Elphinstone. In the opinion of a future husband it was, surely, most desirable that some enlightenment should be thrown on the subject. To question another about a third party is a proceeding from which a delicate-minded, well-educated man generally abstains; but there are certain cases—and a marriage on the point of being solemnised is among the number—where excessive delicacy becomes absolute silliness.

Bruce St. Aubyn, therefore, felt no scruple about getting from Bobby Elphinstone, in his drunkenness, a confession which he would probably never have got from him if he had allowed him time to recover his sobriety.

"Well, if you feel so bad, you had better go to bed," said he, trying to twit him on his weak point; "but, before doing so, you will not, I suppose, refuse to drink a glass of whiskey punch with me?"

"That's the first sensible speech I have heard from the lips of our friend to-day," said Sebastian Leonard, joyously, to Bobby Elphinstone.

"Ha! ha! ha!" laughed Bobby Elphinstone. "The first sensible speech we have heard from his lips, to be sure." And incapable of resisting an invitation of the treachery of which he had no suspicion, "Let's have the whiskey punch by all means," he added. "Lor'! Lor'! How those wines have got into my head! I long to set myself to rights again by drinking some whiskey punch."

"Here we are at Verey's!" exclaimed Sebastian Leonard. "Let us go in."

And pushing Bobby Elphinstone in first, he and Bruce St. Aubyn entered afterwards, both laughing in their sleeve at the folly of the country lad, and both anticipating some most important disclosures of Miss Selina Elphinstone.

CONCLUSION.

MY readers will doubtless recollect that on the first appearance of this work I received overtures from noble and titled families, who wished, at any price, to suppress its publication. I declined every offer, deeming it a duty to let the rising generation of this present enlightened century know to what a fearful extent immorality prevails in "certain circles;" yes, in those very circles where the *fair*, the *frail*, but withal the *wealthy* patrician daughters of rank and luxury, are *most severe*, upon the slightest deviation from rectitude (deviations perhaps caused from "want," "starvation," "famine") committed by the young, the suffering, the equally beautiful but "low born" of their own sex. As I before observed, we determined to proceed with our publication, in spite of all bribery to the contrary; but, as the weight of a feather will turn the balance of a scale, a circumstance (little expected) occurred, which induced me to let my pens dry in the ink, sooner than proceed to publish further the crimes of Anastasia, Baroness Leone. But I am bound in some measure to apologise to my readers, trusting that *many*, if not all of them, possess hearts capable of feeling sympathy and sorrow for a suffering and deeply repentant sister. One evening, a short week or two ago, a note was presented to me hurriedly by a female whose face was concealed by a thick veil. Her voice was low and tremulous, as she said, "Madam, for Heaven's sake read this quickly, and follow me." The missive contained the following words, which were much blotted by tears: "Oh, if you possess the heart of a Christian, follow the bearer to the death-bed of a sinful but repentant woman"—— Without a word I motioned the female to lead the way, and in about a quarter of an hour I found myself in an obscure street, situate in the vicinity of Clare-market; the woman at length stopped before the door of a mean-looking house, and, taking a key from her pocket, opened the door; I followed her into a narrow passage, lighted by a tallow candle, the wick long, unsnuffed, and just expiring in its socket. At the end of the passage was a staircase, very steep and ricketty, up which she preceded me. At the top of the third flight the woman paused, placed her finger to her lips to denote silence, then softly opened a door, and we entered a small, low, gloomy chamber. By the light of a small lamp which stood upon the chimney-piece, and from which issued a strong smell of rancid oil, I perceived in one corner of this close room a small tent bed, with blue and white checked hangings, much the worse for wear and dust. It was easy to perceive that this same bed was occupied, as almost inaudible groans and sighs issued from its tenant, though the old and faded drapery concealed any object from sight. In the middle of this desolate apartment was a small table, upon which were ranged several medicine bottles, a tea-cup without a handle, a well-used pewter spoon, a Bible, and a small prayer-book, opened at the part containing the service for the sick and dying. After the pause of a few seconds the female beckoned me to the side of the bed where she stood, and, withdrawing the scanty curtains, said, "Behold!" Oh, reader! it was a sickening, a sorrowful, a heartrending sight! Upon that squalid bed, in that dingy apartment, void of every comfort, and tended only by a daughter of poverty, in the agonies of death, in the prime of womanhood and unequalled beauty, lay Anastasia, the Baroness Leone. Yes! the dread monster had surprised his prey in the midst of her career of sin and crime. I must draw a veil over the scene which followed my introduction into this abode of poverty and death. She assured me that she felt at peace, having, in that squalid bed, prayed as she has *never* done before since she knelt in innocence in her mother's lap. She told me how one false step had reduced her from affluence to poverty; she implored me to pray for her to that God who rejoices over a repentant sinner. I endeavoured to speak peace to that wounded and chastened spirit. Before the early dawn I closed her eyes in the last dread sleep, and *who* shall dare to say she was not pardoned by the "All Merciful." The mortal remains of this gifted and erring woman repose in the graveyard of a suburban district, and only yesterday I received an anonymous letter thanking me for my sympathy, adding that a plain stone was placed over the grave of Anastasia, with the following inscription:—"There is more joy in heaven over one sinner that repenteth, than over ninety and nine just persons who need no repentance."

Adieu, my reader, at some future period we may meet again.

THE WOMAN OF THE WORLD.

www.ingramcontent.com/pod-product-compliance
Lightning Source LLC
Chambersburg PA
CBHW081211170626
46811CB00010B/3241

* 9 7 8 1 5 3 5 8 1 3 0 6 8 *